FIRE MEETS FIRE

MAYHEM MAKERS

WRETCHED SOULZ MC

MANDA MELLETT

COPYRIGHT

Published 2024 by Trish Haill Associates

ISBN: 978-1-915106-20-9

www.mandamellett.com

Disclaimer

This is a work of fiction. Names, characters, businesses, places, events and incidents are either the products of the author's imagination or used in a fictitious manner. Any resemblance to actual persons, living or dead, or actual events is purely coincidental.

Warning

This book is dark in places and contains content of a sexual, abusive and violent nature. It may not be suitable for persons under the age of 18.

PRODUCTION ACKNOWLEDGMENTS

Photographer Golden Czermak

Model Colt Kube

Cover Design by CT Cover Creations

Edited and formatted by Maggie Kern @ Ms.K Edits

Proof reading by Darlene Tallman

WRETCHED SOULZ MC

PROLOGUE

This is not where I want to spend my night. I certainly can think of any number of better plans, one of which would definitely include a drink in my hand and a girl on my lap.

But here I am. Kicking down the stand, I get off the bike, sharing a chin lift with Legend, who's followed me from the clubhouse. Unlike me, who can think of far better things to do with my time, Legend is bouncing with excitement as though eager to find out the results of his new box of tricks.

As Legend walks ahead into the auto shop, I murmur under my breath, "We shouldn't fuckin' need to be here."

I can't remember a time when anyone with all their wits about them has stolen from the Wretched Soulz. Everyone knows there'd be quick retribution if they were caught, and probably no funeral as their body would never be found. While not overly worried about someone pilfering, we're not lax in security. Well, we're in more danger of being searched by the pigs and need fair warning.

It was a shock to find someone's been stealing from the

shop owned by the club. Walking inside, my spirits are lifted by the obvious success of our business. We build customised bikes as well as providing the usual sales and maintenance service for all models. Evidence of how busy we are is all around me. We've gained quite a reputation, even if some people only like coming to us to boast to their friends how they're not afraid to walk on the wild side.

My mood quickly sours as I pass the containers holding spare parts. You'd think with what people know and rightly believe about the Wretched Soulz MC, that the last thing they'd do is steal from us. But for the last couple of weeks, bits and pieces have been going missing. Not huge things and nothing really valuable, just nuts, bolts, a battery cover and the odd bottle of engine oil. Insignificant, and as such, it took a while for us to notice anything had been disturbed.

Once Weasel, manager of the shop and our road captain, became suspicious, he'd carried out an inventory to check. What he found was that while we maintain and service all models of bikes, everything stolen was for a Harley.

We're Soulz. It's our territory. Our reputation alone should be enough to warn people off. But clearly, not in this case. After Weasel's revelations were greeted noisily at church, Legend was pulled in to replace old or broken cameras and install new alarms. Now, not even a fly could get in undetected. And starting tonight, we'll be staking the place out to see if we can catch our thief red-handed.

Legend, computer guru and all-round tech guy, wanted me to see the magic he'd worked. So I agreed to come take the first night shift with him. It's been a while since my fists have seen some action, so I'm looking forward to deploying them tonight. I really hope our light-fingered guy will put in an appearance. At least that would make my missing out on the good things in life worthwhile.

It's quiet, dark, the moon hidden by clouds tonight. We've only been here an hour and already I'm bored and fidgety. *Fool's errand.* It's probable our nemesis has already realised the error of their ways. I glance at the clock again, only to find the hands have progressed by little more than a minute.

It must be near midnight and I'm on my third beer, when Legend suddenly exclaims, "There. Look."

Placing my bottle down, I sit forward as a shadowy figure seems to be approaching the security fence that's meant to keep everyone out. It's hard to tell much. Their upper body and head are shrouded in a hoodie, and their face hasn't yet been caught on a camera.

"I'll call Claw." Legend reaches for his phone, his finger hovering over the direct dial key that will summon our enforcer.

"Nah. Hold off a moment." There's only one man, and either Legend or I would easily be able to deal with them by ourselves. There's a practical reason for my instruction too. The clubhouse is only a mile away, and the sound of a loud bike approaching might scare our thief off before we can capture them.

"Will you fuckin' look at that?" Legend's eyes widen as he points to the monitor.

My jaw drops as I watch the man lithely scale the telegraph pole close to our fence, secure a rope to the top, then launch himself up and over the high steel fence. Once he's on solid ground, he lets go of the rope, which stays dangling, obviously waiting to be used as his means of escape.

"Guess that's the answer as to how he's been getting in." I'm already out of my seat. I may be impressed with his athleticism, but he's still got a lesson to learn about stealing from the Soulz. My companion starts to copy my action. "Nah, you stay here, Ledge. I can handle one asshole like him." Or if I can't take the not-very-tall and definitely not-very-built figure who's been robbing us, then it's time to hang up my motorcycle boots.

I've honed the ability to move silently over the years. If I don't want you to know I'm near, you won't, not until I've gotten up close and personal. Moving through our darkened building that I know like the back of my hand, I emerge into the yard. There's the thief who's somehow not only managed to open our storeroom door but also defied the new alarm Legend had fitted.

I push the *what the fuck?* question to the back of my mind. It's not important for now. What's more critical is that I end this, and before the thief gets more confident and starts stealing things of higher value.

Stealthily, I come up behind the fucker who's rummaging through our boxes of spare parts, muttering softly as though they're looking for something in particular that's not immediately at hand.

Taking my gun out of my cut, I ease off the safety with an audible and unmissable click.

With a speed I wasn't expecting, instead of freezing, the thief comes straight for me, kicking the gun out of my hand and planting a fist in my stomach.

A split second is all it takes for me to think, *game fucking on.* No one's going to get the better of me and definitely not on my turf. Turning the tables, I go on the offensive, using every dirty street-fighting trick I ever learned.

My opponent has clearly gone to the same school, and for a moment, we're evenly matched, despite that I'm far bigger in size. We both land and block kicks and punches. I'm breathing heavily when, at last, luck's on my side and I get the upper hand.

I sweep the feet from under my assailant, and he lands

heavily on the ground. I come down on him, my fist raised to punch a direct hit on his face, only to pull it at the last moment, as Legend has chosen that precise time to flick on the overhead lights.

"You're a fuckin' bitch," I gasp. To prove it, I sweep the hoodie back off her head, revealing her face.

"Get off me." She keeps struggling.

"Give it up. I caught you stealing from us." And I'm going to make her pay. I don't care if she's a woman. Thieving is thieving whatever the sex.

She refuses to give in, unfortunately managing to attract the interest of my cock, and I harden as she writhes beneath me. I wouldn't be a man if I didn't suddenly have ideas about what retribution she could make.

"Yeah, just keep that up," I growl, unable to keep the leer from spreading over my face.

In the harsh bright light, I see her brave expression change, and her face pales. All the confidence she had while fighting me seems to have fled. Abruptly, she stills as she becomes aware of the effect her movements have had on my groin. She swallows heavily.

Fuck. I'm no rapist. Her palpable fear at the position she's in makes me feel guilty I got any enjoyment from feeling her curves.

"I'll let you up, but you run? I'll catch you and make you regret it," I warn her. When I see the little nod of acceptance, I lift myself away, strangely regretting losing the softness of her body beneath me.

Free, she warily pulls herself up. Once she's standing, she brushes herself off, wincing as she must catch one of the bruises I left.

Par for the course, sweetheart. You left some on me too. Reluctantly, I have to admire her and her fighting skills.

She's about five foot ten, a good eight inches shorter than me. I'd mistaken her silhouette for that of a man as she's got the smallest tits I've ever seen. Her ass is tight and high, and her waist is tiny and pulled in. My cock, which should have stood down now her proximity has gone, jerks as though telling me he likes what he sees.

I should ask what the fuck she's doing, stealing from the club, whether she's got a screw loose, or a death wish. But still amazed as, for a moment, it had been touch and go which one of us would win the set we'd just had, what actually comes out of my mouth is, "How the fuck did you learn to fight like that?"

CHAPTER ONE
HELO

Becoming a thief didn't much bother me. Up against everything else I've done in my life, it's just one more thing in my extensive repertoire to add to my resume. While it's not my acquisition method of choice, I question whether it can be called stealing at all if the people you're robbing from are criminals. After all, I'm probably only taking their ill-gotten gains, or items bought with blood money.

I'm not blind to the risks, though. I'm not pilfering from just anyone. No, I'm stealing from the Arizona chapter of the Wretched Soulz MC—the motorcycle gang with an international reputation for violence and mayhem. I have no illusions about what little mercy they'll have if they catch me. But needs must, as they say.

Whilst I'm never one to turn down a challenge, I'm not doing it for fun. If I could see another option, I'd take it. There might be better ways of keeping a roof over my head, but in my current predicament, keeping the particular ceiling that I've stumbled across suits me just fine. I'll do what I can to keep it that way.

At heart, I'm a daredevil. When the solution to my problem presented itself, I admit I didn't try to persuade myself out of it. Keeping mind and body sharp has long been part of my training. And what better way of doing that than stealing motorcycle parts from a notorious gang? I'm not that reckless. I'm only taking items that are being discarded or are of minimal value, which shouldn't be missed. It can't be unusual for the small shit to go astray, and only an anal-retentive person would keep track of every nut, bolt, or screw. Surely an auto shop run by criminals can't be that well organised? I can't see a leather-clad gang wasting time on detailed inventories. They've probably got drugs or guns to run, certainly things more interesting.

Like before any mission, I analysed my chances of getting into their auto shop and out again without exposure. They might be equipped to keep the day-to-day thief out, and that's if their reputation doesn't deter anyone from breaking into their premises. But they haven't come up against someone like me before, and definitely not someone of my calibre. Bikers? Huh. I could eat them for breakfast.

And if I'm wrong? Well, we've all got to die. Someday. I've risked putting my life on the line more times than I can count. Facing danger has become second nature.

Tonight, just as I have over the past couple of weeks, I first check that the shop's dark and quiet, just as it should be this close to midnight. I move to the telegraph pole that's conveniently close to the razor-wired topped-rear fence. It's near enough for me to be able to use it for what I need to, but not for anyone else to suspect what I'm doing. Then, probably, there's no one else crazy enough to break into the Wretched Soulz premises.

Like any woman who attempts to make it in a male-dominated arena knows, they have to prove themselves better than any man just to keep up. A simple stumble can lead to ridicule and derision, whereas a male companion making the same mistake would just be offered a hand to help them back on their feet. Needing to excel, to be the best, is the background that's given me the skills for what I'm about to do next.

Using several muscle groups in my arms and legs aided by core strength, I shimmy up the pole that has no handholds, as easily as if there was a ladder attached. At the top, I balance, take a small tablet out of my bag, and send the program that will block the MC's alarm system until I reset it. Since I was last here, they've made some enhancements, but I easily take them in my stride. That done, I loop a rope around the pole, running through safety checks to make sure it will hold. Once satisfied, I draw up, lean my weight back a little, then throw myself forward, leaping into the void that will hopefully allow me to land on the other side of the boundary.

I arrive exactly as I've perfected on my previous forays before, two legs balanced on the inside of the fence, well beneath the razor wire, allowing me to gently descend the last few feet until I'm standing on the ground. The rope I leave swinging to help me make the return journey. Later, after I've used it to complete the upward climb, I'll remove the rope, check I've left no footprints, and thus leave no evidence that I've ever been here. Even if the bike gang knows they are being robbed, how will remain a mystery.

My heart rate is only a little elevated after getting over the barrier between me and the premises I'm about to rob. It takes far more than a simple breaking and entering to get adrenaline pulsing through my veins. Nevertheless, I am on high alert as I pause by my escape route, all senses examining the environment, but as expected, I hear and see nothing.

As normal, first, I start picking through the trash they've discarded. My client—I use the word to justify our relationship to myself—has particular requirements. His motorcycle brought back from its current crashed state and restored to factory condition. Not for him are the customisations that the Wretched Soulz are famous for doing. Their customers come in to have a "live to ride" embossed plate fixed over the air filter. Their discarded plain one is absolutely right for what I want. Grinning when I find one that just needs the dents knocked out and some polish to be good as new, I put it into my backpack.

There are slim pickings otherwise tonight though. I'd hoped to find a seal which still had some use, but unfortunately, there's nothing. That means if I want to be able to get on with the job I'm working on, I'll need to take one out of their storeroom. The value is only a couple of dollars, and it's something they'll likely have in bulk.

It's just a minor complication. Picking the lock on the door is child's play and in seconds, I'm pawing through boxes of spare parts, trying to find just what I'm looking for.

"Come on, come on," I mumble to myself, impatiently trying to sort through the jumble inside, the mess confirming they're unlikely to miss anything. While I'd like to be out of there as soon as possible, I don't feel unduly under any time pressure. Those lazy bikers won't be back at work until the sun's well over the horizon, but my bed is calling, and I'd prefer to get home. "Where the fuck are you?"

However safe I feel, I remain alert. My brain might accept I've done this a dozen times before and can be confident I won't be exposed, but my hearing and whatever sixth sense makes the hairs on the back of my neck stick up, never stand down. When all my synapses signal a warning, I pause what I'm doing. The soft, but unmissable sound of a gun's safety being eased off features like a pistol shot.

In less than a second, I've assessed the direction the noise came from. Instead of freezing like any other person may have done, I launch myself around, my leg already in motion, to kick the gun out of whoever's holding its hand. My own hand, fisted and ready, goes into his stomach, expecting to put him down.

I've got this. Automatically I've assessed his height and weight, knowing he's got both those advantages, but I've got the skills and the training. He might now be unarmed, but that doesn't mean he doesn't start giving a good account of himself. Impressed, I up it up a notch myself. To be honest, finding someone of a calibre equal to mine has my blood racing. I haven't had a good work out for months, and as we continue to spar, I have to admit I'm enjoying the situation.

He's obviously using every dirty trick in the book, but hey, I've read the same manual. Terrorists don't play by Queensberry rules, and any soldier has to know how to face them.

I got this, I remind myself. I'm a combat veteran trained by my country, when what can he be but an ignorant biker equipped only with street skills? I can hear his harsh breathing while mine is still steady. I start to smile...

It's been months since I last saw action. Maybe I've grown sloppy, or maybe my over-confidence made the deity look unkindly on me. But suddenly, my feet are swept right out from under me. I land hard, on the ground, my assailant throwing himself over my chest, pinning me down. Winded, I notice how much heavier he is than I am, but I'm already calculating how to get free when I see his fist coming for me.

There's no time to evade it. I suck in air and prepare.

But the punch doesn't land. At the last moment, he pulls back and sweeps the hood off my head, protesting loudly, "You're a fuckin' bitch."

Is that an assessment of my character? If so, it's unfair. He doesn't know me and hasn't enough for an informed view. If it's a comment on my gender, then hey, that's fair. I hope for the latter. While I'm never one to make anything of the lack of a dick, in some circumstances, it plays to my advantage as I note he seems unwilling to hit a female.

Instead of head butting his nose, which would have been my next go-to move—why continue to fight when I could take advantage of his weakness?—I emphasise my feminine voice, raising it an octave. "Get off me," I plead, contenting myself with a few weak struggles.

He might stop at violence, but he's not going to go easy on me. "Give it up. I caught you stealing from us."

He's correct. He has. I can't give him any argument as he's in the right, but that doesn't mean I'm back to plan A. Although he's secured my hands in one of his meaty fists, I brace and position myself. Unfortunately, he reads the signs and my head meets only air as he hastily rears away. My refusal to give in obviously excites him. As a smirk comes to his face, I feel something harden beneath me.

"Yeah, just keep that up." He grinds his pelvis into me and his grin widens.

It's then I feel the telltale signs that my body's going to betray me. Spots start swirling in front of my eyes as my mind shoots back to a different place and time.

I've learned not to fight. It's what they like. Fighting just means more pain and violation and never gets me free. There are too many of them, and I'm too weak. I haven't had a proper meal or more than a sip of filthy water for weeks.

I can't hear any screams coming from the other tents. Maybe their torture has stopped, or maybe they are all dead.

All I can do is lie here and take whatever they want to dish out...

"I'll let you up, but you run? I'll catch you and make you regret it."

His gruff *American* voice pulls me back out of my nightmare before it swallows me whole, momentarily anchoring me to the present. Fighting to breathe, I take a moment to come back to my senses. I'm incapable of doing anything more than giving a nod.

Memories swirling around my traitorous brain have more power to overwhelm me than anything else. As always, my brief mental foray into the past leaves me physically weakened. Remembering when I didn't have the capability or strength to protect myself from the worst knocks my confidence now. Almost cowed, when free, it takes time to stand. To try to disguise how much I'm shaking, I brush myself off, noticing bruises the recent fight must have left. But they're not serious, paling into insignificance as though inflicted by an amateur.

When I feel my heart rate has slowed a little, I raise my eyes and take in my captor. His head is bald with a rounded face and tidy beard. His eyes are the brightest blue I've ever seen, and the crease lines around them suggest he's nearing middle age. He's tall, more than half a foot taller than me, which has to put him at six foot six.

He's examining me too. His brow is creased and his eyes wide open with a look of confusion, as though he can't understand why I've gone from whirling dervish to an approximation of a typical weak female. I can't explain that all my energy has been zapped and I'm hanging on to consciousness by a thread. For now, I'm just relieved I'm still standing.

His lips eventually part and I wait for him to press his accusation of theft, when instead, he poses a different question. "How the fuck did you learn to fight like that?"

In the Army. Well, the service had honed the abilities I'd already had to gain to survive. "The better question would be who forced me to learn."

His eyes narrow and a hardness seems to surround them, making me wonder if he's one of those protector types. "Who?" His shrug belies my thinking, suggesting he really doesn't really give a damn.

Keeping my brain focused on putting together words might help me stave off one of the episodes I know is approaching. It's the only reason I answer him. After a heavy sigh, I disclose, "Maybe it was the foster dad who thought he had a right to put his hands down a ten-year-old's panties. Maybe it was the boyfriend who thought he could sell his teenage girlfriend to his buddies. Or maybe it was the cop who thought he'd exchange the fictional speeding ticket I supposedly earned for a sexual favour."

His expression doesn't even flicker. "Am I supposed to be impressed? Or devastated on your behalf?" He takes a step toward me. "Maybe your sob story would have more effect if I hadn't just caught you stealing red-handed."

I reclaim the distance he'd just closed by taking a step back, and the way the light falls brings his face into sharp relief.

I've faced down enemies in foreign lands, have been captured and tortured close to the point of death. But never have I seen an expression so cold, nor has a scowl sent such shivers down my spine.

He's a danger to me, like nobody else.

Which is crazy. I've gone head-to-head with worse than him.

Who the fuck is he?

I feel pins and needles in my fingers and try to curl them into my hands. Consciously, I make an effort to steady my breathing. Once again, spots start to flicker in front of my eyes.

I'm utterly helpless. There's nothing I can do to prevent it, even if this is one of those rare times when I actually have some warning. I know the inevitable is coming and here, in front of me, stands a man who makes my inner essence scream I shouldn't show any weakness. I use my few remaining lucid moments to stammer out, "Who are you?"

And to process his response as he replies nonchalantly. "Me? I'm your worst fuckin' nightmare."

My traitorous body and mind give out.

CHAPTER TWO

CHAZ

I've never had such a contradictory reaction to a woman before. Not one that's affected my body with diametrically opposed responses. My cock's rock hard, but my fists want to pound her into a pulp. To say I don't understand the effect she's having on me is an understatement.

I hate her for breaking into our premises and making a mockery of what we stand for, and instead of being chastised, how she reacted by fighting as if she was the one wronged. The primordial part of my brain thinks she's the most alluring woman I've ever met, and her willingness to take me on—and let's be honest, it was touch and go for a second as to who'd come out best.

I despise her. *I want to fuck her.*

I stand open-mouthed in shock as she starts to fold right in front of my eyes. Luckily, my instinct takes over, enabling me to catch her before she hits the ground. My cock leaps at the warmth of the woman in my arms, but ignoring him, I ease her way. Annoyed at the tenderness in my action, I step back, dispassionately leaving her lying on the ground.

"What the fuck did you do to her?" Hearing his gruff voice, I swing around as Legend approaches.

Scratching my bald scalp, just as mystified myself, I rapidly run over the past couple of moments in my mind. *Was it my fault?* "Maybe I hit her too hard?" I don't remember getting in a head shot, but for a minute or two, we'd been going at it hammer and tongs, and I really don't know where all my hits landed. I know my jaw hurts from one of hers though. Woman can really throw a punch.

Legend sinks to his knees and shines a flashlight into her face. Suddenly, he puts his fingers to her neck, and then gives a relieved sigh. "For a moment, I thought she was dead."

Perplexed, I crouch down at his side and I can see why. She's unmoving, but her eyes are open. Waving my hand in front of them, she doesn't move, blink or react. It's one of the most unnerving sights I've ever seen.

"She's catatonic," Legend announces after a pause.

"Official diagnosis?" I scoff. First, I feel pleased she's still got a pulse, then I'm annoyed at myself for the concern. Letting my harder side take over, I unsympathetically give a rough shake to her shoulder. "Come on, wake up." But her body's stiff and she doesn't respond. *Had I knocked her out?* She didn't seem fragile while we were fighting. I'd actually had a grudging admiration for her, thinking us well matched before I discovered her gender. If I hadn't seen that, I wouldn't have held back.

Legend reaches for her wrist. The immediate instinct to growl at him for touching her is like a blow to my chest and so out of character. I bite my tongue to keep a vicious comment back. The feeling only worsens as he gently strokes her forehead, making my hands clench. *What the fuck is happening to me?*

Oblivious to my struggles, he frowns. "I don't like this. Perhaps we should get her to a doctor?"

What? And have *another* man touch her? "No fuckin' way," I snarl, then think quickly to come up with a rationale for my comment. It arrives fast. "She's been fuckin' stealing from us," I remind him and myself, biting back the words I want to utter to stop him from touching her. *She's a thief.* "If she was a fuckin' man, we'd be burying him." And with no second thoughts.

A niggling doubt in my head suggests we maybe shouldn't change our modus operandi because of her gender. Some kind of premonition causing a cold chill and hairs rising at the back of my neck warns she could be a danger. But who for? Me personally, or to the club? She's making me act out of character and I've no fuckin' idea why.

"Can't kill her. She's a bitch." Legend waves at her chest, which indeed shows tits. Not much to mention, but definitely female. Again, I want to punch him for noticing. He leans forward and tries to put his arms around her.

"What the fuck are you doing?" I bark.

"She can't stay out here. I was going to take her into the shop. Put her on the couch in the breakroom to make her more comfortable, at least."

Again, that sixth sense warns me, we, or perhaps just I, would be better off having nothing more to do with her. "She's no innocent," I remind him again. "Serve her right to lie here 'til morning."

"Prez?" Legend stares at the set expression on my face. I'm not quite sure what he reads there, but it's enough for him to, *thank fuck,* take his hands off her and stand. "Sorry, Prez. You're right. She broke in." His eyes narrow as if he's just remembered. "And she fucked with our alarms. She might be a bitch, but she's been fuckin' with us. If she dies, then she's brought it on herself."

Still on my haunches beside her, I turn her over—more gently than I'd have done with a man—and start to search, trying to ignore the softness of her skin, and the tantalising sight of her curves. Even the scent coming off her makes me want to take deeper breaths.

Forcing myself to think of her as an unwelcome intruder, I take the backpack off her, open it, and find a tablet, which I pull out and offer into Legend's willing hand. Another quick examination shows other than that, she's carrying nothing of interest and appears to be unarmed. I draw my hands back after my search, rubbing them, as if her touch burned. As I stand, I shake myself like a dog coming in out of the rain, trying to get rid of the strange thoughts and feelings assailing me. *What is it about her?* Perhaps I should fuck her to keep my cock satisfied, then let my brothers take their own punishment out on her. *But would one fuck be enough? What the hell?* I touch the back of my hand to my forehead to see whether I'm coming down with a fever.

Another set of heavy footsteps makes me spin around, watching Iron, my sergeant-at-arms, approaching and coming to a halt by my side. He glances down and gently nudges the prone figure with his boot. There's no response.

He whistles softly. "She's a bitch?" I don't bother to give the obvious answer. Shaking his head, Iron continues, "Ledge told me you'd caught our intruder. Came down to give you a hand." He scoffs. "Seems you don't need my assistance." He's still studying the woman on the ground. "You knock her out or kill her?" His tone suggests it's no matter to him one way or the other.

"She just collapsed." I still have no fuckin' idea why. One minute, she was fighting as hard as any other combatant I've ever faced, and the next, all the fight had seemed to go out of her. I hadn't missed the way she'd paled, nor the rivulets of sweat that had appeared on her face. It was like I'd been dealing with someone else. *Maybe she's ill?* I take a step back, suddenly not wanting to catch anything. *Maybe that's the cause of the strangeness I'm feeling?* I could already be infected. If I am, I'll need to keep everyone away. Covid fucking 19 has nothing on this.

Iron raises his chin, seeming uninterested in the comatose woman on the floor. He nods at Legend. "After your heads-up, I've checked out the perimeter. Saw how she got in." Hearing something in his tone, I glance up to see a look of admiration in his eyes.

I widen mine as I stand. With the help of the new Wi-Fi cameras, Legend and I had had a front-row seat to her entry. "We already know that," I tell him.

Iron snorts. "I know. Legend told me she came over the fence, but when I looked, I had no fuckin' idea how she managed it. I tried to climb that pole myself, but failed. There's a rope still tied at the top and we need to get that down. But unlike her," he spares a glance at the woman still lying on the ground, "I'd need a ladder."

Well okay then. She had to have accomplished quite a feat. Iron's a big fucker, but he keeps himself fit. Which means the comatose woman at my feet must be in even better shape, or maybe it's because she's more lithe and lighter.

Legend chuckles. "Perhaps she's a pole dancer."

It's one explanation. But my unsummoned glare suggests my brain doesn't appreciate the idea of him leering at her as though she's a stripper. Again, unable to explain my unwarranted thoughts, I look down at the subject under discussion. A blink from those previously unseeing eyes gets my attention.

I jerk my chin downward so they notice what I'm seeing. "Maybe she'll tell us herself, now she's coming round."

Legend and Iron step closer and regard her with interest, as I try to tamp my possessive feelings down. Instead, I force myself to remember why I should feel no sympathy for the girl on the ground. She's not one of ours and has made herself an enemy by breaching our land. If she was a man, I'd already have the prospects digging a hole. I don't give a damn the value of what she's taken was only spare change. It's the principle. You do not steal from the Soulz and live to tell the tale.

I'd fuck her, though. Inwardly, I breathe a sigh of relief. *That's the explanation for my strange reactions.* I want her retribution all to myself, well, at least at first, until I get tired of her. Performing sexual favours for me, *for us,* would be a good punishment. She'd have to be willing, of course. We're not a bunch of rapists, but I reckon someone like her could be made to see sense. We've always an opening for an attractive club girl, and perhaps she could show off those pole dancing skills that Legend suspects she possesses—after she's given me a few private lap dances, of course.

Or, better still, she could continue to service me exclusively. While I've never wanted a relationship, the idea of having what would basically be a sex slave with no other complications turns me the fuck on. Not having to share with the brothers has attractions. I'm sure we could come to some arrangement. She must be hurting for money to be so desperate as to steal, and hey, I've more than a few miles under my belt. I know my way around a woman. She wouldn't be left disappointed. I'm still a good-looking guy. I keep myself active, work out and never have a problem getting female attention. I admit it could be down to the president patch that I wear, though I'm arrogant enough to suspect I'd do as well without it.

Idly I wonder whether she'd prefer the alternative punishment I'd mete out to a man over what I'm considering. Death rather than dishonour? Well, hell, she'd change her mind after she's experienced being in my bed. Yeah, I might not be the most humble man.

Seeing she's definitely coming around, I force myself to suppress the instinct to reach down and lend her a hand. Taking their cue from me, Iron and Legend stand at my side, watching as she struggles into a sitting position, her hands clasped to her head as though it's aching, making me feel a small pang of guilt in case it was indeed too hard a blow that had knocked her out. I swallow that thought down. She's no invited guest, and no one could blame me for any damage done.

I stand with arms folded. Iron's next to me in an identical posture, his expression equally impassive. Legend's looking on with undisguised interest as her hands slide down her cheeks and at last her eyes start on our boots, follow our legs, and then land on our faces.

She looks at Legend first, next Iron, then focuses on me.

Her voice doesn't have much strength in it when she says, "I'm sorry."

"Sorry for what?" I growl. "Stealing from us?"

Pressing one hand to the ground, she pushes herself up, first to a kneeling position, then getting one foot under her, then the other, until finally she's standing up. I notice she sways slightly.

It's only then she gives a reply. "For passing out on you." Spots of red appear on her pale face as though she's embarrassed.

Again, I notice she's no longer the feisty female who had almost taken me down. In a moment of weakness, I ask, "You need a doctor?" Immediately after the words leave my mouth,

I'm concerned as to whether or not she'll answer in the affirmative. From the side glances Legend and Iron are giving me, Iron's wondering if I've lost my mind, while Ledge's narrowed eyes try to remind me he suggested that in the first place.

She's a fucking thief, not a princess. If she dies, it's her fault for coming into our yard. If I could take back the words, I would. Luckily, I have no need to.

She shakes her head and lies. "I'm fine." Her voice is weak. She doesn't look *fine*. She's pale, drawn, and appears worn out.

So be it. If she says she's okay, then who am I to argue? No reason to hold back. Ignoring her discomfort, I bark loud enough to make her wince. "Who are you? What's your name?"

She raises her chin defiantly.

My hackles rise. "Why were you stealing from us?" In truth, if a pretty thing like her approached us, asked us for some spare parts, we might have let her have them. Their value was next to nothing, but that's not the point. She hadn't asked. Our reputation won't allow us to let her get away with that.

Despite the foreboding expression on my face and the hardness I know she can see in my eyes, she stays dumb.

"Talk to me," I roar, approaching with my most menacing scowl. It has no effect on her. She doesn't even flinch.

Her face is completely blank, as if she's not heard me at all. Her eyes are fixated on a point beyond my head. It's clear she's determined not to give me anything.

I'm not the only one who can see a closed book. Iron pulls me aside, leaning to speak into my ear. "What are we going to do, Prez?"

Turning my back on the woman, hoping out of sight will get some sense into my head, I allow myself a moment to think. I yawn, realising it's late. If it wasn't for her antics, then I could be in bed and balls deep in a sweet butt by now.

Suddenly rectifying that seems the best idea I've had. Fucking someone else will get her out of my mind.

Speaking as quietly as he had, I reply, "Let's keep her as our *guest* here for the night. Figure out what to do with her in the morning."

Iron grins widely. "I'm sure we can make her 'comfortable'." He puts the last word in air quotes.

He's been my sergeant-at-arms for years, so I'm not surprised he can read my mind. Turning, I take in the pathetic sight of the woman who was fearless only a short time ago. Now it looks like all the stuffing has been knocked out of her. The refrain echoes in my mind, *if she was a man, I'd have no qualms taking her down.* After all my years of being a battle-hardened MC prez, I'm still surprised that there's an innate part of me that feels females should be treated differently. Maybe it's a timeless thing, going back to men being brought up by their moms, or is the "women and children first mentality" so ingrained? I suppose the human race would have died out if there wasn't that protective instinct.

I feel angry that her very presence seems to have me twisted in knots. I persuade myself it's because her gender makes me feel emasculated, as I can't take the revenge on the person who's wronged us in the way that I want. Some perverse instinct pushes me to punish her for being so attractive, and for somehow making me care.

I'm the prez. Woman or not, I can't let any weakness show. Returning to her, I roughly take hold of her arm and start dragging her toward the shop.

She tries to pull back, stumbling as I sweep her along without letting myself feel any remorse. "Wh-where are you taking me?"

I don't answer. Iron smirks, Legend looks perplexed, but neither say a word as I lead our captive inside the workshop. As we enter, some of her strength returns and she starts struggling, but it's not one-on-one now. Without being asked, Iron takes her other arm, pinning her between us.

Our work area is full of bikes and a couple of cars in the middle of being serviced or repaired, but one of the inspection pits is free. With no gentleness at all, I pick her up and throw her down, then follow with a lithe jump.

Iron tosses me a zip tie, and I fasten her wrists to a metal support.

"What are you doing?" she snarls, jerking her restraint and testing it. She's breathing heavily as if the exertion is too much for her. Again, I worry whether she might indeed have a serious brain injury, but stamp down any sympathy fast.

Impassively, I stare back. "You've taken enough of my time tonight. I'm off to get some shut-eye. Perhaps in the morning, you'll find your tongue and tell me what I want. You're not getting out of here until I find out who you are and why you thought you could fuck with the Soulz." I raise my eyebrow, waiting for a response.

Any other female would beg not to be left in such uncomfortable surroundings all night. Any other woman would plead to be set free, or at least start telling me what I want to know. But not her. Despite not having my curiosity satisfied, I feel more than a grudging admiration. *Who the fuck is she? And what brought her into my life?* For a moment, I wonder if for the sake of my sanity it might be easier to cut her loose and let her disappear into the night. But that wouldn't be me acting in character.

I climb out of the pit.

"You can't just leave her here," Legend hisses. "What if she's got a concussion?"

I'm more afraid she's got something far more contagious, as right now I'm having difficultly dragging myself away. That makes it imperative I leave and continue with my other plan for my night.

My confusion makes me snap out a suggestion that I immediately regret. “If you’re so fuckin’ concerned, you stay here with her.” *Fuck no, he can’t.*

Luckily, Legend wants his creature comforts as much as I do. Pressing his lips together, he dismisses my suggestion, then lowers onto his haunches and looks down into the pit. “If you don’t want to stay here alone, in the dark, with the rats, darlin’, then I suggest you start talking. Give us a name. Anything.”

But the woman doesn’t make any motion to show she’s even heard him, let alone being scared into giving any response. Whether she’s making a point, whether she’s injured, or whether the convulsion or whatever it was has worn her out, it’s impossible to tell, but her eyes are closed and she’s leaning against the brickwork as if she’s made herself comfortable.

For fuck’s sake.

Jerking my head toward the door, Iron and Legend take the hint and walk out. I follow, flicking off the lights.

It’s a short ride back to the clubhouse. I try to use the quiet of the night, the roar of the engine and the rush of the ground under my wheels to try and balance my thoughts. Every few yards that I drive away, I feel a pull to go back to her. It’s not just that I have to assuage my guilt about leaving the unknown woman possibly injured and hurting all alone, it’s *her,* and the crazy idea I’m losing something important by riding away.

Fucking loco. My hand twitches on the throttle making my bike jump. Quickly I ease off so as not to alert my companions riding behind that anything’s amiss. Why should it be? We’ve caught our thief and she won’t be getting away. She’ll still be waiting for me in the morning.

Alive or dead.

The thought it could be the latter almost makes me slam on the brakes. I try to shake some sense back into myself. *She's a thief.* If she dies, so be it. It means I won't need to dole out the Soulz retribution.

If she dies, I'll have lost my chance with her.

Chance? What fucking chance do I want? My dick's only hard as it wants some action, and it's not fussy who's the provider. I just need to get laid, that's all, then I'll get that woman off my mind. She's got no tits and I'm a man who definitely likes curves. *Her ass is okay.* Fuck. *Do I need to slap myself around the head to get her out of it?*

It's not far to ride. Moments later, I lead my small pack through the gates and head for my parking slot, kick down the stand and turn off my engine. Leaving Legend and Iron to do whatever the fuck they want to, I make straight for the clubroom and once inside, glance around.

Although, even by biker standards, it's late, there are still people about. And thank fuck there's the curvaceous CeCe who, on seeing me, eagerly stands as if she's been waiting just for me. Futilely, she tries to pull down her too-short skirt, while conversely licking her lips in obvious invitation.

Now that's more like the way my night should be going. Not wanting to lose out to my brothers following in behind me, I waste no time crooking my finger to beckon her over, while simultaneously, with my other hand, indicating to the prospect behind the bar to pass me a bottle of Jack. Both my requests complied with, I take girl and drink and head for my suite.

I'm the president, and while I might live at the clubhouse, I don't slum it. Over the years we've been doing up the place and I've taken full advantage, spreading my personal realm until I've basically ended up with my own apartment—bedroom, lounge, bath and a small kitchenette.

Only pausing to pour a glass of whisky, I watch as CeCe knows exactly which direction to head. By the time I reach the room I sleep in, she's already naked and lying on my bed.

"Touch yourself," I tell her, giving an appreciative grin and bringing the glass to my lips. "Get yourself off."

Again licking her plump lips, she offers a seductive smile then starts fingering her clit, her digits already slick from her arousal. I let the amber liquid run down my throat, both quenching my thirst and bringing a welcoming warmth. As CeCe's skin begins to flush, my cock starts to lengthen. My eyes fixed on her body, I watch as she expertly plays with herself, thrusting her fingers inside her, then bringing them out, making sure that I can't miss how they're glistening. She licks her digits then returns to pleasuring herself. I harden more and start unzipping my pants as her body starts to thrash and unabashed moans come from her mouth.

As she screams, I'm already sliding on a condom. As her body pulsates and she draws in deep breaths, I launch forward to the bed. Pulling her up, I turn her onto her stomach then yank her hips into the position I want. With no warning, I thrust inside her.

"Yes, Chaz. Yes." Her voice is breathy, full of pleasure.

What I've done comes as no surprise. She knows me and the way that I like my sexual encounters—impersonal, both partners finding enjoyment, but basically just a physical endeavour with a mutual desire to get off. Knowing what to expect, she clasps the headboard and braces herself as I start hammering in.

I like rough sex and make no apology for it. The women I go with all know what to expect. Right now, CeCe definitely isn't objecting, proven by the way her cunt starts rippling around my cock.

Knowing she's close means I don't have to put in an effort.

To ensure she's with me, I reach down my hand and pinch her clit in the way that she likes. Then I pause, enjoying the sensations of her coming and squeezing the hell out of my dick. When she starts to relax, it only takes a couple of pumps before I'm filling the latex.

I pull out and go to the bathroom to deal with the condom. After I've flushed and washed my hands, I return to the bedroom unsurprised to find CeCe has already dressed and left.

She knows her place.

Which would be satisfying but for the reason when I came, it wasn't CeCe I imagined beneath me. It was the woman I'd left imprisoned in our shop. And hell if the fact that it wasn't her in reality had left me depleted of cum, but also far from sated.

God fucking damnit.

CHAPTER THREE

HELO

God *fucking damnit!* Why did it have to happen today?

My episodes which caused my medical discharge continue to be the bane of my life. The easy explanation, post-traumatic stress disorder, the harder, what actually goes on in my brain. If there was some trigger to avoid, some way to predict when they'd occur, I could deal with them more easily. Sometimes, like today, I get subtle warnings, other times, I do not. I could be having a normal conversation with somebody and then, lights out. The frequency is erratic as well, adding to the complications of dealing with them.

It's not easy to get over them either. The episodes leave me feeling weak and drained, barely aware of where I am or what I'm doing. I huff to myself. I doubt I'd have been able to answer their questions rationally, even if I was prepared to start talking.

But what kind of people am I dealing with here? They didn't show an ounce of sympathy that I'd collapsed. Sure, they'd offered to call for a medic, but didn't argue when I refused their help. Then, with no regard nor seemingly any care as to whether I'd live or die, the bikers had thrown me in a pit, chained me up and left me alone.

Grinning, I muse medical assistance wouldn't have helped anyway. There's no cure for what ails me. As for my prison, it's not so bad. I've been detained in far worse situations. I even chuckle at the thought of their faces if they only knew, instead of being frightened and alone, I welcome the space to get myself back together. It takes far more than this to make me afraid. I've faced much worse enemies and survived. *Well, kind of,* I correct myself.

Ignoring the bruises from the blows that my worthy opponent had landed, I close my eyes, relax and allow my heart rate to return to its normal pre-episode rhythm, neither too slow nor too fast. From experience, I know that my recovery time is quicker if I don't fight it and give my body time to find its equilibrium again.

But as the aftereffects of my episode fade, I begin to remember the details of what happened before my panic attack. I don't waste time feeling mortified and embarrassed, this is my new normal. Instead, as I become more alert, I start to scan my surroundings, or what I can make out as they've left me in the dark. As my bound hands fumble for anything I can use, I snort at the idea they thought leaving me chained and alone would have any effect on me. They have no idea what I've already been through, and getting out of this is going to be child's play.

It's a mechanics pit. It would be exceptional not to be able to find a piece of wire or something down here, and indeed it's only moments before I find one. Having my wrists zip-tied together is only a slight drawback, as I tackle the padlock on the chain that's fastened me to the hydraulics. It's a matter of moments before I'm free. I stand, shaking my head to rid it of the vestiges of the fogginess that had assailed me, then feel the walls until...

Yes. Steel rungs provide an easy way out of my prison. Relying on balance, I climb without the use of my hands. Once I'm standing in the auto shop itself, I don't even bother laughing. Getting free was so easy, it's not worth congratulating myself. Next step is to find something to undo the zip ties binding my wrists. It's not long before I come across a handy box cutter, and then only a matter of seconds until I'm free.

Shaking my hands out, for a moment I toy with the idea of stealing one of the bikes that are obviously awaiting collection, but firstly, it would be far too dangerous given my condition, and, secondly, I would rather not give the Soulz any more reason to come after my hide.

Frowning, I realise they've taken my backpack which means I've lost the small tablet that doubles as my phone and only means of communication. Luckily, my wallet and keys will still be hidden where I left them outside as I would never make the rookie error of entering somewhere I shouldn't carrying identification. The sides of my mouth change direction as they turn up. I'll be departing here tonight, leaving the MC no clues on how to catch up with me. Which gives me a thought. As they've no idea who I am and no way to find out, I might as well get what I came for, and a bit more besides. It's a damn shame, but now my route has been discovered, I won't be coming back to this place again.

Not wanting to put on a light, and having lost the flashlight I came with, it takes slightly longer than previously to find a few items by touch, and from memory of where they'll be located. No longer having my backpack, I wrap my treasures in a discarded rag. Setting my ill-gotten gains securely under my arm, I then slip through the main door and out into the street, carefully making sure that I avoid the cameras that might detect my escape.

Sparing a smile at the thought of the looks on the bikers' faces when they return the next day to find me missing, I sidle around the side of the lot to retrieve my belongings from their hiding place, then start walking with a spring in my step. One foot in front of the next, rinse and repeat, gradually increasing my speed until I settle into a steady jog.

I've got five miles to go, but that's nothing to someone of my training. In the dead of night when the road is all but deserted, it's enjoyable. As I settle into my stride, my lungs steadily taking in air, my heart pumping in a steady rhythm, I allow myself to take scorn on the bikers for underestimating me. Then I berate myself. I hadn't been prepared to be discovered tonight and had got blasé about being cautious. What I've taken should keep me going for a while, but soon I'll have to find some other way of getting spare parts.

Of course, I shouldn't have been stealing from an MC or anyone in the first place, and the woman I was *before* wouldn't be able to understand the lengths I now must go to in order to keep a roof over my head. I've already discovered I'm not a fan of living on the streets. Yeah, I've been there, done that. And, with my particular issues, it proved to be very unwise. One passing-out episode and I'd lost the few meagre possessions I'd gathered together and was lucky to escape with my life. I don't blame those who stole from me—it's a dog-eat-dog world out there.

Five miles under my belt and I reach the out-of-the-way ramshackle ranch house. I slow my pace and walk on tiptoe as I skirt around the main building to the barn at the back and take the steps up to the loft. If I accidentally wake Harold, well, that would just be the icing on tonight's particular cake. He's cantankerous at the best of times. I don't want to think about how he'd be if I disturbed him.

My accommodation isn't much, an old bed frame, sagging mattress, chest of drawers and a box that doubles as my table. On the plus side, it's dry and I have my own facilities. As I enter the tiny curtained-off bathroom, I stare at myself in the mirror. The reddened skin over my slightly swollen jaw shows me I'll probably have a nice bruise tomorrow, and my half-closed eye will almost certainly be black. But nothing worse than I've had before. What concerns me most is how I'll answer Harold's questioning.

Doing just the necessities before I get into bed, I take a couple of painkillers, then, finally relax. Closing my eyes, I deepen my breathing and hope for a dreamless sleep.

But I should have known that wasn't to be. I wake only a couple of hours later with the sheet twisted around my body and rivulets of sweat running over my skin. My heart is thumping, still in the throes of my dream. It takes more than a moment to convince myself I'm back in the United States, and that the men who tortured me are all dead. For a while, I sit, shivering and shaking, hating myself for being so weak. *They're dead,* I repeat as a mantra.

There's light coming in through the window, signalling dawn is breaking. Knowing I won't be able to go back to sleep, I give up on getting some rest and start my day.

Yawning widely and checking the time, I take a much-needed shower, then dress in my normal uniform of jeans and a tee. Dragging a brush through my short hair, I leave it to dry naturally. As I reverse last night's journey, now descending the rickety stairs, a scent wafting over from the house reveals Harold is awake, and suggests going over there now might be to my advantage.

Hearing my footsteps as I enter the kitchen, the sixty-year-old man turns. What passes for his welcoming smile fades immediately as his eyes land on me and widen. "What the fuck happened to you?"

Shrugging, I walk over to the kitchen counter, pinching a piece of toast as I pass, and getting my hand batted with a spatula on the way.

His eyes now narrow. "If you want some breakfast, you're going to have to pay."

I shake my head. "Board and lodging." I remind him of our agreement, pointing my now half-eaten toast his way. "That was the arrangement."

"Must have been out of my fuckin' mind," he mumbles under his breath. Despite his words, he piles a heap of bacon and eggs on a second plate, and scoots it over the table in my direction.

"You're getting a good bargain. Mmm. This is good." The bacon, as normal, is delicious.

He attacks his own meal, and only when the plate is empty does he question me again, waving a hand at my face. "What were you up to last night?"

"Just out." I raise and lower my shoulders again, unable to admit where I really was. "Someone jumped me."

Obviously having made an assessment and deciding no real damage had been done, he snorts. "I take it they look worse?"

"Oh yeah," I respond, giving the requisite grin. Or, at least, I hope he does. I know I got in a few good licks to the MC prez, but he'd got the better of me when he stopped fighting fair. Not that he knew getting a hard-on while on top of me would trigger my panic attack. If his reaction hadn't sent me spiralling into my past, I would have gotten out of his hold easily.

None of this I say out loud, and after another sharp look,

Harold seems to lose interest in my nocturnal adventures, and turns to his normal topic of conversation. "So how long before you're finished?"

"You want to get rid of me, old man?" This time it's a genuine grin as I crease my eyes and consider my answer. "A few good weeks. And that's if I can source all the parts." Which will be all the more difficult as I won't be able to go back to the bikers' shop to obtain them.

"Weeks?" Harold's eyebrows rise. "Christ, woman, it's going to take you months at the rate you're going. Are you taking advantage of me?"

It was him who'd given me a heap of broken parts and expected me to put them back together. He knows it's a mammoth, nigh on impossible task. So I ignore his grumbling, and finish eating instead. Then I get up to make myself a cup of coffee, refreshing his as well.

Me and Harold coming together was a stroke of serendipity. I desperately needed a place to stay, somewhere off the radar to regroup. He wanted his son's crashed motorcycle restored but hadn't the money to pay for it, and it just so happens I'm an amazing mechanic. But when I was first confronted with little more than a twisted frame and a heap of broken parts, I was dismayed. I wasn't surprised the professionals had quoted him extortionate amounts to put it back together—honestly, the best thing would be to count his losses and purchase a replacement instead.

His story, though, broke my heart, and is what drives me to do the impossible. Turns out Harold's son was knocked off his bike when an eighteen-wheeler lost control a couple of years back. He ended up as damaged as his beloved bike, hanging on to life by a thread. For two years, he's remained in a coma. Harold has nothing but hope to repair his son, so he's intent on repairing his motorcycle, as if that's the charm to bring him back to life. Who am I, or anyone, to be qualified to tell him his thinking is ridiculous?

Harold feeds me and houses me in exchange for my work, and however much he gripes at me, I think he's glad of the company. On my part, I've become fond of the prickly older man, and enjoy our sniping repartee.

His son's medical bills have wiped him out, so he's got no spare cash for parts. He thinks I source them out of my own funds, but as I've no access to money, I have to get creative. It's not just that it suits me to continue living at this sanctuary that keeps me safe, although I doubt my mission has much chance of success, I respect Harold, and fully intend to do my utmost best to get this bike up and running. And maybe, like him, I, too, am invested in the hope that its restoration does have magical properties.

Harold's staring at me, his brows drawn down in a V. "I'm seriously worried you're never going to leave."

I grunt. "In your dreams, old man. Why would anyone want to stay with a grumpy grandpa like you?"

He bangs his fist on the table. "Less of the fuckin' old. And I've not got enough years to be your fuckin' grandpa." His eyes shutter, then open suspiciously. "Have I?"

Laughing, I wave him off. "Not unless both you and your dad procreated before you were each sixteen."

A grin comes to his face. "Not that I know of." He tries to attempt a lecherous wink but just makes me laugh again. He pulls my empty plate toward him and places it on top of his, then points a finger my way. "I cooked. You clean up." He waits a beat for me to incline my head in agreement, then he gives a rueful shake of his. "Next time I bring me home a woman, I'll settle for one who can cook and keep house."

"Keep your complaints to yourself, old man," I retort.

"Where else would you find a mechanic who'd work on your mess of a bike?"

He stands and offers a parting shot. "I'm off. One of us has got to work."

I smile at his back. Harold, like me, tries to live off the grid. He grows a variety of fruits and vegetables and has a small holding raising his own chickens, pigs and cattle. It's a ranch, but not one that stretches for hundreds of acres. If you can call having the time of his life work, then he toils damn hard. But he loves what he's doing. The fact he keeps himself to himself and doesn't often venture out gives me an additional sense of safety. It's unlikely that anyone will find where I am from him.

Apart from the sorry story of his son, I know he's known loss. While there are no pictures around the house, I found an old tin box in the barn. Having nosed through, I found photos of him with a younger man looking so much like him he had to be his son, and more photos of the son with a woman and a young child. A yellowed newspaper clipping explained the car accident where his wife and daughter had met their demise involving an Arizonian monsoon and an out-of-state and ill-prepared driver.

Harold never mentioned the loss of the rest of his family. And like he hasn't asked me for my back story, I've never queried his. Of anyone, I know the right to keep secrets.

Finished with my chores, I collect my overalls and head down to the barn where the bike is kept. On the way, I find I'm reminiscing about how I met Harold. He'd been in town for supplies he couldn't provide for himself, and I'd had one of my episodes right outside the store.

People can have many reactions when I'm incapacitated. Some walk away in disgust or embarrassment, thinking I'm drunk. Others may try to help but have no idea how. I forget how often an ambulance has been called, only for me to dismiss them when they arrive. Harold was different. He chased away the deviants who'd decided it was a good time to steal my backpack and instinctively knew what to do by staying by my side until I returned to my senses. Then after I answered in the negative when he'd asked if there was someone to call, or someplace he could take me, he'd ushered me into his truck and had given me a ride. We'd come straight back to his ranch.

I instinctively trusted him. Somehow, we both recognised each other's demons. I didn't need to hear his screaming nightmares to know he was a fellow PTSD sufferer, but what trauma he or I hid, we kept to ourselves.

I never had family, but if I had anything to compare him with, I'd say he's acted the role of a grandfather. A lonely man, I think he was pleased when he found an excuse to keep me around, despite how much he protests to the contrary.

We both know here isn't where I'll spend the rest of my life, but I'm so thankful and grateful to him for now. It's why I'm doing the best I can on the almost impossible task of restoring his son's bike to factory condition, and doing it as cheaply as possible.

Of course, pilfering what I can is not only exercising my warped sense of helping out, but also keeping my skills intact.

My conscience? Well, you can't really steal from criminals, can you?

CHAPTER FOUR
CHAZ

As I wake, I'm aware I'm sporting an uncomfortably rock-hard cock. It's more than just the morning wood that assails most men. It's the vestiges of the dream I'd just had and lingering memory of the woman I met last night, well, more accurately, of her ass that I'd imagined I was hammering into. When I recall her mouth came into play in some parts, my hand reaches down and squeezes the base of my throbbing cock.

Damn it. I'm a man in my forties not a schoolboy who can't control himself. Trying to get my unruly appendage to calm down before I make a mess of my sheets, I force myself to pull my focus away from her physical attributes and instead on the fact that the woman in question is now a captive of ours. Or dead.

Nah. Something tells me whatever happened to her wasn't fatal. Of course, that could be wishful thinking as she's got certain attributes it would be a waste not to explore. No, she'll be awake and... I grin, picturing how spitting mad she'll be when we visit her this morning. Then I frown. We'd been well matched in that fight until I came down on top of her. I'd been prepared to be sent ass over tit as she got out of my hold, but instead, she'd frozen.

Why? She'd been giving me a good run for my money before she'd suddenly stopped. At the time, I'd taken it for the gift that it was rather than putting much effort into wondering why. But now, in my bed, I go back over what had occurred.

She'd frozen, paled, gone shaky. She'd tried to recover herself, but then she'd fainted. Or gone comatose.

I must have just hit her too hard. For all her skills, she's a woman, and they're not called the weaker sex for nothing. For a second I feel guilty, then remember she was stealing from us. If she hadn't wanted to get punched, then she shouldn't have been fighting. Briefly I wonder whether Legend was right, and we should have gotten her medical treatment. I consider again what if we return to find a dead body, then decide that would at least remove a complication from my life. Not only wouldn't I have to deal with her, but I wouldn't have to work out why just one sight of the woman made me dream about her last night.

I can't recall hitting her hard enough to cause a concussion, unless her skull's like an eggshell. No, what I remember is her expertly blocking punch after punch, forcing me to change my approach and come up with some decidedly ungentlemanly blows. I'd enjoyed the competition until... Again, my eyes narrow as I think back. What had caused her to go still after I'd taken the advantage and gotten her on the ground? Had something about me being on top triggered her? My cock had definitely gotten hard. Rethinking the event is not helping me now as I try to ignore that unruly appendage.

The answer hits me like the ice cold contents of a bucket of water, and the woman herself had given it to me. I'd recalled the conversation I'd all but forgotten. *She's been abused all her life.. She'd admitted a past that forced her to learn to defend herself.*

Fuck, Any idea of her making reparation for her theft by way of her body may have to be put aside. I'm no rapist. I'd rather kill the bitch than force myself on her.

Shit. That only confirms that maybe I'm on the right track. But I'll never know until she tells me the answer.

I start to plan what I'll do when I next see her. Will I immediately let her out of her prison? Nah, where's the fun in that? I'll torture her with the thought she'll never get out unless she confides exactly who she is and what she wants, and what the fuck is wrong with her. She had the audacity to steal from the club, and no one fucks with the Wretched Soulz and gets away with it. She's got some punishment coming and I've just got to work out what. And it will be me that doles it out. The thought of one of my brothers laying their hands on her makes me see red.

What the fuck is wrong with me?

Throwing off the sheet, I make my way to my shower, rubbing one out as soon as the water flows hot, hoping now my cock's been relieved I can start thinking rationally. But any easing it provides me with is only fleeting. Just the thought of seeing her, of questioning her, of possibly getting my hands on her, if only to shake some sense into her has me ready to go again within moments.

At last I admit I haven't looked forward to something as much as seeing her again in years. My heart rate speeds up, my muscles are quivering, and I'm almost as excited as the first time I put on my cut. Of course, I could be ill and on the verge of a heart attack, which would be a far more reasonable explanation other than a random bitch having gotten me riled.

Ignoring the urge to relieve my cock for a second time, I switch off the shower, dry myself, and complete the rest of my morning rituals on autopilot, my mind totally focused on *her*. I'm still barefooted and just zipping my jeans when a knock comes on my door.

Opening it, I find Mac who's been a member for the past couple of years. After a year of prospecting and answering to the name Shitface, we relented and agreed on a cut down of his surname for his final road name. Though we now do have another Shitface as a prospect, it was too good a name to give up.

"Whatchawant?" I mumble, fastening the button to close my fly.

"Bull called me. Tried to call you—"

Turning, I roll my eyes. My phone is on the nightstand, obviously uncharged. "What he want?"

"He went to check on the bitch you caught yesterday, but found she was gone."

Gone? "What do you mean she's fuckin' gone?" I roar, my hands reaching for him and grabbing the sides of his cut. Thoughts of how I was going to get payment from her now pushed out of my head.

"Whoa. I'm just the messenger." Mac holds up his hands and blanches.

Knowing I'm taking my anger out on the wrong person, I let him loose. "Fuck it!" I brush my hands over my bald skull. "Get out of here, Mac."

I'm so enraged, I'm likely to do him serious damage if he doesn't get out of my sight. I slam the door as he goes, and plant my fist against the wall. In my head, I'm envisioning how I left her secured. *What did I do wrong? How the fuck did she escape?* She didn't have a phone so couldn't have called someone to get her out of there. How could one slight woman get out of both zip ties and chains? One thing's for certain, I've underestimated her. My rage is tempered slightly with admiration as my anger turns inward.

I'd been too cocky thinking I had the upper hand, and despite her fighting skills saw only the weak female who'd ended up comatose on the ground. If I hadn't been swayed by her tits, or lack of them, and ass, maybe I'd have considered securing her better.

Well, one thing's for sure. That will be the last we'll see of her. She's not likely to come thieving again. Pinching my nose and trying to take deep breaths, I try to convince myself that it's a good thing. We'll tighten security, make sure neither she nor anyone else could ever again steal from us, and chalk it up to an experience best left as fodder to fuel my cock in the depths of the night. Yeah, it's a good thing. Now I don't have to worry about punishing her, and being gone, maybe I'll be able to forget the strange reaction I had to her.

But as I pull on my t-shirt, I wonder why I've got this feeling of having missed out, of lost opportunities, and that perhaps I'd have liked to know more about her, and most of all, how she felt to sink my cock into her.

I shake my head, knowing there are questions I'd have preferred answered. Like why, when she successfully got onto our premises undetected, why she didn't try to take more expensive stuff? She could really have fucked us up if she wanted. She hadn't even touched the petty cash left overnight. *Or not yet.* I make a mental note to get Bull to check. Knowing she'd paid her last visit to our premises, who knows what she'd taken with her when she escaped?

And what, exactly, had caused her to pass out? If it was my very male reaction to her, there's a part of me that's frustrated I've lost my chance to track down all the men who'd ever hurt her.

What the fuck?

I place the back of my hand against my forehead. Nope. No fever. Nothing to explain my unusual interest in someone who, if they'd been of the opposite sex, would probably already be dead, or at least regretting the day their mother gave birth to them. As for going after anyone who'd laid their hands on her, I very much doubt there'd be anything left for me to clean up if she'd gotten there first. Damn, that woman can fight. *And there goes all my blood draining south.*

Putting my phone on charge, I take a burner out of the drawer. I hit the keys and dial a number. As soon as it's picked up, I snarl, "Did she steal anything else?"

Recognising my voice even without caller display, Bull responds, "Yeah. Just petty stuff like before."

"Cash?"

"Nah. Money's not been touched."

That's something at least. "Got any suggestions how we can find her?" Bull might have something I haven't thought of. While I'm in charge, I'm not one of those men who think I've got all the answers.

"Legend's digging into what he can, but we're not hopeful we can track her. Might have to mark this one up as a loss, Prez."

"You coming back?" I'd debated going to the shop myself, but if my men can't pick up any clues, I wouldn't know what I could offer. Bull, being my VP, is one of the best.

Bull seems much of the same mind. "Yeah. Not much I can do." He pauses. "Fuckin' shame. I wanted to see the bitch who almost got the better of you."

"I put *her* on the ground," I correct, while thinking I'd perhaps been lucky. But there was no way I was going to admit to that. Not to my VP, or anybody.

I end the call, exit my suite, and head down to the clubroom, making my way to the inner sanctum where Legend holes up. Without knocking, I open the door and step inside.

It's gloomy in here, blinds are pulled, and the main light comes from the bluish glare from his multiple screens. Cigarette smoke fills the air, and as I inadvertently suck it into my lungs, I cough. The sound alerts him to my presence.

"Prez." He stubs out his cigarette. He glances down at his screen, then up again, his eyes narrowed. "She got away."

"I heard." Pulling out a chair, I sit down. "Any clues?"

He rakes his hands through his shaggy hair. "Been doing whatever the fuck I can. Don't like losing her, Prez."

You and me both.

He points to a screen. "Been tapping into whatever CCTV I can find. All I can tell you is that she left on foot. Went around to the back near that telegraph pole where presumably she'd had some kit stashed." He turns the screen around, and I see the woman reappear, and she's sliding something into her pocket. "I've looked everywhere for a bike, car, scooter, any fuckin' mode of transport she might have used, but I've not been able to find anything." He taps at his keyboard for a moment. "It was quiet that night, so I'm searching all the cameras I can find on the roads leading away from the shop. If I see anything, I'll try and track it down. Maybe a process of elimination, but anything will help."

It sounds like a lot of work, but I'm grateful he's doing it. Seems, he too, wants her found. But then, that's Legend. He's like a dog with a bone when he's got a lead to follow, and he keeps gnawing until it's done. Satisfied he's doing all he can, I start to stand.

"Well, I'll be buggered."

I pause half bent. "What you got?"

He turns the monitor around to face me. There, approaching a junction is a hooded figure exactly like our thief.

I watch as he taps and advances the footage. She crosses over, then proceeds down the darkened road leading away from the suburbs.

"She is on foot," he says, unnecessarily.

"Where the fuck is she going?" I ask, probably rhetorically.

But Ledge answers me anyway. "There's nothing down there for miles." He pulls up a map. "She's already a mile away from the shop. If she had a vehicle, she'd surely have hidden it closer." He continues studying the map. I watch him and see the instant his eyes widen. "The only place down there is a small farm. Harold McPherson's place. After that, there's nothing but scrub and desert for fuckin' miles."

My eyes meet his. As realisation sets in, both of us start grinning broadly. "That's the fucker who wanted us to restore a motorcycle."

It was. He'd approached us sometime back about a restoration project. But after being told how much it would cost, we hadn't seen him again.

"Could be a coincidence." I'm trying not to get my hopes up.

"Worth checking out. Want me to go see McPherson?"

My normal response would be, yeah, and take so and so with you. But I want, *need,* to go myself. Simply because I've nothing else on, I rationalise, and, of course, I want to get justice for the club. I deny that it's because I've any particular interest in catching up with the woman again. *Yeah. Right.*

"I'll come with you," I state. Seeing him widening his eyes, I pull myself straight and head for the door.

He's right on my heels as we enter the clubroom.

"Unck Caz!" a piercing voice shouts.

Knowing what's coming, I sink into a crouch, catching the little tyke before she can crash into me. I tickle her before asking, "What you up to, Maria?"

She giggles then pulls back. "'elping Momma."

"Well, get into the kitchen and help Momma and stop making a nuisance of yourself." Her father, StoryTeller, approaches and admonishes her.

"Unck Caz lubs me."

"Unck Caz," I stop myself, realising I'm copying her, cough, then try again. "Uncle Chaz has places to be, honey."

Sorry, mouths StoryTeller, but his laughing eyes don't show any apology.

"Come on, trouble. Let's go find your Mommy." Pothead, who's got a soft spot for StoryTeller's little daughter, holds out his hand to her.

Seeing StoryTeller gives me an idea. Though he's been grounded to the clubhouse for the last three years, he was previously a nomad, my travelling enforcer. If we find the mystery woman, this time, I won't be underestimating her.

"Up for a ride, StoryTeller?"

"This got anything to do with the excitement last night?" He raises an eyebrow.

It's obviously common knowledge which doesn't surprise me. It's hard to keep any secrets around here. "Yeah. We think we might be able to find the bitch."

He grins. "I'm all up for meeting the broad who got the better of you."

"She didn't get the better of me," I growl, turning my back on him and exiting the clubroom, ignoring the snorts of laughter from the man behind me.

I go to my bike, wait for the others to get to their rides, then start my engine. In less than ten minutes, we arrive at the small ranch house that sits in the midst of a small farm.

Immediately after our engines are switched off, I hear the gentle mooing of cows, the cackle of hens, and the barking of a dog. A grey-haired man pushing a shit-laden wheelbarrow comes around from the side of the barn. As he sees us, his eyes widen comically.

No one expects the Spanish Inquisition. For some reason, the Monty Python words go through my mind, and I chuckle. I expect finding Wretched Soulz on your doorstep is just as chilling. Especially if you're hiding anything.

Leaving his wheelbarrow behind, with short nervous steps, he approaches us. "Uhm. Can I help you, fellas?" His brow creases as though he's searching for a reason for our visit. "Got some fresh eggs if that's what you need."

"Don't need produce, old man." I swing my leg off my bike.

"Not fuckin' old," he murmurs with a frown, but his expression changes to one of unease as he sees StoryTeller and Legend also dismount.

"We're here about the motorcycle you talked to us about."

It takes a moment for the penny to drop. Well, it had been a year or so back he approached us. Now his eyes narrow. "Couldn't afford your prices then, can't now. If you're touting for business, you've come to the wrong place." He makes as if he's going to turn away.

I take a step closer to him. "Not hurting for business, but turns out we could make some space. Come to renegotiate."

Cautious eyes return my stare. "What do you really want?"

Okay, so he's not buying my story which in itself makes me suspicious. I can't imagine Harold's got anybody else to restore that pile of junk, not at a cost he could afford. Unless, either it's no longer a priority, or he's got someone else to do it. And on the cheap. Momentarily, I wonder who the woman was stealing parts for. It wouldn't be Harold himself. He'd said a year back he was no mechanic. *Has she got a man? Is it him who's fixing Harold's bike?* Stamping down the irrational twinge of jealousy, reminiscent of how I felt last night, I clear the red from my eyes, force a friendly smile onto my face, and concentrate on reeling him in.

"As I recall, we didn't actually look at your bike. Just gave you an estimate off the top of our heads. Why not show it to us and we'll see if we can come to a mutually beneficial agreement?" I keep my tone casual.

"Not much to see." He huffs. "I told you it was a mess."

"Nevertheless. As one biker to another, why don't you show us what you got?"

It's impossible for any of us to miss the nervous look he sends toward one of the barns. StoryTeller walks past me and starts to head that way.

"Hey, this is private property." Harold runs after StoryTeller, but he's brushed out of the way. He turns to me, looking like he's about to complain, but withers under my glare.

Likewise ignoring him, Legend and I follow StoryTeller. Harold comes along, snapping at our heels, moaning all the way—shit like how he's too busy and ain't got time for this now. He even tries to block our progress, but my arm pushes him aside.

The barn door is old, misshapen, and takes a hefty pull to finally open with a protesting squeak, sending a hen fluttering up with an indignant squawk. As soon as sunlight hits the interior, one of my objectives can be seen, the Fat Boy. It's not quite the disaster I'd been expecting, and it certainly looks like someone's been doing some work on it. However, there's no sign of whoever that is, or the woman I'm seeking.

Pressing my lips together, I step forward. Last time I'd heard of this bike, it was little more than a frame. Now, while on stands rather than wheels, it has a V-Twin engine attached. While nowhere near done, it's in the process of being lovingly restored. As a professional, I can admire the work.

"You doing this yourself?" I swing around to see Harold's face.

He blinks twice before saying, "Can't afford anyone else to do it."

I note his answer could be taken in more than one way. StoryTeller bends to take a closer look, then catches my eye and grins. When he beckons me over, I look down. There's a rusted part which was one of the ones listed as being missing from our scrap pile.

There's no doubt in my mind that Harold's fixing his bike with parts from our shop. My question is, whoever was undertaking the work, why had they gotten the woman doing his thieving for them? What hold did they have to make her do it?

It's time, I decide, to take off my kid gloves.

Suddenly, I have a hand around his neck and Harold pressed against the wall. "You think you could steal from the Soulz and get away with it?"

"What?" he blusters. "I've stolen nothing in my life."

"StoryTeller," I start without taking my eyes off the man I have restrained. "Take that fuckin' engine apart and remove anything that came from our shop."

"You can't do that!" Harold cries out. "That's weeks of work. And the parts are all mine."

"Liar." Now it's my forearm pressed against his throat, crushing his airway and his face starts to turn red.

"No, no. Not lying," he manages to spit out.

It's then that I hear the sound of a gun being cocked. "Leave him alone. It's not him you want."

CHAPTER FIVE

HELO

There's never been occasion for anyone to accuse me of being a coward. I won't stand by and let someone else be threatened and hurt for something I'm responsible for. As I'm also not suicidal—even though some days I'm not too sure why I bother to get up and continue living—I climbed up into the rafters once I saw the bikers approaching. I've got the advantage and am in charge of the situation. As I steady my hold on the gun, I see the exact moment when their leader, Chaz, if I recall his name correctly, looks up and sees the predicament he's in. His narrowing eyes and slight flush to his cheeks shout out it's a situation he doesn't like.

Hidden by the beams, I'll be hard to hit, while I'm able to pick them off one by one. I demonstrate that now. When Chaz doesn't immediately back away from Harold, I fire a warning shot at his feet, kicking dust up over his shoes. To give him his due, he doesn't flinch, just looks down disdainfully at his now dirty footwear, then he turns his cold eyes up to meet mine, and one eyebrow rises in question.

I got this. Confident, I call out, “Harold. Back away and go to the house.”

But the older man’s lips compress and he gives a vigorous shake of his head. “Not leaving you here with these assholes, girlie.”

Girlie? Under the circumstances, his moniker for me almost makes me snort. But I’m annoyed that he uses this time to show his chivalry.

“Go to the house, Harold,” I repeat.

But he shrugs and just stands there steadily. *Fuck it.* Souls recognise souls, and while I have to force myself to see the benefit in climbing out of bed every morning, I’m fairly certain Harold feels the same way, surviving only by pinning his hopes that I can bring his son’s bike back, and therefore his son out of the coma’s hold. Knowing there’s only a slim chance of success, he probably values his life as little as I do mine.

I give up trying to persuade him, narrowing my focus on the men standing below. I might not have a lot to live for, but if I’m to go out, it will be on my terms. Rock steady, I wait on the alert for any movement toward a weapon or for one to slip out and take a back way to try to find me. *Never underestimate your enemy* is a lesson that’s been ingrained. Rather than considering I’ve some members of a motorcycle gang who are only brave when in numbers and riding their intimidating metal beasts, I treat them exactly as I would a group of highly trained special forces. Though nothing about them at the moment particularly impresses me. They seem at a loss as to what to do.

The other man who’d been there last night taps Chaz on the arm, then speaks into his ear. The man spoken to nods, and while keeping one eye on me, addresses Harold.

“Where’s the other fucker?” As he speaks, I notice the third person, the man I've not before seen, cautiously looking around.

Harold is rightfully confused. "There's no one else here."

"The mechanic," Chaz snaps. "The man restoring the bike?"

At last Harold seems to find some amusement in the situation, and barks a laugh. He points up to where I am. "Oh, that fucker is her."

After taking a moment to digest that information, and having shared a raised eyebrow conversation with his companions, Chaz leaves Harold and walks front and centre, putting himself directly underneath me. His eyes focus on the sturdy wood I'm resting on as though calculating what it might take to bring me down. This barn's not newly built and I'm lying on thick timber, I doubt even a hail of bullets would do much damage to it.

Clearly seeing the same, instead, he resorts to words. Shading his eyes from the beam of evening sunlight that's angling its way in, he moves his head side to side. Unlike Harold, his moves slowly, thoughtfully. "A coward and a thief," he eventually announces scornfully. I've been injured and hurt in too many ways to count, but words have never hurt me. I don't respond, just wait for him to continue. He doesn't disappoint. "Why don't you come down and face us?"

"So you can take me captive again? No thank you. I think I'll stay where I am."

"Captive?" Harold blusters. "What the hell has been going on? Is this anything to do with that black eye you got last night? Did these fuckin' bikers hurt you?" Even from here I can see his fists clench, and realise he's going to get hurt unless I find some way to defuse the situation, or he obeys me and clears out of the way.

I'm opening my mouth but Chaz gets in first, raising his

brow as he turns to face Harold. "She didn't tell you?" His expression and tone suggest there's a wealth of shit that Harold might not know, and now he shoots a glare up at me, as Chaz says casually, "Oh, her crimes are many. She's been stealing from us. Caught her red-handed yesterday, so yeah, we offered our hospitality—"

"Fucking amateurs." I snort. "They couldn't hold me, Harold."

But instead of sharing my amusement, Harold shifts uncomfortably foot to foot, then he grimaces. The old man's not stupid. He's put two and two together fast. "Helo's been getting some parts for me. She was getting them off a scrap heap." His eyes reach up to meet mine accusingly.

"I was," I confirm.

About the same time as Chaz repeats, "Helo?" He smirks widely. "What kind of fuckin' handle is that?"

It's the name I earned though I don't know why I should confirm it, instead directing my next comment to Harold. "They're just pissed I got into their premises." Chaz's face hardening is the affirmation that I'm right on the money. I continue, "See, if they were sensible, instead of coming after me for trespass, they'd ask where their weak points were in their security. I could have taken something of value, or stolen one of the bikes."

The man who wasn't there yesterday, barks a laugh. "She's offering us advice?"

Before Chaz can answer, I call back down, "Don't see why not. My expertise in return for the parts."

"We've got cameras where you entered already," Chaz points out, showing how they were on to me yesterday. "And we've plans to heighten the fence and put more razor wire on top. No one's getting in that way anymore."

"And you think that would stop me?" Already I'm running through the other options I'd explored.

Chaz rubs his neck as if he's getting a crick from looking up. "Come down and talk to us man to," he coughs, "woman. And maybe we'll be interested in any weaknesses you can point out."

Yeah, and I was born yesterday. I know you don't trust men like them, and coming down from my perch would give them the upper hand. Up here, no one can get close to me without getting a bullet in their head.

Chaz rolls his head to relieve his ache. I have to admit, I'm impressed that he seems to be thinking about the situation and not simply screaming and yelling. He already knows I'm not a good little girl who's going to simply do what I'm told. Instead, he eyes Harold with a narrowing of his eyes.

I'm sure he's wondering how much I'm invested in the old man and calculating the odds of being able to take him with them. But I'll shoot anyone who touches him.

Then, the president of the Wretched Soulz surprises me. Instead of making a move on Harold, or issuing more threats against me or him, his lips turn up in an approximation of a smile, and instead demands, "Five hundred dollars and we're quits."

To be honest, while well over the top, what he's asking isn't extortionate if it gets me off the hook. Problem is, I've not got the money. Well, not where it's accessible, that is.

Harold glances upward and frowns as he thinks. His eyes flick between me and Chaz. Finally he exhales a heavy sigh and grumbles, "Keep them here, Helo. I'll go get it."

"No, Harold. Harold?" But as I call out, he's already striding off and his only response is his raised middle finger. I grimace. *Damn it.* That's one more debt I'll need to add to what I owe this grumpy bastard. On my part, if he's really gone to get the money, and there's nothing in me to doubt it—Harold's not the type to come back all weapons blazing—I think he's given in far too easily. Nothing about this suggests Chaz is a man to be trusted. Quits? I don't believe him for one minute. Nothing is ever that simple. It's a trick to get me to come down from my perch. Nah, he won't be satisfied with his money. He'll want his pound of flesh as well.

"Hey, biker boy," I call down. Chaz, who'd been staring thoughtfully at the door through which Harold had exited, again looks up. I don't need to see his hands fisting to know he doesn't like the name I just called. "You going to swear on your fucking Harley that if Harold pays you the money that will be the last of it?" I use a warning tone to let him know I won't be messed with.

His face reddens, that beam of sun emphasising the colour. "I believe we're the wronged fuckin' party here." Again he seems to analyse the situation, examining me on the beam and then the rest of the barn. I can almost see him calculating whether he can get one of his men to sneak up behind me, but then clearly correctly dismisses he can't. I'm the one holding all the cards.

Obviously, there's a chance I'll eventually need to come down if they stay and lay siege to my position, but I'm banking on they've got better things to do with their time. Eventually, with a slight grimace, a shake to his head, then, after he cups his hands to his cheeks, draws them down and away. I watch the tension leave his body and realise he can't be bothered to fight. Then, when we all hear the sound of footsteps, he swings around.

As Harold approaches with a bundle of notes in his hand and his face set in a frown, Chaz makes a gesture to the man who was there last night.

"Legend, make sure it's all there."

Without hesitation, the man relieves a glaring Harold of the money and rapidly swipes through as he counts the bills. Once satisfied, he gives a chin lift toward his prez.

Chaz turns around and points to the door. Legend makes a move in that direction, but the other man holds back, leaning over I see his lips moving at Chaz's ear. Watching carefully, what he says has Chaz stiffening again, and a stunned look appears on his face as if asking him whether he's serious. He listens to him speak in an undertone a little more and while I strain my ears, I can't make out any words. It's enough to make Chaz snort a laugh. As if it's a signal, both men look up.

Chaz calls out, "You want to make that money back? Find another way into our shop and you can have a refund. You hear me, little girl?"

He gives me a moniker meant to taunt me, but it's not going to work. Try as he might, he can't deny once again I've got one over on him. His attempt makes me grin, and it takes a moment longer than necessary to process what he means. Then it's my turn to laugh. "You want me to check your security out?"

One side of the MC president's mouth turns up. "I'm challenging you to find another weak spot."

"Which you can't," Legend, who'd reversed his decision to exit, dismisses the possibility while giving his prez a sideways glance.

Hmm. I can't deny that the challenge excites me, particularly as I'm certain I'd end up winning Harold's money back. But I'm not stupid and sense a trap. They'll be watching out for me and it wouldn't be good for my health to place myself back in their hands. Still... The prospect intrigues me. Perhaps not for a while, but when they least expect it, I could give it a try.

They haven't bothered to wait for my response. Chaz beckons and the other gang members move out. The man whose name I didn't catch is the last to leave with one final look and a shake of his head in my direction. I wait until I hear the sound of three bikes start, then concentrate until the roar of all the engines have faded. For good measure, I pause a minute or two longer to make sure none have come back.

Then, finally, I put my gun into my belt and descend from the rafters to where Harold is standing with an apoplectic expression on his face. He's as angry as I've ever seen him.

Wincing, I apologise as profusely as possible. "I'm so sorry, Harold. I didn't mean to bring trouble to your door. I promise I'll pay you back." Somehow, eventually.

His cheeks puff out. "Fuck it, girl. I'm not concerned about the money. I'm worried that you've got the Wretched Soulz on your back. Why the fuck did you go and do something so stupid?" He kicks at the dirt. "If I had the slightest idea that's where you were getting the parts, I would have stopped you. Have you a fuckin' death wish? You don't mess with that club." He starts to list all the reasons I shouldn't, and the shit they're rumoured to have done. How the area is probably littered with bodies of those who've crossed them. How I've probably never come across their like before.

I wait him out, letting the words flow over me.

No. But while I haven't come across the Soulz previously, I've come across far worse.

What I've been through makes the Soulz look like choirboys. I won't underestimate them though, but I'll have to be smart.

His final point is harder to argue.

"You could have fucking passed out up there, girlie."

CHAPTER SIX

CHAZ

Sitting, perusing the club's latest set of accounts, I glance up when a knock comes on the door. In one smooth action, I close my laptop, sit back and fold my arms, while simultaneously calling out for whoever it is to enter. To be honest, I'm glad of the interruption. While a necessary evil, I find the day-to-day running of the club boring and I'd about reached the point where the numbers were blurring and no longer making sense.

"Ah, StoryTeller," I greet the newcomer, a smile curving my lips. My grin broadens as I see the two bottles that he's holding. "Come on in and take a load off."

Before he sits, he hands one beer over to me. "Am I interrupting?"

"Fuck no." Then when guilt assails me, I am, after all, the prez and signed up for this shit, I add, "Well, yeah, but nothing I can't pick up later."

StoryTeller chuckles softly. He's heard me moan about the mundane work before. He knows doling out a beatdown to some deserving fucker is much more my style. After opening his beer by using leverage against my poor abused desk, he raises a leg and rests his foot against the wood. He leans back, takes a swig, then focuses his eyes on mine. "Sheri's pregnant again."

Again? Hell, can't StoryTeller catch a break? Or, is this what he wants? To be tied down even when there are plenty of woman in the sea? Images of the woman I met a week or so ago flit through my head. It's all too often I find myself thinking about her, having to stop myself getting on my bike and riding back to that farm which appears to be her lair. Then I remind myself that whatever pull I felt toward her was just because I found her lack of fear for the Soulz and her actions intriguing. Sure, I can use my memories of her as fuel for my spank bank, but I've no desire to see her again in person. *Or shouldn't have.* Helo. Where the hell did she get that name? I give myself a mental slap and regard the man in front of me.

For StoryTeller, it had been different. Finding Sheri had grounded the man I'd never thought would come in off the road. He'd been nomad for years until he'd met her. Their first child had been an accident, a result of a coupling under forced circumstances, though Maria, the kid who was born nine months after, was, even in my view, quite delightful. As the only offspring of a club member, she's spoiled rotten and a complete handful. I don't envy her parents. But it's clear StoryTeller adores her.

Having delivered his proclamation, StoryTeller's face is blank as he waits presumably for some kind of response. What is he expecting? Permission to bring another kid onto the compound? My blessing, congratulations? Or is it commiserations he's after? What do I know? I've spent my life doing my best to avoid complications that give you responsibility for eighteen years after.

After more than a couple of beats have gone by, I manage to

find something to say. "And that's… good?" I'd faltered between saying the opposite first.

A snort bursts forth from StoryTeller and he grins wide. "Fuckin' ace," he confirms. "Though I can quite see how you wouldn't understand."

Scratching my jaw, I realise he's right. I don't comprehend. My life revolves around making the best life possible for my brothers. Protecting them takes all my time. A woman would be a distraction. One kid, let alone two, would be impossible. How could you cope when you're pulled so many ways at the same time? As for StoryTeller? He's clearly already handed over his balls to Sheri and their daughter.

A son to follow in his footsteps, I could see some attraction in that. But… "What if it's another girl?" I grin, interested in how he'll cope.

He shrugs and chuckles. "Just have to make sure my double-barrelled shotgun is loaded."

The idea doesn't seem to bother him in the least. But then, he's never fazed, even when Maria twists him around her finger in the clubroom. I've seen him seriously pretending to have a picnic with her while carrying on a conversation about transporting guns with Iron. Being a dad seems to come naturally to him. I suspect he'll be fine with two.

If he has a son, I might even be envious. What man doesn't want someone to continue his line? To pass on what he's built, knowing he'll be leaving a legacy, and that he'll be remembered into the future.

But, for a son, I'd need a woman. I scoff at myself. Best I focus on grooming one of the younger members when it's time to find someone to step into my shoes.

"Congratulations," I find myself saying belatedly.

He accepts with a chin raise, then smirks. "So, what's going on with that woman you've found yourself?"

"I don't know what you're talking about," I snap back. "I've no fuckin' woman." I deny everything even though I know exactly who's he's asking about. As if I haven't just had my head full of her.

"No?" He's unrepentant. "You found a thief but couldn't keep hold of her, then she made you, and the rest of us, look like fools when she got the upper hand in the old dude's barn. She had you by the balls there, Prez."

My knife is out of its sheave and quivering tip down in the wood before the last word is out of his mouth. "Don't push me, ST."

But instead of being cowed, the fucker laughs. "Not often someone gets the better of you, Prez."

Not often? Never more like. Well, not until her. And isn't she full of surprises? A seasoned hand-to-hand combat fighter, an escape artist, a crack shot, and someone who doesn't stand down. She'd be such a challenge to bring to heel. And there it goes. Thinking about how exactly I might tame her gets my cock revving to go. He doesn't seem to give a damn that my mind sees a huge red flashing light over her head, telling me to stay far away. It seems he likes a feisty woman and shows it by chubbing up every time she crosses my mind.

StoryTeller's watching me carefully. I force myself to show no expression on my face and refuse to shift in my seat to ease the predicament thinking about her has again caused.

"Doesn't seem like she's going to take you up on the challenge you issued."

It doesn't. I should be pleased, not disappointed. It's been seven days since we confronted the oddly named Helo at Harold's, and since then, there's been no sight or sound of her, and no evidence she's been around. And we'd know. Weasel's been watching his stock like a Hawk. What the fuck kind of handle is Helo anyway? I've spent far too much time wondering whether it's short for Eloise or something. I've no fucking idea why I'm bothered by it anyway. Even if my dick got its way, babe or good girl would do when I was fucking her.

Shit. There's my boner again. I'm not a kid. I'm a man in my mid-forties and should be able to control myself. That bitch has got trouble stamped all over her forehead. I'm glad I hadn't seen her again even if my dick is not.

My thoughts make my voice gruffer than I want. "Of course she hasn't." As StoryTeller's eyebrows rise, I rush to correct any misassumption. "We scared the fuck out of her. She won't be back."

He doesn't need to know how much part of me had hoped she'd take up the gauntlet I'd thrown down and try to break into the yard again. Oh hell, why don't I just admit it? She intrigues me, and I want to know more about her. I still feel slightly guilty about how she passed out, wondering whether I hit her too hard which is stupid. If she'd been a man, I wouldn't give a fuck. I'd successfully hidden my feelings, but I'd been relieved when we'd seen her the next day that she didn't seem to be suffering any lingering effect. Well, she didn't go comatose and fall from the rafter so I presume she was okay.

StoryTeller grins. "She was something, though, wasn't she?"

I apply my best poker face and hope that he doesn't know how close he is to the mark. I guess where he's concerned, a woman has changed his life, and now he wants the rest of us loved up and locked down. Ain't never going to happen to me. Firmly I repeat in my mind, my only interest in Helo is making sure any loopholes she found in our security have been tightened up. And, perhaps, that I still think her becoming a sweet butt would be better compensation than the five hundred dollars I charged. She could service all the brothers... *Fuck no.*

"Is that all you want?" Losing patience more with myself than with him, he bears the brunt as I snap, "Some of us have got work to do."

He chuckles, shows me his finger, then presses his hands down on the arms of the chair. He's halfway to standing when there's another knock at the door.

"Enter," I call out, not sure whether I appreciate yet another interruption. The answer's certainly no when Legend bursts in and I hear the words that come out of his mouth.

"Got info about that thieving broad." He pauses, then helpfully adds, "Helo." As if there was any other bitch stealing from us.

StoryTeller, *goddamn him,* sits himself back down. His folded arms posture and the smirk on his face tells me he's not moving despite me gifting him one of my fiercest stares. Without appearing to be over-interested, I beckon our information guru to take the second chair in front of my desk. "What you got?" I half want to know, half wish I never had to hear that name again. Oh fuck, I'm kidding myself. I want to learn everything he's found out.

Now he's inside, Legend seems in no hurry to share whatever intelligence has come his way. Instead, he turns to the other man in the room. "How's the family, ST?"

"Fuckin' catch up later," I growl. "Ledge, what do you want? And, ST, why are you still the fuck here?"

StoryTeller just grins and makes no move. I could put on my prez voice and tell him to get lost, but he already suspects I've got a special interest in the bitch, so I decide to let him stay. Only so I can show absolutely no reaction to anything Legend has to say.

Legend clears his throat. "I was interested in the broad who got through our security, so I sent the handcuffs she got out of to Mayhem in LA. I was hoping he'd find some DNA or fingerprints that might identify her."

That's caught my interest. Mayhem's a man with a questionable past which we've only been able to guess at. Rumours abound that he originally worked for the FBI, but no one's had confirmation. Initially there were concerns he'd been planted as a spy, but he's proved his loyalty to the Wretched Soulz over and over. Legend's good once you give him the information to work with, but Mayhem's the man to go to if you've only got the bare bones. Which, in this case, was all that we had. I wave at Legend to continue.

Opening his laptop, Legend wakes it, then turns the screen my way. "Let me introduce you to Queenie 'Helo' May. An Army helicopter pilot, a Night Stalker no less."

Sitting forward, I try to reconcile the service picture in front of me with the image I carry in my head. While the uniformed woman is more put together than the one that I met, there's no doubting they're the same person. StoryTeller, leaning over to see, lets air whistle through his teeth.

Before StoryTeller can make any comment, I ask, "Not serving anymore?"

Legend shakes his head. "Medical discharge." As I open my mouth, he continues fast, "And that's all she wrote. Everything else was redacted."

"Night Stalker?" StoryTeller looks impressed. "There aren't many women pilots, and to join that team you have to be one of the best." As a former SEAL, he'll know what he's talking about.

"What's with all the redacted shit?" I ask.

Legend shrugs. "Mission gone bad? Or a successful one they don't want anyone to know about. Who the fuck knows?"

StoryTeller looks like he's still getting his head around her role. Sweeping his hands through his long hair, he shakes his head. "Whatever it might have or have not said, woman's a fuckin' hero. I've had occasion to thank the fuckin' Night Stalkers before. Their flying skills and nerve are exceptional."

Which explains her bravado. And while I hate to think it, the reason she blacked out could have been why she was discharged.

Legend snorts. "After a career like that, she's probably missing the adrenaline rush. Could explain why she broke into the shop."

There's nothing to disagree with in his statement.

Fuck, pushing boundaries, challenging myself, is probably something I'd do if I had to drastically change the way I live. I'm a biker as I like living on the wild side, putting one finger up to the world, telling it I'm going to make the most of my life, whatever the fuck it wants to throw at me. I'd rather go out early then die with a pipe and slippers at hand, with nothing to reminisce about except for a wasted and boring life.

I don't know how long Helo served, but jeez, Legend's right. What an adrenaline kick it must have been every time she took that helicopter up, flying over enemy lines. I consider my bike to be an extension of myself, knowing its limits and pushing myself and it to them. Is that what Helo felt like when she was flying?

Take my bike away and I'd be half the man that I am, and desperate for other ways of thrill seeking. Is this what Helo feels like?

Fuck it. Now it's not just my cock that's attracted to her. Everything about her intrigues me—her mind, her ability, her bravery, and despite her lack of physical ones, the mental balls she must have.

I've never looked at a woman and felt the need to tame her. Let's face it, most patch chasers will fall at a biker president's feet. But Helo? Hell, someone like her would take a lot of chasing. And for once, it might be worth it.

I'm fucked. If there was a chance to keep her off my mind, I've now lost it.

I'm barely able to restrain myself from leaping on my bike, racing to Harold's, confronting her and doing what I can to make her mine.

And that's the very last thing I can do. I'm the club president. I've far better things to do with my time.

CHAPTER SEVEN

HELO

Harold hasn't spoken to me for a couple of days, but I preferred his silence to all the shouting he'd done after the bikers had left. I couldn't refute that it was all my fault that I'd brought the wrath of the Wretched Soulz down on both our heads. I had no reasonable explanation to give him, not without admitting what a charity case I really was. How could I tell him I'd not even the few dollars needed to pay for second-hand parts? I'd thought I'd found a good alternative option, but apparently outlaw bikers are far better at inventory than I'd expected. Who would have thought?

Now Harold's out by five hundred dollars and I've no way to repay him. While I'd be willing to try my hand at anything, without any form of transport, it is going to be hard to get a job. I can't access my funds as any use of a bank card would send out a glaring signal to show exactly where I am.

But Chaz had offered a way for me to earn the money back.

Yeah. Stupid I'm not. Test their security? They just want to take me captive again, and I doubt that a second time I'd get away so easily.

Harold's made it clear his view is I should never go back there, and while that's the sensible option, it's the challenge that I can't get out of my head. I'd never be able to live a normal life with a nine-to-five job. I crave excitement and danger. My brain survives on calculating odds and deciding on courses of action.

Do I trust them to give me the money should I find another way onto their premises? Like fuck I don't. They're outlaws.

Harold might not be talking to me, but I often catch him looking my way, unable to hide his suspicion. I'm sure it's to prevent me succumbing to temptation and returning to their lair. I have reassured him that the lack of parts isn't holding up the rebuild. Currently that's true. I'm spending time smoothing dents out of the tank and fender.

Of course both of us expected another visit from the MC, but as the days go by, quickly adding up to a week, there's been no sign of them. Up to now, I've been sleeping with one eye open, but while not completely letting my guard down, I've started to relax. Maybe the extortionate price Harold had paid had satisfied them. What I'd taken in total couldn't have added up to more than fifty, maybe at a push, one hundred dollars.

Of course the guilt that he had to pay anything hangs heavy on me. Harold asks nothing from me other than I restore his son's bike, feeding and housing me for free. It was never my intention to cause him extra expense. Somehow, sometime, I vow to repay him. But as to where or when, well, that's all in the air for now. While it's in my nature to fight, I can't do anything until I've identified my enemy, nor without any tools, and especially not with an affliction that can cause me to lose consciousness at the drop of a hat. For now, all I can do is regroup.

But staying still is boring. I'm a risk taker. I've had to be. There is many a special forces officer who owes his life to my skills in putting my helicopter into places it shouldn't really go, skimming the mountain sides with barely an inch of clearance, making my team draw in a collective breath as though by doing so the rotor span would be narrower. You don't get to fly as a Night Stalker without being prepared to put your life on the line. Every flight behind enemy lines has the chance of ending in disaster. I live for the adrenaline buzz. And while I might no longer be able to fly, I need to find that somewhere else. If not, what have I got left?

That's partly why I don't bemoan the situation that keeps me away from my home and on the road. Keeping my head down and off the grid is a challenge in and of itself, making sure I stay one step ahead—and alive.

Here, working for Harold, sometimes feels too safe, and my desire to pit my wits against the Devil, combined with the sense of injustice that Harold got ripped off, makes my mind toy with the idea of getting back into the MC's yard, and thinking of ways to beat their presumably by now upgraded security.

If I fail and I'm caught, they can preen and congratulate themselves. Whatever they do to me, someone else has already done worse. If I succeed, well, as long as they live up to the bargain they made, Harold won't be out of pocket.

I'm bored. I'm not used to long spells of inactivity, so it's not really surprising how I keep thinking of what I would have done were I the MC and wanted to keep out people like me. Then, I put my mind to wondering what loopholes there might still be.

The Devil may well find work for idle hands, and that might be what's driving me. But the very next night, I'm not surprised to find myself jogging that five-mile stretch of road that leads back to the Wretched Soulz.

When I get close, I get off the road, making my way across the rough ground to the rear. The light from the moon is enough to show me where the new cameras have been set up. Where I got in before has indeed been closed off with higher fencing, more razor wire, and, looking closer, a pressure point sensor to see if anyone gets too close to the pole. These boys are clever and not to be underestimated, but not as smart as myself.

For one thing, checking the angles of the cameras, they've left me an option to explore, which, obviously, I take advantage of. It's actually child's play to get in.

Once inside, I use my previous knowledge to turn off the alarms. This time I'm not going for discreet. It's a case of go big or go home. This time, I've decided to make a lasting impression. A fucking great calling card that tells them Helo was here. I haven't quite decided what yet, but the ideas will come.

Picking locks is nothing new to me, I can do them in my sleep. Within a minute, I'm in the shop itself and choosing my target. Allowing the beam of my flashlight to rest on each of the bikes that are in the process of customisation, I finally settle on one that looks almost finished. It's a glorious Road King which has obviously come in for a custom paint job, and wow, I'll take off my hat to the artist. The work's about as good as any I've ever seen.

This is the one.

Quickly finding the right key hanging up on the board, and after disabling the bike's alarm and lock, I carefully kick up the stand, then wheel it outside into their front parking lot. *Now that's going to make an impression.*

My hands twitch to turn the key in the ignition and take off down the road. The only thing that comes close to flying a helicopter is riding a motorcycle. You're at one with the elements with only your skill keeping you alive. Though I may be impulsive, and a rule breaker at times, I'm not stupid, so that key stays unturned. I do swallow hard at the reminder of what I've had taken away from me. *Once I wouldn't have hesitated to take it out for a ride.*

Concentrating instead on the only other option to bring me pleasure, I anticipate the livid expressions of the bikers when they see I evaded the security they presumably thought was tighter than a gnat's ass. Glancing at the lightening sky and the dawn just breaking over the horizon, I bring my legs under me and settle down for the wait.

My intention was never to steal a bike, just to demonstrate how easy it was to liberate. Like taking candy from a baby. And while I can't ride it away, I don't want anyone else coming along and taking advantage, so I'm going to stay on guard. Propping myself up against a wall, I get comfortable while musing I've spent many a night in far worse places than this, and at least the night air isn't full of the sound of shots or screams.

Of course, that was the wrong thing to think about. *Don't go there.*

Taking deep breaths, I make a conscious effort to keep my mind from revisiting the past, focusing instead on the magnificent view of the sun rising, the rays gradually strengthening and lighting everything in their path. I smell the air, tinged with oil, rubber and gas from the shop behind.

I'm here. I'm in the US. I'm in Arizona.

I breathe in, then breathe out, rinse and repeat. Gradually my demons fade back to where they should stay, in the past. They're helped on their way when my ears pick up the sound of a motorcycle engine, at first faint, then gradually getting louder.

Game on.

My lips curve into a half-smile, and although I remain sitting, I roll my shoulders as I prepare myself.

At first just a speck in the distance, the bike draws nearer and nearer. The Sportster seems to speed up as it approaches the shop then squeals to a halt. Looking like it's only at the last moment the rider remembers to kick the stand down, he throws himself off, a gun appearing in his hand.

"What the fuck?" he asks, at first spying the bike but not myself. He's a prospect, I notice, as his back is turned toward me. I watch as his mouth drops open and his upper lip curls back.

Holding his gun in both hands, he starts to cautiously approach the shop. As he inches toward the open doors, I decide to save him the bother and reveal myself.

"Hey," I call out, deliberately keeping my voice feminine and low.

He jumps as if scalded, and I don't like the way his hands shake as he trains the weapon on me.

"Whoa." I hold up my hands. "I'm unarmed."

He stares at me, then at the bike, then at the door. "Are you alone?"

"Yup." Keeping my hands in the air, I confirm, "It's just me."

He stares through the open door behind me, sensibly too cautious to go and investigate the truth of my words on his own. Then, with his left hand, he liberates a phone from his pocket. He taps a number and raises the device to his ear. "Prez. It's me. That flat-chested broad you've all been speaking about? Well, I think it's her. She's here at the shop. Looks like she's stealing a bike, and I got here in time to stop her."

Bristling, I glance down at my breasts. I'm not very well-endowed but to call me flat chested is just mean. Raising my eyes, I glare his way. "Not fucking stealing. If I had been, you'd never have found me."

"Yeah," he says into his cell. "I'll keep her here."

He'll keep me here? I suppress a snort, knowing I'd have him unarmed in seconds if I'd any intention of getting away.

"Prez is on his way," he growls, then waits as if I'm supposed to quiver in my boots.

"Great." My shoulders rise, then lower and I relax back against the wall. "That's who I wanted to see." I hope he'll make good on his bet. I hate being in debt to Harold. "Can I put my hands down now?"

He gives a cautious nod but growls, "Keep them where I can see them."

Taking that means I can relieve some of the ache, I lower them to my lap, my eyes on his, analysing whether he sees this as a threat. He doesn't. *He should.* If I had been armed, I could have rolled, drawn my weapon, fired and killed him before he could finish blinking his eyes. But he's oblivious to how much danger he's in.

Reckoning we probably have a good few minutes to wait, I decide to defuse the situation before he gets a cramp in that hand holding the gun, or coughs or sneezes. His finger is on the trigger.

"What's your name?"

His cheeks flush. For a moment, I'm not certain he's going to say anything, obviously not wanting to share information with his prisoner. He gives a deep sigh and lets out through gritted teeth, "I'm Shitface the Second." Well, I've got my reason for his hesitation. No, I wouldn't want to admit to that either.

And, the third...? I snort. "What, as in you were named after your dad?" I'm unable to stop the grin that widens my mouth.

"Not after my fuckin' dad," he snarls, then gives the explanation. "Soulz named a prospect Shitface a couple of years ago. Renamed him when he patched in, but the handle kind of stuck, so I'm the one who's inherited it now."

I have no idea how to respond to that, so, I settle for, "Well, Shit. It's nice to meet you." I can't help but smirk. It's no different to the hazing that goes on in the Army, but at least I got a better moniker out of that. "I'm Helo."

"I know who you are," he grunts.

Ah, yes. The woman with no boobs. I suppose there have been worse phrases used to describe me and better ones. *The thief who broke into their premises. The bitch who made fools of their security.*

He takes a breath as though he's going to start questioning me back, but before he can, the dull roar of multiple motorbikes gradually increases in volume. Ignoring both the prospect and his gun, I get to my feet to face them as they arrive. I'm unsurprised to see Chaz at the head of the line. Shielding my eyes against the low early morning sun, I recognise Legend with him, but there are also a few others I've not met before.

Now am I a curiosity, or do they really need so many to take me? The latter thought makes me snort. I manage to compose my features by the time Chaz has kicked down his stand and dismounted his sled.

He takes off his gloves and slips them into his pocket while studying me with narrowed eyes. I meet his stare without flinching, then two of his long strides close the gap between us.

His eyes are cold, his cheeks tinged red with either anger or the wind. His voice is steady, though there's an underlying vibration that belies the effort he's taking to restrain himself.

"So you're thieving again," he states, then sneers. "Presumably you can't help yourself. And escalating, I see." He nods toward the gleaming machine I'm still standing beside. "I suppose I'm fuckin' lucky the prospect decided to get some work done early else I'd be down one customer's bike."

I knew this was how it was going to look, so I need to set him straight. "I liberated it. I wasn't going to steal it."

He snorts loudly, half turning to catch the eye of a man wearing a VP patch, before looking back. "Yeah, and a bear doesn't shit in the woods."

I shrug. "I was sitting right here when your prospect turned up. Believe me, if I'd wanted to take it, I would have." The drawn down V between his eyes suggests he's considering my words. "You asked me to check out your security." Adding a shrug, I continue, "Thought this was a good way to make a point. I could have left it here for you to find in the morning, but instead, I stayed to make sure no one else would take it."

"Can't believe a fuckin' word that comes out of your mouth, bitch," his VP growls.

"Stealing parts is one thing, Prez. But a fuckin' bike?" Another man looks and sounds disgusted. Staring harder, I can see his patch reads SAS *Sergeant-at-Arms.*

"Lucky I came around." Shitface puffs up his chest and preens.

At my glare, he takes a step back. Seeing the angry faces and hearing the murmuring, I know I've got to get on top of this fast. "I did exactly what you challenged me to do. I could have left a note but decided this was a better way to get your attention. Your security needs tightening up, otherwise it won't be me out here babysitting an expensive bike. It will be stolen for real."

Chaz folds his arms. "You got a fuckin' death wish or something? Sure, I challenged you to find a way inside, but not set you up to steal a ride—"

I advance on him. "Now just wait a goddamn fucking

moment." At my approach, he lowers his hands. "If I wanted to filch a bike, then that's what I would have done. And by now, I'd have been in the next county, hell, the next state, and you'd never know where I had gone."

"I don't believe you."

"Well fuck you." I throw the keys to the bike I'm still holding down at his feet. "I suppose you're sticking to that line so you don't need to hold up your side of the bargain and give back the five hundred dollars."

"Tired of this bitch, Prez," his sergeant-at-arms remarks in a lazy tone. "I say we take her back to the clubhouse and teach her some manners. Make sure she doesn't fuck with us again. Or just put a bullet between her eyes now."

Chaz blinks his way, then again his cold eyes find mine. As he cocks an eyebrow, one side of his mouth rises. I suppress a shiver seeing his sergeant-at-arm's suggestion is an option that appears to carry appeal. Looking at the men surrounding me, I know one-on-one I could take them, but I'm not stupid enough to think their numbers couldn't overpower me. And once I'm in their lair, heaven knows what could happen.

My blood runs cold at the thought of what happened the last time I was in a male sanctuary. Clenching my fists, I try to remain in the present, and come to realise that I've got to give them something to get them to believe me.

Like most people, I don't enjoy admitting to a weakness. My muscles contract and my mouth thins. "I couldn't steal your bike. I can't ride it."

The VP snorts. "Oh that's rich. You can't fuckin' ride?"

"Figures a bitch wouldn't be able to." The prospect I'm now starting to have no problem thinking of as his moniker is getting on my nerves.

Gritting my teeth, I expand, "I can't ride a bike, drive a car, or fly—"

It's the VP who barks a laugh. "You ain't got wings or balls so I'm not surprised."

But Chaz waves him down. He's looking intrigued. "Why not?"

"She never fuckin' learned," one of the others whose name I don't know remarks.

Again Chaz turns to hush him, and again that querying eyebrow rises my way.

Annoyed that I have to admit it, I huff. "You saw how I was the other night. I have these... episodes where I pass out. I don't know where or when they're going to hit, so it's far too dangerous for me to be in control of a vehicle."

Completely opposite to any reaction I'd imagined, Chaz's face softens. "So that's why you were medically discharged?"

His query might sound innocent, but its reaction on me is anything but. Forcing my voice to remain casual, I ask, "What do you mean?"

"Come now." He scoffs. "You really think we didn't find out who tried to rob us? You're Queenie 'Helo' May, Night Stalker helicopter pilot."

No. My eyes widen, and I feel the blood rush from my face as I take a step backward. Then I take another.

"Wait," Chaz demands, clearly seeing I'm about to run. "Helo," he snaps, when I just shake my head in response. He moves quickly and is in front of me, his hands landing on my arms.

I could get out of his hold, but I don't even try. There's a buzzing in my ears as my brain begins to work through all the ramifications. Calculating risks, analysing them, and working out my next move.

"You alright? Stay with me."

The words slowly filter into my brain. Gradually refocusing my vision, I see the president of the Wretched Soulz MC looking at me with narrowed eyes, no longer angry, but concerned. Pushing my initial panic away, I realise I need more information, clarification on what his revelation really means for me.

I swallow a couple of times as my throat has gone dry and finally manage to speak. "H-how did you find out my name?"

Facial features relaxing slightly, he answers me, "Thieves who run away leaving fingerprints and DNA should realise they'll be found out."

I'd thought I was dealing with an ignorant motorcycle club, not the freaking FBI. Alarms bells start clanging loudly in my head as my body begins to get flooded with adrenaline.

I might not have expected an MC to be able to find out who I am, but I sure expect whoever's after me has the expertise or contacts to do exactly that. And to have triggers set for any such search.

My days in Arizona are numbered, as well as, quite possibly, my days on this earth.

Chaz is studying me closely, and I'm surrounded by his men. If I make a bolt for it, I can't bank on being able to outrun them. I've got to get them to let me leave.

"Chaz," I say his name, hoping to make a personal appeal. "You don't know what damage you've done. You have to let me leave. I've got to get out of state—"

He's faster than I expected, swiftly adding two and two together. "You're on the run from someone and you think we've given you away," he interrupts, summing it up precisely.

Air leaves me in a heavy sigh as I gently raise and dip my head. He sweeps his hand over his brow, then stands unmoving, staring at me. With nothing else to do, I wait for his decision, hoping he makes the right one. There's no way of knowing how quickly my location will be traced, or whether there's now someone coming to find me. I may only have hours. I can only pray that I've got days. Every minute I'm standing here is allowing my enemies to come closer.

"Where will you go?"

I can't answer, so I shrug. I've no money, no transport, only my legs to rely on. I'll need to detour back to Harold's to pick up my pack containing my meagre belongings, then get the hell out of Dodge. It's not like I haven't done it before.

Pursing his lips, Chaz doesn't remove his eyes from my face.

I'll get no sympathy here.

I rise on my toes, anxious to start heading off into my uncertain future.

CHAPTER EIGHT

CHAZ

From the very moment I arrived, I didn't believe that she intended to steal the bike. If she had, she'd have been long gone, and we'd have had a cat's chance in hell of getting it back. If that had been her objective, Shitface would have been very unlucky to arrive in time to catch her, and if he'd attempted to stop her, I've no doubt I'd have found him in a heap on the ground.

It's not even that I now know she's a Night Stalker. It's my own take on her, my intuition that she could give any man in my club a run for his money when it came to street smarts. But Iron and Bull would have thought I'd lost my mind if I hadn't played along, putting her on the spot, letting her come up with reasons why we should believe her. I had enjoyed the word play with her. Until...

Until, *fuck it, damn it,* until she'd confessed as to why it would have been impossible—or at least, very unwise—for her to have ridden the bike away. The desolation in her eyes stole my breath.

Because it's not fucking hard to understand how devastating that would be. If I couldn't ride my bike, I don't think I'd survive. I live for the open road, the freedom of the wind rushing past. And I'm just a biker. I would think as a fearless, revered Night Stalker, being told they could no longer fly would be crushing. How could I not feel sympathy for her? I have to clench my hands against my sides to stop from reaching out, pulling her close and hugging her, knowing instinctively someone who's survived and excelled in a man's world wouldn't want to admit to weakness, nor need the comfort I itch to provide.

That's when I started to put together that she was running for her life. Who the fuck could be after her? I mean, *who?* I'm having difficulty processing her having to stay under anyone's radar. Unless it's the law. Tapping my finger on my chin, I think for a moment. That has to be the most likely reason for her to be concerned about anyone checking her out. Any number of the alphabet teams could have been alerted.

What's she most worried about? Is it because she doesn't want to be locked up? I'm not quite sure they've yet built a prison to hold her, and apart from the petty theft enacted on us, I can't see her as a hardened criminal. The way I read her is she wouldn't be scared at the thought of escaping authority. She'd take it as a challenge, pitting her wits against theirs. Like breaking into our shop, it would be an adrenaline rush. No, from the way her face paled, her problem's more visceral, a matter of life or death.

Maybe an ex? But again I find that hard to believe. If that's the answer, even I wouldn't like to meet the motherfucker who could take someone like her down. Any man brave enough to live with her would need to keep her happy or always sleep with one eye open.

An abuser? Again, I'd have thought anyone messing with her would soon find he's picked on the wrong one. But I can't forget the way she froze when I had her under me, and there was no denying her struggling had turned me on. And that, like a switch being thrown, had turned her off. Slave traffickers? Has she come to the notice of the wrong people? She might be able to take one person on, but could be overcome by numbers.

Or perhaps it's something from when she served.

Or maybe... I purse my lips as I look at her. Maybe it's all in her head, a result of some injury. Perhaps she's just paranoid.

Whatever the answer is, I've got this strange desire to help her.

I'm not a man who's ever been accused of being empathetic. Someone in my position can't afford to be. If a brother's in trouble, I might sympathise, but I'll look at the situation calmly, identifying any risk to the club. I'll provide help and support, but I'll never get emotionally involved. In Helo's case though, I feel her pain, can feel the anguish at not being able to ride.

I know I don't understand the extent of it. How can you live life on the fly when you've got no transport to escape with?

I'm torn about what I should do. I don't know whether it's my dick talking when I remember how I've been attracted to Helo, but that's precisely the reason that I should let her walk away. I just need to think of StoryTeller to realise I'm right to keep my distance. Just look at him now with not only his old lady but his two-year-old wrapping him around her little finger. My role is to protect my club, to make it a safe environment so people like StoryTeller can enjoy their families. It's not to be distracted with a woman of my own, and the club girls are adequate for keeping my dick amused.

But when I try to dismiss her, when I think about walking away, my gut joins my cock in screaming I'm making a mistake. I try to rationalise that it's just curiosity that I don't want Helo to disappear without finding out her answers. That I don't want her leaving until she's helped us failsafe our security. Of course I'm not worried that her legs won't carry her far enough to escape whoever's looking for her. Why would I be?

I'm also not known for being indecisive, and one raised eyebrow from my VP shows he expects my answer. Quickly, my brain comes up with an option that I believe sounds reasonable. "You're coming back to our clubhouse. There are things we need to discuss." *Like why you bring out emotions in me that I'd considered long lost.*

Bull snorts, Iron swings around fast, staring at me with narrowed eyes, while the woman herself takes a step back, looking a combination of perplexed and worried.

"Why the fuck should I do that?"

Because I can protect you. Luckily, I prevent those weird words from coming out of my mouth. "Because we're not finished with you yet. I want to know exactly how you accessed the shop, bypassed our security and managed to wheel out a bike." *There.* I feel like fist pumping the air because I've made some sense.

"I can give you that info right here and now."

"You could," I agree, scrambling to come up with more. "But you could also work with us to keep people like yourself out of this, and our other businesses in the future."

"A bitch as a fuckin' security consultant?" Iron barks. He sweeps his hands back over his bald head and for a second, his piercing eyes stare at me. "Now I've heard everything."

I'm more interested trying to read the expression on Helo's face, but what I see makes me think I'm not likely to take her on in a game of poker. She could be carefully considering my proposal or already have dismissed it as a joke. She could also be plotting my death.

While my eyes are on her, I hear Bull telling Iron that this is no normal bitch, that her training and skills, as already demonstrated, might indeed have something to offer the MC. For a second, I want to hug my VP for seeing things my way, then want to slap myself upside the head. See? I'm already letting a bitch get to me.

I'm about ready to rescind my offer when her features suddenly unfreeze, forming a frown which is accompanied by a little shake of her head. "You want the bounty."

For a second I'm nonplussed then I realise what she must mean. I feel heat come into my cheeks at the realisation she thinks so little of us, of me, before I accept she's only our reputation to go on, and by preference, we'd rather appear like demons than angels.

There's a tinge of ire in my voice as I rush to set her straight, snapping, "Ain't going to fuckin' snitch on you. Don't fuckin' care if you're wanted by the feds."

Bull coughs loudly, getting my attention, then he nudges me, indicating he wants to talk to me privately. Following him, I let him lead me a few steps away. Leaning to speak into my ear, he says, "You make a good point about the feds. Before we let her into our house, don't you think we ought to know why she's keeping her fuckin' head down? If our digging has revealed her location, we could already have heat on our tail. Not sure I want to be caught harbouring a criminal. Or not when it's not one of ours."

No MC wants the feds' attention. They're always just one step away from slapping a RICO indictment down and the whole club ending up in prison. I stiffen, berating myself that my VP has had to give this lecture to me. I should have paid her the five hundred dollars I promised and let her walk away. He's utterly right about not inviting trouble into our house and fuck it if that's not what my dick wants to hear.

Iron joins us with a frown on his face. "Hear your concerns,

VP, but look at the girl. Sure, she knows how to defend herself, but I don't like the thought of a woman being on the run with no transport." As sergeant-at-arms, he's all about safety. But even though I should be relieved he's thinking along the same lines as me, I can't help eyeing him suspiciously, wondering what his interest is in her.

What the fuck is wrong with me?

"Look at her." Iron jerks his head over his shoulder. Both the VP and I turn our heads. We catch her in an unguarded moment, when for once she's looking unsure of herself, scanning her surroundings as if she's waiting for someone to suddenly jump out. "Remember how she just passed out for no reason? If she has one of those attacks, she'd be vulnerable. Anyone could take advantage of her. I agree with Prez. Let's get her back to the compound and give her some breathing space."

"We could dump her back at MacPherson's." Fuck, I hate that that practical solution came from my mouth, but it would make sense. And, maybe, in the long run, be beneficial to my mental health.

"Nah." Bull defiantly folds his arms. I suppress my sigh of relief. "There are a lot of unanswered questions. For one, I'd still like to know who she's running from."

"Find that out and we might be able to help," Iron insists.

The VP snorts. "I was thinking more about heading off trouble coming our way."

Pinching the bridge of my nose, I allow myself a moment to get my head straight. I'd be a piss-poor prez if I ignored what my righthand man had to say. Lowering my hand, I roll my shoulders. "Okay. Let's see what she has to say." Turning around, I look for Shitface. Spying him, I order, "Prospect, get this bike back inside, and start doing your fuckin' work." I take the few steps that brings me in front of the woman. "You, come with us into the office."

"Why?"

"You don't want to come to the clubhouse, so you can answer some questions here." I read her reluctance and try to sweeten the deal. "And it does seem I owe you five hundred dollars. I've got that in the office."

I watch as she seems to eye up her chances. She'd given me a run for my money one-on-one, but her gaze peruses Bull and Iron, and then encompasses the other members of my crew standing close by. After a moment of calculating the odds which are clearly stacked against her, she dips her head, and starts to move into the garage.

She knows where the office is. Of course she does. With the number of times she's robbed from us, the shop's become her second home. I've no hesitation in taking Weasel's manager seat behind his desk. Iron grabs a chair, and places it in front of the desk for her, while Bull stands behind her with folded arms.

Again with a cursory glance to consider her options, she takes the seat that's been offered. I take a moment to study her. This is no ordinary woman, and I try to see beyond the short blonde hair that frames her delicate face, and focus away from her athletic form. I'd have previously said I'm a tits kind of guy, but despite her lacking a lot in that area, there's something about how she's put together that makes it hard for me to concentrate.

She's no simple piece of ass. No, she's one of the legendary Night Stalkers. That she's got nerves of steel is a given. There's no point in me coming straight out and asking her for information she doesn't want to share. She's been trained to withstand interrogation and torture. Push too hard and all I'll get is name, rank and number. And only if she's prepared to give me that.

If I want information out of her, I need to be clever. So instead of shooting straight for the heart of the matter, I ask her something easy to answer and deigned to make her relax. "How did you get in this time?"

Her cheeks puff then relax, as if she was expecting something harder, and her lips curve up. "I noticed an animal had started digging a burrow close by the fence. The earth was loose, easy to scoop more of it out and enough for me to squeeze underneath." She pauses and grins. "The cameras don't pan that low, so I crossed to the shop on my belly, undetected."

I have to do no more than raise my brow toward Iron, who gives me a sharp nod. "I'll go check it out."

As he leaves the office, there's no twitch on her face that would suggest what she's told me is a lie, no expression of awkwardness that she's going to be found out. I don't doubt for a moment she's telling me the truth.

"We need to put cameras at ground level?" I ask.

She chuckles softly. "Or get the existing ones to pan lower."

I give her an appreciative chin lift, showing I've conceded her point. Though the information is useful, I doubt we'll have many more thieves like her turning up. Not ones who aren't deterred by the Wretched Soulz logo above the door that is.

I analyse her face, and while I want to try to find out who's after her, Bull is right. If it's the feds, we'll have to think carefully about helping her. But if it's not? Well, a promise of our assistance to get whoever it is off her back might tempt her to stay around longer. Just to help us make our ship watertight, of course.

"Any other observations on our security?"

Her eyes sparkle. "Any sign of that five hundred dollars?"

Chuckling, I open the desk drawer and unlock the cash box, taking a wad of bills out. After counting them, I slide them across the table to her. Without checking the amount, she slides the money into her pocket. For a moment, I expect her to bargain for more before she shares her info, but no, she starts to speak.

"Your locks are standard, and you need better ones," she begins, and then goes on to list a few other observations she's made. She's got a few good points and I notice small raises and dips of Bull's head, showing he's mentally noting them.

With the money in her pocket and our obvious acceptance there are things we could improve, I see her settle back in her chair, crossing her legs but unfolding her arms. She looks more at ease than I've so far seen her, so it's now I can start.

"Who's after you?" My lazily toned and out-of-the-blue question will hopefully catch her off guard.

It doesn't work. Her back straightens again and she shrugs.

"Woman, you speak to us, we might be able to help," Bull states gruffly from behind her.

Still no response, just a hardening of her eyes.

"Is it one of the alphabet agencies?" I probe.

That gets her brow furrowing, and she gives a rapid shake of her head with a dismissive smile. "Definitely not."

I hear Bull's audible exhale, and my heart rate eases as well. If no one in authority is after her, it's more likely there's an ex who we can take on.

"Who is it, then?" Bull, having been reassured, asks gently. He comes around to the side of the desk, leaning forward and placing down his forearms.

It's him she looks at. "I'm not being obtuse. I don't exactly know who's after me." The words are softly spoken, and she grimaces after they've come out of her mouth.

Bull's eyes flick to mine, then back to her. "But someone is? Someone you know with the resources to find you?"

I don't mind her attention turned away from me as it seems she's responding to Bull more than myself. Any jealousy I'll deal with later, but for now, I want to know what we're dealing with. Yeah, we. She's got my help whether or not she wants it. Why? I'll analyse later.

She might be watching the VP, but she's not answering. Bull pushes again. "If you don't know who, what makes you think anyone has it in for you? Must be pretty serious if you're living off the grid." He pauses, swallows, then notes, "You must have a veteran's pension, yet you're hurting for just a few bucks. You've already told us you think this phantom person has resources, so surely you have some clue, if they do exist, who it is."

A few moments pass and I don't think she's going to answer. When she does, she doesn't use words. Instead, she pulls down one side of her t-shirt. I hear Bull's gasp first until she turns herself around, presenting me with the shocking image of her left shoulder. It's a mass of healing tissue, no longer red and raw, but showing enough to let me know how painful the original injury was. I hiss in air through my teeth and Bull does much the same.

"Blowtorch," she explains undramatically.

"In your job?"

She snorts softly. "I wish it was. No, this is just a taste of what he, they, want to do to me. I got away. This time."

Moving away from his sentry post, Bull stands, props his ass against it and faces her. "Why use a blowtorch?"

Her voice sounds monotone, but fire sparks in her eyes. "To remove my Night Stalker tattoo."

I can't help my breath exhaling on a hiss. Sure, we remove the tats of traitors, and I've seen how painful that is, but more than the physical torture, for us, it's the tangible loss of brotherhood. Like our, luckily few, turncoat members, she's lost her badge of honour, something that she fought to earn and reflects what she is.

Bull, likewise, looks shocked, but it's him who recoups

first. "If you don't know who, then surely you've got some reason of why?"

Suddenly finding her hands interesting, she stares at them lying in her lap. I notice they're twisting together, the only outward sign she's agitated. "It's classified," she says softly.

Leaning back in my chair, I first fold my arms, then exchange a glance with my VP. "A mission or op?"

The slightest movement of her mouth shows me I'm on the right track. I look again at Bull, who shakes his head. It's clear he's assuming the same as me, that we're unlikely to get more out of her at this point other than, as I suspected earlier, her name, number and rank. But fuck it, that injury to her shoulder shows the real danger she's in. It wasn't a bullet, though, apparently, they'd gotten close enough for that. It's a sign someone wants more than her death. They want her to suffer.

Well, they won't be getting another chance to get close. While I don't understand this powerful need to protect her, and though I know if she knew my thoughts she'd laugh in my face, something tells me she's mine to care for and look after however much she protests.

There's absolutely no doubt I want to know more about Helo. *Or Queenie,* I muse, recalling her real name. I'm not sure it suits her. She doesn't look regal to me. She looks like a warrior. That makes me think about the parents who named her, and her family. Why hasn't she gone to them?

Without realising I'm going to speak my thoughts aloud, I find myself asking, "Queenie? That your real name or another nickname?"

Having surprised her, she can't hide the pain that sweeps briefly over her eyes. Quickly bringing herself back under control, she scoffs. "Oh no, that's all mine."

"Family name?" Bull asks, quite reasonably.

When her eyes come to mine, I raise a brow. Shaking her

head, air leaves her lungs before she refills them to ask, “You really want to know?”

I shrug. She’d answered my question. I’m pretty sure that’s her legal name. I’ve got that power over her now which is what I wanted.

I think had I pressed, she might have kept it to herself, but with a roll of her eyes and with absolutely no self-sympathy, she tells us how it came about.

“I was an abandoned baby, found in a dumpster in Queens.” Her shoulders rise, hover, then fall back to their original position. “It had been a cold night so was touch and go whether they could save me. I think the medical staff were more worried about that then being very inventive when it came to names. I doubt they expected me to own it long anyway.”

But she fought and survived. As I suspect, she’s been doing all her life.

“And May?” Bull enquires. “Is that from your adoptive family?”

She gives a delicate snort. “That was the month I was found.”

“Original,” I say, while thinking that’s a fucking sad story. No parents who’d spent months agonising what to call their child, no family name to give her, let alone people who wanted her.

“And the rest of the story? Adopted into a loving family?” I prompt.

The scorching look tossed my way shows I couldn’t be further from the truth, but her button-upped expression suggests that’s all the information she’s going to impart.

CHAPTER NINE

HELO

I've got more than enough reasons to be wary of men. Even before... Well, I had to survive in a male-dominated world, had to show I was the best just to get by. There's something about Chaz that draws me in. Somehow, he gets through all the boundaries I've set, and I don't understand why. I don't know why I ran my mouth. Normally, I tell no one my early background, but then they normally don't ask. Names are accepted without explanation, and in the Army, before I became Helo, I was just called May. But for some reason, though I was looking at the man wearing the VP badge, I spoke to Chaz.

I didn't tell them to get sympathy. I've lived my past and survived it, and it made me into the woman I am today, or who I was anyway. Now I turn my glance Chaz's way. It seems like he wants me to elaborate further, but they should get the picture without me having to spell it out. An unwanted baby abandoned to die doesn't necessary lead to a happy ending. Especially when no one wanted a kid already addicted to heroin and who had to be weaned off that shit before having a chance at life. Adopters who'd turned their backs had had a lucky escape as I'd remained a sickly child for the first few years of my life.

I'm wondering why I'm telling them anything at all. After giving them ideas about what was wrong with their setup and how they could improve their security, I should have insisted they let me leave and then get on with figuring out the rest of my life. I'm really not at all sure why I'm sitting here. They've not even offered a cup of coffee to me.

This wasn't how I expected my day to go. Sure, I knew they'd be annoyed and want info from me, but I hadn't realised they'd have had me investigated. And that, even though I was comfortable at Harold's, meant I was going to have to leave. I'm not looking forward to coming up with some explanation for letting the old man, and his hopes for his son, down. Neither am I embracing the thought I'll, yet again, have to start all over with nothing to my name except a pitiful few dollars and a rucksack of worn clothes. All to stay one step ahead of whoever blames me for being alive.

Sometimes I wonder why I try so hard to survive, why I keep breathing and don't just let them end my life. It's the pigheaded side of me that says it was a miracle I already climbed out of the darkest pit of despair, and the effort that took shouldn't be wasted.

A lapse of judgement had once allowed them too close as the remembered agony of my shoulder can attest to. I suppress a shudder recalling it was sheer luck that had allowed me to get away, but my instinct had been to run and fight for survival. A Night Stalker doesn't give up. I'd had the advantage they thought they were dealing with a weak female, not a battle-worn soldier, something they'd ignored despite knowing my rank.

Why am I still sitting here? Now the third man has left, two against one are odds I can deal with. Fuck knows how soon my trail will be picked up now my DNA and fingerprints have been checked. The sooner I get a head start, the quicker I can find a new refuge, or at least a place to temporarily hide out.

For some reason, it's hard to get myself moving. The thought of heading off into nowhere again and starting over is making me weary—and angry, with the bikers and myself. If I hadn't gotten into their auto shop and hadn't been arrogant enough to think criminals wouldn't care, then I could have stayed at Harold's fixing his son's bike. Though, it's a pipe dream to think of being able to stay in one place. That's a luxury I've never experienced.

As a child, I moved from one foster home to another, getting more and more fucked up until no one wanted the disturbed unruly child. Then, in the Army, I went from base to base, and then in different areas on tours. Since coming back Stateside, I've been forced to keep moving around.

I'm sick of it.

I served my country, suffered for it, and what have I got to show? No friends, no family, no roots and no prospect of settling down.

I don't know how much of my thoughts have been showing on my face, but it's enough for Chaz to lower his tone, saying softly and cajolingly, "Tell us what's going on, Queenie. We might be able to help."

Queenie. How long has it been since anyone called me that? Normally I'd insist on my hard-earned handle, but what's the point if I can no longer fly? It just makes a mockery of all I've achieved. As Queenie, perhaps I can strive to make a new life, one equally as fulfilling as the one I've lost.

I'm tired, physically and mentally. The thought of confiding in someone is tempting. But I can't. I, too, soften my voice. "There's no point telling you anything, you won't be able to help. At worst it will put you into the sights of people you don't want to be on the wrong side of."

Joint chuckling comes from both of the men, Bull adding an amused snort. "We're the ones feared, sweetheart, not the other way around. Not many people are brave enough to take on the Wretched Soulz."

That may be so, but they've no idea who'd they'd be up against. I might not know who exactly, but I'm pretty sure whoever it is is using ex-US Special Forces to carry out their dirty work. And I don't want to share my story. These men might have more sympathy for my enemy than for myself.

"If you want to help, you can give me a lift out of town." To the state line might be best, but however far I can go would be a good start.

Chaz stares at me for a moment, then his eyes lift and find Bull's. They have a conversation consisting of chin lifts, head jerks and grunts. Having been around men for a long time I'm not surprised when Bull nods and, without explanation to me, exits the room. *Leave us alone and maybe I'll get more out of her.* I interpreted.

Once the door closes, Chaz wastes no time asking, "How about I agree I'll help you if you tell me all that you know?"

I don't know how I recognise it, but I can see this stern abrupt man is bending for me. I don't think he's normally got much patience. A motion catches my eye. His fingers are strumming a silent rhythm on his desk, showing underneath he's agitated. I admire the fortitude he's displaying. This probably isn't a man who suffers fools lightly.

What I don't feel coming from him is any animosity, which is strange. He should consider himself the wronged party. While I don't feel comfortable enough to share my whole story, I am driven to give him something.

Putting my hands on the arms of the chair, I push myself to

my feet. This is a conversation I need to have moving. I pace to one side of his office then back, and give myself a moment before I speak, assessing how much I can divulge without harming national security. Then, inwardly, I laugh at myself. *Why the fuck am I still worried about that?*

First, I assuage my conscience. "I had to run. I've no access to my money. I soon found using it gave them the ability to track me. Eventually, I ended up here. Harold found me, took me in, and we came to an agreement. I fix his son's motorcycle, and he provides board and lodging. For the first time in a long while, I could hole up and regroup."

"You're a mechanic?"

Without conceit, I reply truthfully, "If it's got an engine, then I can fix it." To his credit, he shows no sign that he doubts me. When he gives an imperious wave of his hand, I continue, "You refused to help Harold—"

Interrupting, he scoffs. "That bike was a total write-off. Yeah, we could put it back together, but it would have been cheaper to buy a new one."

Unable to argue with that, I give him a brief version of Harold's story. I see his face go through a variety of emotions as I explain how the old man's linking the restoration of that bike to his son regaining consciousness. Instead of sneering, I reckon Chaz is feeling empathy with the man who's more dead than alive, compassion for another biker losing out to a bigger vehicle on the road.

When I finish, Chaz puts his hands to his face and rubs his cheeks thoughtfully. "You think his son will pull through?"

Grimacing, I shake my head. "Extremely unlikely. But getting his bike fixed is allowing Harold to come to terms with the situation gradually."

"You don't think it's better for him to face reality?"

"What's reality, Chaz?" I counter. "Who can say there's nothing in Harold's dream for his son's recovery? Miracles have happened before."

He stares at me thoughtfully, then raises and lowers his chin, then observes astutely, "But MacPherson isn't paying for any parts that you need."

"Harold's bankrupting himself keeping his son alive. The medical costs are astronomical. I thought I'd try and do as much as I could without asking for money."

Chaz snorts. "So instead, you stole from us."

I shrug. "Yeah, but even you know the money you demanded was ten times the value of what I took. Most of the shit came off your scrap heap."

"Nevertheless, you stole from us and thought you could get away with it."

As his tone is calm and not at all angry, I chuckle softly. "I didn't give a motorcycle gang much credit for stocktaking."

"Club. Not gang." He's not disrespecting me, so I raise my chin, acknowledging the correction. Suddenly, he sits forward. "Tell me, what's the main driver? You wanting to put a roof over your head or were you sucked in by MacPherson's sob story?"

I take the seat again. "Until you went searching for me, Harold's was a great place to stay. I was able to keep busy, and if I had one of my attacks, then I was safe."

"Safe except when you were up on a beam in the barn shooting at us. What the fuck would you have done if you passed out then?" As I look down at my hands, his head moves side to side. "Fuck, woman. You've got less sense of self-preservation than a biker."

My lips curve. "I was a helicopter pilot in multiple war zones, so..." I don't bother completing my sentence.

Chaz stands now. He walks around the desk, leaning against the front of it with his arms folded across his chest. Standing emphasises his build, but he doesn't intimidate me. It's not desire or justified anger which I read on his face. Instead, he seems to have a genuine interest in me.

"Tell me what happened," he cajoles in a gentle voice. "I presume you crashed or something? Got injured and left with fainting problems you now have."

"It's classified," I remind him.

"Woman," he snorts, "I've probably dealt with more classified information than you have, though it might not be at national security level. Brothers wouldn't last long in an MC if they didn't know how to keep their mouths shut. It's why prospects have to show us they're trustworthy before they patch in. Might not deal in State secrets, but what I carry up here," he taps his head, "could end up in people doing serious jail time."

I don't have to try hard to believe it.

It's his gentle tone. If he'd demanded, I'd keep quiet. There's something about him that makes me believe if he says he'll carry my secrets to the grave, I can trust him. And for some reason, after all this time, I'm ready to share my story. Placing my head into my hands, I rub at my temples, trying to summon words to use that will give him the bare facts without making it too hard on his ears. What happened still plays like a constant loop in my mind, invading my waking thoughts and plaguing my nightmares. It was hard to live through at the time, and sometimes I wish I hadn't survived. I glance up at him, seeing him watch me gather my thoughts, and patiently giving me time. What is it about this man? Anyone else and I'd have raised my middle finger and told him I wasn't going to say anything. But Chaz?

Fuck knows why, but I want him to understand my story. Maybe I'm just tired of running.

Eventually his patience starts to run out, and I see him fidgeting. It gives me the impetus I need. Turning to stare at the Wretched Soulz logo on the wall, I let out a long breath, and begin to give up my secrets.

"I can't tell you where I was, or why." I notice he's stilled again at my opening words as I check that he accepts the secrecy that surrounded my last mission. His lips thin, but he doesn't pry. "I flew a Black Hawk." That part's easy. It's a matter of record, and up to that fateful day, an occupation of which I was proud. I loved my work, loved the adrenaline, the feeling of a job well done when I dropped off or rescued whoever needed transporting, or when we entered the fray ourselves to take down the enemy. Every time we flew was exhilarating. For a moment, my thoughts are lighter as I think about the good times, then I swallow twice before I go into the details of my last flight. "The call came in. A team of SEALs needed extraction." All in a day's work, nothing unusual about it. "Unfortunately, there was a sandstorm enroute. My co-pilot, Karen, wanted to delay takeoff." My voice trails off as memories fill my mind.

"And you didn't?" Chaz interjects to prompt me.

"I took note of what he said."

"He?"

A half-smile comes to my lips. "Yeah, Karen was his handle, like Helo was mine. Well-earned as he was a Karen about everything. A serial moaner if you like." I shrug. "He'd gained his nickname long before I met him, it suited him. But in many ways, he balanced me. I could be too gung-ho. There were times I could do with being more cautious."

"And this was one of those times?"

Raising and dipping my chin, I agree. "Probably. I thought

there was a chance we could have flown around the storm, but Karen was risk adverse, or as much as a helo co-pilot was allowed to be. Our departure was delayed by an hour." Sixty minutes which changed everything. Three thousand six hundred seconds that ended my war. Again, I swallow, trying to moisten my throat. "The delay had consequences. Once in flight, we lost contact with the SEALs, but carried on anyway. We had no way of knowing how long they'd been out there, and it was likely their radio batteries might have failed."

Chaz shifts awkwardly. "That sounds risky."

In hindsight, it was. Even at the time, I had an uneasy feeling. Grimacing, I confirm, "Yeah, but what could we do? Leave the team there, or carry on and get them out?" It's a rhetorical question, and I don't wait for the answer. For me, both at the time, and now, it was a no-brainer. It didn't matter that Karen, Bosh, my crew chief, and Jaxson, my aerial gunner, all felt the same unease. No one objected to continuing the mission. We weren't going to leave any man behind. Night Stalkers aren't quitters. Even now I recall that with only raised chins, grunts and nods, we'd discussed and simply agreed on extra vigilance.

Lost in the past, I relate the bare facts to Chaz. Explaining how the flight had already been tense as we approached the target area. I'd circled once, getting the lay of the land. In this mountainous region, there was no place to set down. No problem, we'd employ the SPIES system, a single rope with rings to which special harnesses would be attached to winch up the men from the ground, but first Bosh and Jaxson would fast rope down to make sure none needed additional assistance. Without communication with the SEAL team, we didn't know what we would find, whether we were also recovering dead or injured.

A flare had gone up from the ground. Grinning at Karen, I'd said, "They're almost home", not knowing my thought was premature...

"Queenie?" Chaz prompts, noticing I've been lost in my head.

I blink, for a second needing to take in the shoddy but practical office I'm sitting in, the whack of the rotors fading away. Unable to suppress a shudder, I relate what happened next. "We were in position for the extraction. Bosh and Jaxson were ready. They'd already unclipped their harnesses. The missile warning system went off." I swallow rapidly, bile rising in my throat now, just like it had then.

The loss of directional control and my inability to maintain stable flight immediately told me our tail rotor had been hit. I didn't need to think of the devastating consequences as they were already happening. The aircraft began to spin out of control and I could do nothing to stop the rapid descent. Combined with the wailing of the alarm, I could hear the screams and thumps as the men who'd been preparing to exit lost their battle to hold on to anything and were tossed out.

There was nothing I could do.

There was nothing Karen could do.

It seemed to take hours, but it was a matter of seconds until we hit the ground.

Chaz clears his throat, and again, I come back into the present with a start, unaware of how much I told him, and how much I'd kept in my head. It must have been enough as he sums up succinctly, "You were hit. You crashed."

I glance down at my hands, seeing they're shaking badly, grasping them together to try to get them to stop. My whole body ends up trembling as I confirm, "We crashed." I try to pull myself together, consigning the memories of the terror I'd felt to the past. It wasn't the crash. Fuck knows we'd gone through enough simulations in our training. At the time, I'd been calm, the professional in me fighting to minimise the damage and give us and the SEALs we were there to rescue the best chance.

Chaz's hand moves as if to comfort me, but thinking better of it, he takes it away. I take a breath into lungs that feel starved of oxygen then force myself to resume my story, relating it in a monotone as though describing something that happened to someone else.

"The Black Hawk came down hard on one side. I knew immediately Karen was gone. He'd cracked his head against the side window and his eyes were wide open and staring. I was trapped, pinned by the harness and the cyclic." My mouth's gone dry. I work to get saliva into my mouth. "It wasn't long before I was freed, but it was by no rescuer. That's when I found out Bosh had fallen to his death. Jaxson was badly injured but alive."

"The SEALs?" Chaz asks, as my voice trails off.

"They'd been ambushed." I thump one fist into the palm of my other hand. "If we'd taken off on time, we'd have been able to save them. Four were still alive, but they'd lost two more of the team."

Chaz doesn't ask what happened to us. The answer we were captured was obvious. His eyes narrow and his jaw clenches. "How long?"

"Six months," I say calmly, trying to hide the sheer and utter hell of twenty-six weeks of being held captive. Hope of a rescue receded fast as days all rolled together in a never-ending cycle of torture and misery, replaced by the despair that there was only one way this could end—death—and the wish that that would come sooner rather than later.

Chaz turns and goes back behind his desk. His hands disappear from sight, then reappear holding a bottle and two shot glasses. He pours out two generous portions of amber liquid.

I take the one he slides toward me. Sniffing it, I know it's probably top-dollar scotch. Not my favourite spirit, but right now, I wouldn't turn down anything alcoholic. Remembering the crash is bad enough, but that's the point my nightmare started.

"They blame you for the crash?" he asks, after downing his own shot. "About the delay? Could you have rescued them if you'd taken off on time?" He pauses, then offers, "Do you think it's one of the SEALs who's after you because of their capture?"

If only it was that simple. He needs to give me time to compose myself if he wants to hear more. This is the part that's hardest to speak about.

When I don't answer, he takes it as confirmation of what he's just suggested and gives a quick shake of his head. "I don't get it. How could you be blamed? Firstly, you could have taken off on time and lost the helicopter due to the storm and never arrived at the pickup point. Secondly, I don't know much about flying, but I doubt even the most experienced pilot would have been able to survive a missile strike like the one that affected your craft. Who the fuck could blame you in any of that? And why would it be so important that they are now threatening your life?" He pauses, then continues, "It doesn't add up, sweetheart."

It doesn't. My mouth works but I don't know how to tell him the rest. But he's waiting for something, so I give him the basics. "Only two men apart from me survived. All of us were in a bad state. One, in particular, had been worked over pretty badly and was a mess when he returned to the States."

"What had happened to the others?"

"Tortured and beheaded." I shudder as I say the words and again raise the glass of whisky to my mouth.

"You were tortured?" Chaz asks, his face contorting with rage.

How can I reply? My eyes meet his, allowing him to see something of the truth in them.

I wasn't beaten or threatened with the loss of my life. They didn't see the point, believing a woman couldn't have knowledge worth extracting. My captors had very different ideas what to do with an enemy female.

I'd rather have died.

CHAPTER TEN
CHAZ

Christ. Her story has cut right through to my cold heart of stone. I've heard sad stories before, almost all of my brothers has one of their own, and I've listened to them without much empathy. Helo? Fuck. She's not had it easy from the day she was born, but not one word she's uttered has been one of complaint.

How did I dare have thoughts about taming her? She's far too good for me. I'd only taint her. But even though I've now more reasons for staying away, something still draws me to her. Something that makes me want to see the Queenie she's hidden under that hard-as-steel exterior.

I'd sent my VP away, in some ways to test whether she'd open up to just one person, speak to me, let me know what's going on inside her. Then again, I'm selfish. I want everything about her to be mine, including her secrets.

She's staring past me now, her eyes unfocused, her jaw tight and her lips narrowed. It's not hard to see it was that stupid question that came out of my mouth that affected her. Of course she was fucking abused and tortured, and from the sound of it, she's lucky that she's alive. First, she survived the helicopter crash, then for some reason, her captors kept her breathing. The rationale behind that, I don't like to think about, though I can read the truth of it in her eyes. I'd suspected she'd been abused, but I could never have dreamt how bad it was.

She got out of there, but definitely not unscathed. I'm sure she's suffering from PTSD and that's what makes her have the episodes, which means she can't be in charge of anything mechanical in case she passes out. Though she's now safe on US soil, someone is trying to kill her. What the fuck's up with that? Who could it be? The SEALs who survived, or maybe the family of one of those who had died? But why? Why blame her? It doesn't make sense though I've lived long enough to realise not everything in life has a reason, or all action grounded in logic. That she can't tell me more details of where, when or who suggests she was involved in some kind of black op.

I'm so full of admiration for her. I can imagine how fucking hard it is for a man to become a Night Stalker, let alone a woman. I doubt many reach the grade, and wasn't it only just recently, they started allowing females in? She must be a trail-blazer, and would have to be the best of the best. I'm actually in awe sitting opposite her. Though it's obvious the Helo sitting in front of me is not the one who owned the air. Instead of the warrior I envision her to be, I'm faced with a woman haunted by demons. I find myself wishing I could put a smile back on her face.

Having that kind of job ripped away from her probably equates to me losing my club. She's strong just because she keeps moving forward, even though she's got a nemesis trying to hold her back.

Unusually for me, I'm at a loss for words. I know I'm insanely attracted to her but feel the tables have turned. She's a true hero while I'm just a pretend one. I feel like a fish out of water, and when my phone vibrates with a message, I grab hold of it like a lifeline. Seeing the message is from Legend, I tap with my finger to open it.

Legend: There's a two-million-dollar bounty out on Queenie 'Helo' May.

Not knowing how the hell I manage it, I keep my face completely impassive while my brain whirls. *What the fuck?* Apart from that injury to her shoulder, anyone could be forgiven to have doubts there was anything other than demons in her head chasing her. This is proof she's told me nothing but the truth, and ups the ante considerably. She had mentioned a bounty, but I had no idea how much.

This isn't just one person searching for her. There's no knowing who's taken up the challenge. That's some serious change, which means whoever's after her isn't fucking around. With a sum like that I can just imagine how many assholes will start crawling out of the ground trying to find her. Does she know the size of the price on her head?

Under my eyelashes, I consider her carefully. Would she have told me as much as she had if she knew how much betraying her was worth? How can she know who to trust? Or is she just tired, and would welcome the opportunity to stop running, paying only a token tribute to keeping herself hidden. For some reason, I hope to hell she hasn't given up.

But two million dollars is enough for me to contemplate momentarily just what an amount that high would be worth to the club… it would be a new ride for everyone for a start. New clubhouse too, perhaps. The temptations are endless.

She's a bitch to whom we owe nothing. The opposite, she owes us for fucking with the club. To my brothers, I owe everything.

Could I turn her in for the money to give my brothers a

better life? My heart thumps in my chest, and a sour feeling roils in my gut. I couldn't do that. For some inane reason on this occasion, *because of her*, I can't put my club first.

She's a hero for fuck's sake. A woman in a million, a woman of the like I'll probably never meet again. It's me that's not worthy to have her in my bed.

There and then I determine I'm going to help her, whatever the ramifications are for me as Prez. Quickly I tap out a message to Legend.

Prez: Keep that info to yourself.

Legend: K

But it's one thing to decide to give her assistance, quite another to plan how I'm actually going to keep her safe. One thing you can take to the bank is I'm not going to let her out of my sight. Fuck her desire to go to the state line, with no resources, no transport. Even someone as skilled as her wouldn't be able to protect herself. Not against assholes who only see dollar signs and not her not-classically-beautiful but-characterful face.

But how to keep her? My brain begins to whirl through various options until I decide persuasion is probably the best. If only I can come up with a proposal that she won't be able to turn down. Telling her she's staying will have the opposite effect, and as for suggesting she can't look after herself, well, my jaw already aches in anticipation.

While I've been thinking, she's been content to stay silent. As she rubs her strained eyes and covers her mouth to hide a yawn, I remember she's been up all night. Not unusual for a Night Stalker, but even they have to rest sometime.

Sounds filter in through the office door, the increasing noise level in the shop telling me more brothers are arriving to start work. It's time to make some decisions, and an idea begins to form in my mind.

"If I take you to the state border, what will you do then?" I jerk my head to indicate the lightened sky outside. "It's daylight, surely you'd be better travelling in the dark?" Night Stalkers fly under cover of darkness. She'll be programmed to think there's safety in that. From the glint in her eye, I've caught her attention. Taking advantage, I press my point. "You were awake all fuckin' night. Not a good start when you're taking off, not knowing where you're going to lay your head or where your next meal will come from."

Her lips press together as she considers my words. After a moment, she says, "I can't go back to Harold's. Knowing they could be so close..." She shudders. I doubt MacPherson would be much good in a firefight, and somehow I know she wouldn't want to put him in danger.

I rap my fist on the table as if I've suddenly had an idea. "I'll take you to the clubhouse. You can get your head down for a few hours—catch up on the sleep you should have had last night. Get some food in your stomach and give some thought about where you want to go. You can wait until night falls." I've no intention of letting her leave then, but it buys me a few more hours to persuade her she'd do better to stay. I sweeten the pill, and scoff. "No one will look for you on an MC compound."

My words don't convince her. "If your enquiries left a trail, that would be the first place they'd come for information."

"Do you think we'd let an outsider get close?" My tone is sneering. Then I rethink. If Legend doesn't keep his mouth shut, some of the brothers actually might. All they'd see is what they could do with a share of that reward, while to me she's worth so much more. Hell, not many of them even know she's a Night Stalker, although StoryTeller might have been spinning his tales by now. I've got to give them a chance to see her as someone worth saving and not just a thief who stole from us in the night.

Practised, I don't let one iota of my thoughts show on my face. My sneer, accompanying my statement, remains pasted in place.

After a moment, her eyes rise and she frowns. "Why on earth would you want to help me?"

I shrug. Knowing I can't tell her I believe meeting her was fate, that somehow whatever passes for God in my world sent her my way. To reward or torture me? Well, that I can't yet say. So, I scramble for a reason that sounds plausible. "You helped us when you found the flaws in our security. And some of our members are ex-services. They'd have no problem giving some space to one of their own."

"You?" she asks. "You served?"

My shoulders rise and fall. "Army, but I did my four years then got out." The Army and I weren't a good fit. I preferred giving orders to taking them and rules be fucking damned. The MC was a much better fit.

Queenie stifles another yawn, seems to think for a moment, then her shoulders slump. "I'm not quite sure why I should take sanctuary with the men who outed my presence in Arizona, but I suppose you're right. It is the last place anyone would think of looking for me."

"Accidentally and possibly outed," I correct. "There's a chance that no one's watching that closely for you." Slim chance, I would think, considering how much they want her as evidenced by the size of the bounty. "But you'll be able to rest better if you play it safe and you couldn't be safer than on an MC compound." *Unless my brothers got wind of the amount on her head.* I cross my fingers again, hoping Legend has kept his mouth shut.

I probably trust our data expert more than most. This isn't

the first time he's been asked to keep information close to his chest.

She's wavering, I can see. Her contorted grimace and raised hand show she's unsuccessfully trying to stifle yet another yawn. Taking my chance and giving her no more time to think about the wisdom of entering my den, I stand and retrieve my bike key from my pocket. "Come on. Let's take you back."

As though complying with a senior officer's order, she follows me out. As I lead her through the shop, various heads turn our way, but the look on my face shuts any questioning down. It's only when I'm outside that I realise there's no other transport available except for the bikes. Briefly I toy with the idea of asking the prospect to take her on his, but a burning sensation in my chest makes me direct her to mine instead.

CHAPTER ELEVEN
CHAZ

While it might look like I subscribe to the notion of never having a woman as a backpack in case she gets ideas, in reality, I don't take passengers because I'm just not overly fond of anyone riding behind me. In the past when I've taken brothers in cases of emergency, I've hated the change to the bike's handling. So as I throw my leg over the saddle, right my sled, and kick up the stand, I'm already gritting my teeth, anticipating the dip of the suspension as she gets on behind. But as she places her hand on my shoulder and expertly slides on, showing this is far from her first time on this mode of transport, instead of annoyance that I'm not riding alone, I feel an unexpected burst of jealousy.

Whose bike has she ridden on before?

Rather than unbalancing me, the bike settles with the weight of us both as if her presence has caused it to reach an equilibrium it hasn't before.

I thought I'd direct her to steady herself with the handholds instead of me, but when she immediately goes to curl her fingers around the impersonal anchors, I reach back and pull her hands tightly about my waist. The rightness of the sensation takes me completely by surprise.

Frustrated with myself, almost angrily, I punch at the start button, hoping the familiar engine roar will knock some sense into me. I perform a lifesaver to check there are no vehicles approaching, then pull out onto the road. In my rearview, I see Bull pulling out behind me. My lips curve. He's my VP, and however short a journey, won't let me ride alone.

Helo doesn't tense as we draw away. There's something about her relaxed posture and the way she's hanging on that makes me believe if I turn my head, I'd see a great big fucking smile on her face.

Having her ride pillion is so far from uncomfortable that I'm hard put to stop grinning. *She feels right.* But that's totally wrong. Neither she, nor any other woman, belongs there. I like my bike as I live my life, riding alone.

I'm half-relieved, half-sorry when the short journey ends. Helo gracefully dismounts like an expert, then shades her eyes from the sun and regards the building in front of her. It's not much, an industrial type construction that we've converted and made our home.

After backing my bike into its parking spot right next to the door, I take her elbow and guide her inside.

It's morning and the smell of bacon still lingers which hopefully means there's still some cooking going on. My lips curve as Helo's stomach rumbles loudly. It's a no-brainer to head to the kitchen where, *thank fuck*, StoryTeller's old lady is manning the stove.

"Unca Chav!" Maria comes wobbling across, grabbing onto my legs with hands which look suspiciously like they're covered in syrup.

Carefully, I extract myself and send her back to her mom.

Sheri laughs and leans down to wipe the little tyke's sticky fingers. "Sorry, Chaz." She grins at me, then brushes off her own hands as she notices the woman at my side. Her eyes widen and I can see the wheels in her head turning, interpreting her thoughts, as *she's no sweet butt.* I must be able to translate it correctly, as she approaches with a smile. "Hi, I'm Sheri."

Helo hesitates for a moment then introduces herself. "Helo." As she speaks, she reaches forward to formally shake Sheri's hand. I notice, despite the recent wind in her face, she's paled, and wonder whether she's even more exhausted than I first thought as she points down at the toddler who's now plonked her butt on the floor and asks, "Yours?"

"For my sins, yeah." But Sheri's fond expression and soft tone belies her words.

With thumb in her mouth and staring up at the newcomer, even I admit she looks cute. I find myself wondering whether Helo's the maternal type, but then know I don't need to ask whether she wants kids from the look of longing I see on her face as her eyes focus on the child. *Uh-uh, no way.* I've always kept my dick covered up and have absolutely no desire to propagate a next generation. But Helo's expression looks too much like me or one of my brothers when we eye up a coveted bike. *She'd want a baby.*

The thought of impregnating her makes my cock twitch, while my brain tries to remind it of the responsibility that comes with that. It means being faithful to one pussy and being cockblocked at every turn. But even that doesn't stop it thickening. I'm concentrating so hard on making the damn thing stand down that I'm only half aware of Helo suddenly falling, and unable to do anything until she's prone at my feet. I never had a chance to try to catch her.

It takes a split second before I spring into action. As Sheri's mouth drops open, I sink down to my knees, belatedly cradling her in my arms, making sure her head is off the ground, and feeling for any lumps she might have gained during her less-than-graceful fall. Remembering it wasn't long last time before she started to come around, I rock her gently and softly stroke her forehead, not wanting to move her in case she's damaged herself.

Coming close and peering down, StoryTeller's woman is concerned. She takes hold of Helo's wrist and starts feeling for her pulse.

Realising she's going to start going through her repertoire of diagnostic skills if I don't stop her, I quickly explain, "She has these episodes." I keep my voice low. "No medical assistance required. She'll come out of it soon enough."

She gives me a quizzical look. "Well, if you do need me..."

"I'll let you know." Having a nurse resident on the compound comes in handy, even if her skills aren't needed now.

Satisfied, Sheri turns to console her daughter. "It's okay, Maria. The lady's just not feeling well."

"Has she got an owie?" Maria's high-pitched voice asks. "'Cos Unca Chav could kiss it better."

From the innocent mouths of babes—for a second I consider lowering my lips onto hers, not because they might have some magical healing properties, but because the idea is attractive all by itself. But I'm no prince wanting to wake a sleeping princess. I like my women awake and very aware.

Her eyelids flutter, focus slowly coming back into her eyes. Gentler with her than I was last time, I slowly help her to sit, keeping my arm around her. I notice how she blinks and her face reddens when she notices the woman and child staring at her.

"You hurt?" If my voice is gruff, I can't help it. I hate seeing such a strong woman as her brought down.

When she shakes her head, I stand, then sweep her up into my arms.

"What are you doing?" she squeals.

"Taking you somewhere you can lie down." My unspoken addition *and away from prying eyes* isn't missed by her. While she tries to protest her legs haven't stopped working, she seems to appreciate my desire to give her some privacy.

I might not know very much about Helo, but I've been around my brothers who had a worse time than I did when they served. Most have an underlying self-confidence and strength, and hate to display any weakness, or fuss being made if they exhibit PTSD signs. I doubt Helo's very much different.

The clubroom is virtually empty at this time of day, so I carry her through, shushing her when she tries to get me to let her loose. I don't give a fuck she's capable of walking on her own two feet. I like the feel of her in my arms. If she was one hundred percent, I've no doubt she'd find ways to get free from my hold, which probably includes emasculating me. But as she's still groggy, she doesn't struggle too hard.

Without really having thought about it, I take her straight into my room. It's only when I'm in there that I realise my mistake. The bed's unmade from when I left it this morning, and not only that, but the sheets definitely need to be changed. I'd had a sweet butt in it for a couple of hours before chucking her out.

To my consternation, the used condoms are still tied off and lying where I'd dropped them on the floor.

I put Helo down in front of the chair and tell her to sit while I change the linen. She eyes the bed and other shambles with a curve to her lips.

"Chaz, I'm dead on my feet. I can sleep anywhere. Just pull

the covers up and I'll lie on top of them." Her hand failing to hide exactly how wide her yawn is shows me it's rest she needs more than pampering.

I watch as she efficiently bends and takes off her sturdy boots, then simply loosens her belt before lying down on the comforter with a sigh. She props herself up on her elbows to ask, "Does that door lock?"

"Yeah. It will lock behind me, and only I have the key." I don't add most of my brothers could easily pick their way in if they wanted to, and the lack of that addition means my reassurance works.

Her chest sinks as a sigh of breath leaves her. Momentarily I wonder whether it's a sign of trust she's giving to me that she appears relaxed in my bed, or whether her recent episode has emptied her tank. My lips twitch as I strongly suspect, weak as she appears, should I try to take advantage and get handsy with her, I'd soon find myself on my ass.

As if confirming, although she appears otherwise, like any good soldier, she's still on high alert, one eye cautiously opens. "You still here?"

I can't admit I have a strong impulse not to leave her, and I don't understand what drives it myself. It's not to ensure her safety. She's in less danger here in my room, in this clubhouse, then she would be anywhere else. It's like there's something elemental drawing me toward her, wanting to immerse her into my life. These totally alien thoughts cause me to wonder if again I've been subjected to some virus or nerve gas.

Now her second eye opens, and I feel like an ass. She must be tired, both from being awake all night and her last episode taking it out of her. I should leave her to sleep. While I'd like nothing better than to stay with her, on her part, trust only goes so far.

She's magnificent—her job, her role in the masculine

world, her acceptance of risk that few civilians would ever contemplate. No wonder I admire her. Before I leave, something drives me to take a step closer and show my appreciation by saying in a low voice, "Thank you for your service."

Her head raises fast off the pillow as she again balances her weight on her elbows. "Don't say that. I had a fucking job many people would die for. It wasn't work. It was pure fun, in control of a machine that could bring death or save lives. I was a thrill seeker, and the Army allowed me to be what I wanted to be. So don't thank me."

How can I explain I'm not thanking her for doing her job, but for the way it all ended? One day, she was in control, living her dream, the next, she had no say in whether she'd live or die, and no way to influence the matter. Deciding it's best to stay quiet rather than try to put into words the admiration and compassion I feel for her, I raise my chin then lower it.

She nods in return, then leans back on the bed, and her eyes close. This time it looks unlikely they'll reopen.

I pause for a moment, watching her, then, realising that's a bit creepy, quietly leave. The lock snicks reassuringly behind me.

I stand, my back against the wall outside the room for a moment. Part of me is surprised she didn't wait to relax until I left, and there's a warmth in my chest when it dawns that it demonstrates to some extent she already trusts me. Before descending the stairs, I lean my head against the wall, as I become conscious that she's partway won my trust too. Although my words and actions might have looked otherwise, there wasn't a moment when I'd thought she'd intended to steal the bike. There's just something inherently honest inside her. And, while I wouldn't be a good MC prez if deviance didn't run through my blood, she must have recognised when I do give my word, I mean it.

CHAPTER TWELVE
CHAZ

Eventually, I push myself away from the brickwork when my thoughts start going in directions I don't want them to go, as my brain points out I've never been intrigued or interested in a woman before, or not beyond what she can sexually offer me. I still can't work out whether she's the best or worse thing to happen in my life, but for certain, she's making me consider things I never have before. Making an effort to blank her from my mind, I clomp down the stairs in my usual fashion, pausing at the bottom step to see who's in sight.

Bull's there, of course. He followed me back from the shop but hadn't entered the clubhouse and was unaware of Helo's recent collapse. Beard, our treasurer, is also here, though fuck knows why, as is Claw. My eyes roll as there's only one reason they're hanging around. It's clear to see what Bull's done with his time, gathering the troops and gossiping.

He swings around as I approach. "You make her pass out again, Prez?" He makes a show of sniffing under his arms. "Maybe you need to use better deodorant."

After showing him my finger, I glance over to see Sheri standing in the kitchen doorway wiping her hands on a towel. As my eyes narrow at her, she shrugs as if she couldn't see why it would be a secret.

I turn back to Bull in time to see him wink. "You get her settled..." he pauses to give me a knowing nudge, "in your bed okay?" I don't know whether to be annoyed or proud of the speed at which he thinks I can work. I've only been gone a few minutes.

"I don't take fuckin' advantage of comatose women," I snap. "Anyway, she's crashed. There'll be time to talk to her later."

My VP turns serious. "You get much out of her after I left?"

I don't want to share her secrets. Or not just yet. "Not a lot," is all that I give him. Then, before he can accuse me of losing my touch, I add to pacify him, "We talked enough for me to earn her trust in so far as to get her back here to get some rest. Once she's recovered, then it will be time for an inquisition."

He looks unconvinced, as if I'm losing my touch, but shrugs as though my non-answer will for now satisfy him. When Mac approaches with something on his mind, Bull gives me a mock salute and goes off with him.

I glance around, looking for Legend, hoping I'm right to trust him to keep his mouth shut. I should be the only one he's told that she's got such a big bounty out on her, and to keep her out of harm's way, that's the way it has to stay. None of the men in front of me are giving off any vibes that I may have brought home a payday. Although I do overhear some comments about how that thieving bitch owes something to the club, and some suggestions of how she could make recompense which make my hands fist.

Grimacing, I can't blame them. Only I know the full truth

about her, and while it doesn't condone her stealing from the club, I'm prepared to overlook her minor misdemeanours – they weren't more than any of us would do if driven to find some way to survive.

I might be the prez, but the club's run on democratic lines, and there could be some brothers who'd prefer to have the money in our coffers. While I hope most wouldn't want to sell a woman out, they'd be right to say the only thing we really know about her is that it was our shop she robbed. It worries me that my brothers might only measure her worth in what she could bring to the club. At the moment, they're talking about sex. But if the truth got out, I worry about whether I'd be able to control them. They haven't caught the same sickness I have.

It makes it more crucial that I talk to Legend, but he's not in sight. The door to his office is open and his desk unoccupied, so leaving that talk in abeyance, I turn on Claw, hoping to get the talk in the room away from the woman currently occupying my bed. "Why aren't you laying down ink?"

The enforcer grins. "Finished my client early and not got anyone else booked. Clarise is dealing with walk-ins."

"While you hang around getting the gossip." Again the VP winks and I wonder if he's got some ailment that's given him a twitch in his eye.

"Must be losing your touch if you've got time to be here," I observe, my gaze returning to Claw.

Taking no umbrage, Claw snorts. "I've got a list a mile long. Just had a cancellation. I was curious..." The shake of my head and growl has him changing the subject. "Hey, now you're here, Prez, and Beard as well, can I pick your brains about something?"

As long as it's something other than Helo—for now I want to keep what I know about her to process myself—he might as well. I've no idea when Legend will be back. Nodding, I beckon him and the treasurer to follow me into my office.

"So what's with our thief?" Beard pulls at his facial hair, grinning broadly.

"Not what you wanted to talk about. Or do you just want to waste my time?" I give them my best prez's stare.

They share glances, but as it turns out, they do have a reason for a discussion. Despite today's cancellation, Claw's actually drowning in work and wanted to talk through some figures about taking on another ink slinger. When Beard agrees the financials make sense, we then start talking about some of the tattoo artists we met in Sturgis, which leads on to us reminiscing about our road trip last year. I even get out my whisky and we have a few shots. Once the conversation's reached a natural end point, Claw and Beard make their exit and I decide I better go upstairs to check on my guest.

Stepping out into the clubroom, I realise time's gone faster than I thought as there's been an influx of brothers signalling the workday has ended. StoryTeller isn't around so I don't expect to see his old lady or kid. He usually disappears around this time to get his youngster fed and presumably put to bed. Pussy whipped for sure. Me? I'd rather have a relaxing drink with like-minded men than deal with a screaming kid.

Pothead has a joint in one hand, and a beer in another. Legit seems deep in an animated discussion with Fire. Skunk's by himself which isn't unusual. I mentally note all the men who are here while looking round for the man that I want. Ah, there he is. I catch Legend's attention and beckon him over, waving him into my office and closing the door.

Hardly waiting for him to get his ass on the seat, I ask the burning question that's been playing on my mind all day. "You told anyone else about the reward for information about Helo?"

He looks at me sharply and gives a vigorous shake of his head. "Fuck no, Prez. I was waiting to hear what you wanted to do." He shifts a little awkwardly. "I can dig deeper for information on the contract if you want that."

What the fuck is he asking? "You think I'm going to sell her out?" My eyebrows rise.

With a grimace, his head again moves side to side, then stares ahead as if a picture in his mind is more in focus than his actual surroundings. "My brother was a SEAL. They got themselves into a sticky situation and needed extraction fast. Way he tells it, those Night Stalkers deserve the reputation they've got, putting themselves into impossible situations just to get people like him out of danger. They're brave, resourceful, and will do what they can to never leave someone behind. He owes his life to people like Helo." He pauses for a moment, then adds, "Fuck, it could even have been Helo's crew that got him out." The palm of his hand hits the desk as his attention returns to the here and now. "So no, I can't believe you'd sell someone like that out. But..." He half turns his head to look at the door before turning it back. "I'm not stupid. That money could mean a fuck of a lot to some of the members of this club. And some who may not have reason to be grateful to someone like her."

Someone who's been fucking with us, I realise without him having to spell it out. My head tilts as I look at him. I knew I could trust him but hadn't realised he'd be so personally invested. I also know what he's saying. While we stick our middle fingers up at the law and at society's rules and are more likely to take the side of the underdog, the men riding with the Wretched Soulz are still human, and just as likely to have weaknesses and flaws. If it was a brother involved, there would be no question. We protect our own. But Helo's nothing to us. Worse, she's a thief and they all know it. They've no loyalty to her, and while others might think like Legend and that her former career should be respected and rewarded, a couple of names come to mind who might prefer the money in their pocket instead. Fuck, from what I overheard earlier, it could even be more of them.

"Keep it on the down-low, Ledge," I instruct him.

He raises his chin deliberately as if scoffing he'd ever do anything different. "She going to be hanging around?"

"Life's dealt her some bad fuckin' hands. Feel she deserves some breathing space." It's not an answer, I know, but I really can't say anything else. Part of me wants her to stay close, while another part is screaming I should keep far away from her.

Legend's cheeks puff out as he inhales and holds a breath, then deflate as he speaks. "So it's about time for her luck to change." He gives me a quick grin. "Could be you've met your match, Prez."

I glance at him sharply. "Got no idea what you mean by that. Now get the fuck out of here."

As Legend chuckles, stands, and exits the office, I realise I know only too well what he was hinting at. There's a beast inside me that wants to roar, *she's mine.*

Running my hands over my smooth skull, I feel like roaring *fuck* at the top of my voice. *I* want to be the one who gives her a fresh start, who chases away her demons and make it safe for her to live her life. Then I chuckle to myself. I might not know much about Helo, but I doubt she'd admit to needing anyone's help.

It might well be the time for the winds to change and blow her in a new direction, but there are so many reasons why I can't be by her side. First, I'm the prez, and I'm never going to take an old lady, and second? Well, there's that fucking great price on her head, and what happens if that knowledge gets out?

There are two dangers. If they haven't already, someone's going to take that contract, and if their search for her leads them to us, my whole club could be in danger. And for what? A woman who stole from us. Could I really ask that of my brothers?

And if they knew, they might want the money for themselves. Two million dollars is a huge test of the loyalty my brothers show to me, when they've fuck-all reason to show her any fealty.

But perhaps they would, if I made her my old lady.

Fuck! I am not going there. No way, no how. I snort loudly. I've not even taken her for a test ride. Hell, we might not be compatible physically, and even if we were, I'd never be content with just one pussy. As for being tied down, someone wanting to know all my comings and goings? Yeah, I'd need someone meek who'd say "yes, sir" and let me be. Someone like Helo wouldn't be happy being kept out of club business. Hell, no, she'd probably want to take charge.

No. No old lady for me. I've lived forty-five years without entanglements, and I'm not going to throw away my freedom now.

Perhaps if I can keep Helo here, the brothers will begin to see what I see. That she deserves the same respect as any other veteran in our ranks. Her country might have spat her out, but the MC can give her a safe place to land.

But what could her role be? A mechanic, perhaps? Maybe one of them will see her merits and step up where I can't.

Leaning forward, I start banging my forehead against the desk. My hands clench so hard I'd draw blood from my palms if my nails were longer. *Let anyone touch her?* Over my fucking dead body.

I'm their prez. If I say she's under my protection, they'll have to be content with that. Sure, that's worth more than a cool two million. I roll my eyes. For that money, they might take my *Prez* patch.

I stand so fast, my chair topples over. Without bothering to right it, not wanting to tarry and be subjected to more of the same thoughts going through my mind, I stomp out of the office.

Weasel waves, trying to get my attention, as I storm through the clubhouse, but my raised hand and pace shows I'm not going to be stopped. I'll get to him later. Skunk steps in my way, but moves aside fast when I glare and shake my head. Iron looks up and laughs, while Bull, catching my eye, does that winking thing again. I'll really have to ask him if he's got a problem.

Having successfully navigated the increasingly loud and rowdy room, I reach the stairs and climb them, now certain the racket will have woken Helo. I pause in front of my door, knocking twice on it, before inserting the key and opening it. On my bed she's stirring, still in the process of sitting up and rubbing sleep from bleary eyes.

Her words come out partly smothered by a yawn. "Is it time to go?"

No, it's fucking not. Never if I get my way.

Crossing the room to her, I stare down, noticing she's got a little more colour in her face than she had earlier, but the way she's rubbing her temples suggests that her head is aching. That makes me remember she fell hard on the solid tiles. Diagnosing she probably needs something to take the edge off, I grab a bottle of water from my mini fridge and extract a pack of painkillers from my nightstand. She smiles gratefully as I pass them to her, presses out a couple of tablets and swallows them down.

I had thought about taking her downstairs and introducing her around, hoping that meeting her, seeing her as a person, would help the men welcome her into their ranks. Before any word of the size of the bounty leaked out, I wanted them to discover for themselves what I've found. That Helo is an inherently honest person, and could be useful to keep around. Or, at least, not hand over to be killed.

But looking at her now, while I have no doubt she would rally if I asked her too, I'm not sure it's the right time to introduce her to my brothers' boisterousness. They can be loud at the best of times, so I make a swift change to my hastily thought-out plan.

"Just wanted to check if you were alright. You're okay to stay here if you're still tired. I'll bring some food up in a while."

She glances out the window. As my eyes follow her gaze, I notice, as she probably has too, that the sun is low in the sky. "It *is* time for me to go," she remarks. She seems to have a one-track mind.

At the thought of her disappearing from my life, my heart misses a beat, and I want to scream no. Somehow I'd persuaded myself that I could keep her. But how can I explain to her I don't want her to leave if I don't know the reason myself? It doesn't sit right that she'll vanish into the night and I'll never see her again. And with that fucking bounty on her head the chances of her staying safe are next to zero.

For a moment I wish to fuck she'd never stolen from us and put herself onto our radar. If she'd kept to her lane, we'd never have known about her, never had to satisfy our curiosity as to who she was, and she'd have been safe staying with MacPherson. I'd never have met her and my equilibrium wouldn't have been disturbed.

"Later," I suggest, buying time. "There's no need to hurry. It's better if it's full dark and there's less traffic on the road."

She winces as though hearing this isn't what she wants, but if she wants help to boost her on her journey, relying on me is all she's got. "You'll get me a ride?" If I have to, I will, so I nod. "Will I be able to go via Harold's so I can collect my bag?"

"Sure." Yeah, it's entirely possible. Doesn't mean it will happen though. I want to try to persuade her to hang around.

Strangely, even with her lying on my bed where I've had so many women before, while I find her sexually appealing, the urge to get my dick wet isn't what's driving me. Instead, there's a connection between us I've never experienced with anyone else, and a knowledge that simple sex would complicate things and possibly ruin it, I'm wary of admitting that's my ultimate goal. Her consent will need to be earned, not just cajoled, and I'll need to deserve it. I've never been nervous about fucking a woman before, but I am with her.

Suddenly I feel awkward standing there, though fuck knows why. This is my room and my bed that she's in. Normally that would give me liberties over any woman lying there, but not her. I feel strangely discombobulated like a schoolboy on a first date, not knowing what's expected or how to behave. Mentally I slap myself. She's no date, and I've no intentions like that with her, so why do I feel this impulse to stay while at the same time having the burning urge that tells me to run away?

She's giving me no signs that she'd like to take advantage of the position she's in, but even if she was willing, I can tell she wouldn't just be a quick fuck. All I can offer her is something I've never suggested to a female. Friendship. I'm in uncharted territory.

A few moments pass as we do nothing but look at each other. It's strange, as if neither of us wants to break the silence, nor bring to an end this strange impasse. Finally, words escape through my tongue-tied lips.

"I'll...er... go rustle up some food." *Fuck, that's not me. I never stammer.* But then, I've never had someone so strong, so beautiful, so fucking admirable and unobtainable, lying in my bed.

The worrying of her lip by her teeth shows me she's not a fan of the delay, so I edge backward out of the room. Again I pause outside the door trying to get my thoughts together, trying to understand why she makes me so confused, and how she brings all the protectiveness from inside me. She's the last woman on earth who needs a man to stand up for her, or that man would need to be a giant. Is it something of a challenge that I want to be the person she leans on? The man who she can depend on to keep her safe.

Why can't I see the slippery slope that? If I followed my impulse, I'd be in danger of falling in. I'm lying to myself. Friendship be damned. I'm getting dangerously close to wanting a woman in my life but only if it's her.

Best thing for both of us is for me to get Shitface to give her a ride to the state line, and then forget all about her.

My fingers curl into my palms. Yeah. That's a plan. I give a sharp nod. Resolve made. As I straighten my back and determinedly step down the staircase, I'm preparing to issue instructions to the prospect. He can get her food, then get her out of here. I never need see her again.

And I won't regret it.

I falter on the third to bottom step as I realise the clubroom is noisier than normal for this time of day. Normally there's someone assing around, but mainly they don't get crazy until a few more beers have been downed. Tonight it's pandemonium, brothers all speaking at the same time, and each trying to be heard over the other.

"I'm getting that Fat Bob I've always had a hankering for."

"I want the Road Glide."

My head swivels left and right as if I'm watching a tennis match as various requests are called out around me.

I'm staring straight at Legit when he states, "New pipes will do for me."

"A new fucking clubhouse!" Fire shouts. "That's where we should start."

A horrible feeling comes over me, and I search for Legend to find him waiting to catch my eye. He shakes his head rapidly and holds up his hands, his gesture conveying, *nothing to do with me.*

Then, like the parting of the Red Sea, brothers step aside, allowing me to see we have a visitor. Without him uttering a word, it all becomes clear.

I wouldn't be the prez of a Wretched Soulz charter if I hadn't the brains to think quickly and come up with rapid solutions. Summing up the situation in a flash, I prepare to play this cool.

"Well met, Bro. Well met." Slugger, the titular head of the Wretched Soulz, stretches out his hand to me. "You've got yourself a fuckin' winner this time, haven't you?"

Playing dumb, I dutifully pull him in for a man hug and back slap. "Welcome, Prez." When I step back, I admit, "I haven't a fuckin' clue what you mean."

His eyes gleam like a man who's got a secret to share. "Mayhem didn't catch up with you?" As he names the IT expert of the Las Vegas crew, I recall it's him who's been helping Legend, and it's him who's clearly got a loose mouth. But without waiting for my response, Slugger informs me as eagerly as a child informing their parents about a good report, "That bitch who's been stealing from you? She's worth two million dollars."

I let my eyes widen as if this is new news, swinging around sharply at the slap on my back to see Bull's eyes gleaming at me. Then I turn back to Slugger needing to somehow buy time. "You're fuckin' kidding me."

"Nah. God's honest truth. You boys are gonna be rich."

With my mind working a mile a minute, I turn back to him, trying to keep my real emotions hidden. "Well, that's just great." I let a wide grin stretch my face, hoping it doesn't look like a skull's grimace.

It's not the first time I wish Slugger hadn't appeared in my clubhouse.

Ask any Soul and they'll tell you that each charter is run separately and there's no one at the head, no mother chapter nor national prez. What man would be stupid enough to have that target on his back? But all members know that bullshit is a ruse to keep Slugger protected. With no home base, our dear leader, or Alpha as some call him, travels various charters, in my view, sticking his nose in where it may or may not be wanted.

Not that he isn't a man I want on my side, but he can be a loose cannon, and it's not always possible to know what he's thinking or what he's going to do next. The fact he's obviously already announced our windfall means I've limited options on what I can do. Especially, when looking around me, I see the excited, eager faces. How could I disappoint my club?

How could I betray Helo? She's a woman who's already been through so much. She's already almost given her life for her country and even now I'm not sure how much she actually sacrificed—she's been left with severe PTSD for fuck's sake. I'm ninety percent sure if I had time to talk to my brothers, they'd understand how little she deserves being literally sold as though her life can be measured in a few new Harleys. Or make that fifty percent. Maybe.

I'm not sure I could chance it.

I couldn't live with myself. Or more correctly, I wouldn't want to live in a world without her in it. Already she's come to mean so much. *More than my club? My brothers?* Fuck no, never that. But I need to buy time. If I let Slugger have access to her, I'll lose her for good. I'm sure if I have a proper chance to explain the situation I can get my brothers on board, bring them around to my way of thinking that giving her up is exactly the same as the sex trafficking which we all abhor.

But there's no way of talking to them right now. Apart from Legend who's glaring daggers at me, everyone else seems to be caught up in the idea of how we'll spend our new funds. As for Slugger, I know he'll be calculating how much he'll ask for himself.

If I bring her downstairs now, into the midst of all this, someone's going to do something that I, at least, will always regret.

I've a good poker face, and now I use it. Still with my lips curving upward, I raise my chin at Slugger. "Carrying a value like that, she needs to be secured. I'll go get her then we can put her in the basement where she won't be able to escape."

Again, Bull's palm meets my back, while Slugger snorts a laugh.

"Fuckin' like the way you think, Brother."

CHAPTER THIRTEEN
HELO

It's probably counterintuitive that I feel safe in this outlaw bikers' clubhouse. Instead of sleeping with one eye open, once I'd heard the door lock behind Chaz, I'd let myself relax and catch up on some zzz, not only replacing those which I'd missed last night, but also several nights before that. While I trust Harold, he's not particularly security conscious, and anyone could just walk into his place. I'd been surprised to find that in Chaz's bed I slept like the dead, though undoubtably part of it was physical exhaustion brought on by the embarrassing episode I'd had once again.

After Chaz had woken me, though, I couldn't go back to sleep. My anxiety about my identity being discovered returned in full force, and after using his bathroom—tidier than I expected a man like his would be—I was more than ready to put this place in my rearview, and mentally swearing because he was making me wait. But I'd hold him to his offer of a ride, anywhere, in any direction, as it would be further than I'd get on my own two feet.

I'm not naturally a patient person. I'd rather be doing something, anything, other than waiting, but the Army had curbed my impatience to some extent. While I used to hate hanging around before we went on missions, wanting to throw myself into the fray of things rather than putting them off, I learned the best results came from careful planning, and waiting for the best time to present itself.

It's not easy waiting. Sounds come up from the clubroom below. I find the increasingly loud voices disturbing, warning of multiple men down there, far more than when I entered earlier. I've listened hard but can't distinguish any of the words. They all mingle into a cacophony of sound. As my heart rate speeds up, I force myself to remember the woman and her daughter who I'd met earlier—surely they wouldn't be around if there was any danger? I might not have talked to her long, but in no way did she seem cowed or fearful of her situation, or worried about the appropriateness of having such a young child around.

I know I'm being crazy. I'd lived my life in the Night Stalkers' world, and you can't get much more masculine than that. While on active duty, I'd never thought twice about being capable of holding my own in what was a predominately male environment.

So why's my heart racing now, adrenaline pumping around my body as if telling me I need to run? Deliberately slowing my breath, I manage to slow the blood rushing through my veins, while acknowledging the devil on my shoulder who reminds me of when men were definitely deleterious to my health.

Hearing male voices drinking and having fun used to have me not hesitating to join them, being well able to down beer and horse around just as much as them. But those six months, those twenty-six weeks, broke me. My hands clench.

I'm Queenie 'Helo' May. I'm a fucking Night Stalker, top of my game.

I'm a broken woman, no longer able to drive, ride or fly.

Try as I might, I can't slow my heart down, nor can shake the feeling of impending doom. This no longer feels like the sanctuary that allowed me to sleep. I'm on edge. I'm trying to fight sinking deeper into a mental dark hole of my own making when a brisk warning knock sounds at the door before it's pushed open. A wild-eyed Chaz enters.

My initial thought is that I'm grateful for the company to get me out of my head, the second does nothing to restore my equilibrium when I see the expression on his face. For the first time since I've met him, he doesn't seem sure of himself. His hands brush back over his bald head, then he does that again. His mouth opens, then shuts without any words coming out.

I watch as he takes a shuddering breath and draws back his shoulders. Then he bows forward, putting his hands on his knees, murmuring unintelligible words under his breath, before finally, he straightens, his mouth firm, as he obviously comes to a decision.

"We've got to go now," he snaps.

I've heard that tone before, used it myself, normally in a matter where delay was a matter of life or death. He hasn't brought the food that he promised, and my stomach's decidedly empty, but his expression warns me not to mention that.

I don't know him well enough to blindly follow him. "Why now?"

His eyes still and become dark. His chest expands, then deflates, and the words that he utters sound like a plea. "Trust me?"

If it was a demand I give him my faith, then I'd have baulked against such instruction. But that undeniable question mark at the end shows me he's giving me a choice. I'm bemused. When he left, there was a calmness about him, a confidence that all was well in his world. Now he's back, that certainty seems to have deserted him. He seems unsure, uncertain, and for a second I can't understand why. Then the only answer I can think of occurs to me. While I wouldn't expect a hardened MC prez would be overly worried about the fact, his behaviour suggests my past has caught up with me, and he needs to get me away.

Could I have underestimated whoever was after me? Could they pull together enough of a crew to threaten an MC? Of course, knowing the size of the bounty offered for me, that I have underestimated is probably fact.

Whatever the question, the answer is clear. Chaz is suggesting nothing I don't want. I've got to get away from here.

Maybe it's stupid to put my trust in one man. Chaz could be taking me *to* my enemy instead of away. But there's something about his agitation, his urgency to leave that transmits to me. He wastes no time. After I give him a rise of my chin, agreeing to go with him, he throws my backpack at me, then as he opens the door, signals me to stay back until he's checked it's all clear.

Are they already in the clubhouse? It's the only explanation that comes to mind. Just the thought gets adrenaline rushing through my body as my heart starts to pound. Not fear, but anticipation, much like hearing the sound of the rotors starting to turn, knowing we could be lifting off and facing anything.

My hands don't shake. My nerves are rock steady as I go into action mode. Following Chaz's example, I quietly step out of the door and follow him along the hall in the opposite direction to the stairs. Without being told, I quietly ease down the fire escape stairs which brings us to the rear of the building, then carefully skirt the brickwork until we're out front where the bikes are parked.

Chaz signals me to stay back while he gets his bike out of line, then, when he gives an urgent summons with his hand, I rush forward and throw myself on behind him. He waves to the prospect manning the gate and instructs him.

"Close the gate behind us and don't let anyone else out. You do and you won't be getting your fuckin' patch."

Shitface's eyes widen at his strange instruction, but snaps to attention as his prez starts the bike and quickly gets into gear, twisting the throttle so hard, if I wasn't holding on, I'd have been in danger of sliding off the back.

I glance behind as we hit the road and see the prospect has done as instructed.

I tap Chaz's shoulder as we pass the turn that would have led to Harold's, but he ignores my touch and the wind whips away my frustrated shout. I've no option but to be driven away into the unknown without clothes, toiletries or anything.

Fuck my life.

Accepting it must be too dangerous to go get my shit, I let my heart rate gradually slow to match the thump of the engine. I'm just relieved to be moving away from any threat. When I see an object fly past and just have time to note it's Chaz's phone, I realise he's doing all he can to ensure danger remains behind. There's no way to track us.

Miles fly past accompanied by the roar from the exhaust. I lose sense of time as the road rushes beneath us. At first, I'm exhilarated, enjoying the ride even though I'd rather be controlling the bike. There's something about motorcycles that give the illusion of freedom that I miss from the sky. But as more time goes by, I start to feel my ass getting numb and wonder how far Chaz intends to take me before dropping me off. For the first few miles, he'd constantly been looking in his rearview, but then when he turned off the main road, made so many twists and turns I could almost believe we were going back to the place we started from, I could feel the tension leave his body.

We ride and ride, keeping to secondary roads and past signposts which don't help much to give me a final destination and it's then that belatedly my brain kicks back in. *Why did Chaz prevent his brothers from following him?*

Damn it! Has he discovered the bounty on my head? Is he now riding to deliver me to my nemesis? Did he delay his brothers as he didn't want to share the reward?

As the wind whips through my hair, that's not the only thing starting to chill me. *Would Chaz really betray his club like that*? What do I know of the man? He's a criminal living outside the law but the one thing I thought he'd possess in spades is loyalty, to his club if no one else. If he knows of the bounty, would he really keep that to himself?

Two million dollars would be enough to set a man up for life, or, at least, for a very long time. Perhaps he's been looking for an out from the club and I came along at the right point in his life.

Glancing around his shoulder, I see the bike's pushing a steady eighty miles an hour. Unless I want to kill myself, I'm his unwilling passenger for now. The one plus is that he's taking me far away from the place I could have been reported to have been last seen. The danger could be that he's delivering me to the exact people I don't want to see.

Moving closer to hug him tighter, as if I'm enjoying the ride, I can feel the bulge against my stomach that suggests he's carrying a gun in his belt. Although it would be too hard to explain my wandering hands were I to try to prove it, I'd be surprised if he didn't have another in an ankle holster. I'm carrying one myself. Like normal, underestimating a female, the assholes hadn't searched me.

Confident I can disarm him without him suspecting a thing, I decide to let this journey continue. If he thinks I'm going to blindly trust him, he's got another think coming. I'll wait until we get to our destination then he'll see how wrong it is to mess with a Night Stalker.

It would be a shame if I have to kill him. But even the most perfect looking skin of a fruit can hide a rotten core.

After a couple of hours, he pulls over to top off his tank. Suspecting he might not have chosen this place as random, my hand hovers close to my ankle, ready to draw my weapon, but the place seems deserted. No other vehicles have come to this out-of-the-way service station. Testing him, I tap his shoulder.

"I need the facilities."

"Sure." He kicks down the stand as I dismount. Then he gets a look at my face. This man isn't stupid. "Er, Helo. I've not kidnapped you."

"Haven't you?" I swing around. "Then where the fuck are we, Chaz? And don't kid me this is a shortcut to the border."

His lips press together. "I'm taking you somewhere safe."

My brows rise. "Okay. But where?"

His brows draw down in a V and his eyes harden. "Somewhere no one will find you. I promise you that."

"Where?" I repeat, ignoring his rising temper. "You asked me to trust you and so far I've done that. But I need more information other than just follow you blindly."

"For fuck's sake, woman. I'm in this as much as you are now." His head jerks toward the shop. "If I don't give you information, you can't share."

He thinks I'm going to contact someone and give myself away? My eyes widen. If I knew where we were going, there's no one I can call in any event. I do need to pee, so I turn and walk away, if only to give myself a few minutes to think about what I should do. Stay, and let Chaz take me where he wants to? Or extricate myself from the situation and head off on my own?

If I take the latter option, I'll have to beg, borrow or steal to get food and clothing, but that's nothing I haven't had to do before. As I wash my hands, I consider it. I'm out in the middle of nowhere, and to be honest, I'm sick of running. While the weirdness of the journey means I now don't trust Chaz further than I could throw him, if he is taking me to claim the reward, then it would give me a chance to face my enemy head-on. It would at least be good to discover who wants me dead so badly.

Maybe I can end this once and for all.

Wondering how much of a fool I'm being, I go back outside, and obediently situate myself back on the bike.

Dusk falls and the skies grow dark. Soon the way is only lit by the headlight. We've passed no houses for miles and now the road starts to narrow and wind up through trees.

This is definitely nowhere near the state line, and there's no bus to be caught or taxicab in sight.

Chaz turns onto a rutted track, dropping our speed to a crawl, then, finally, comes to a halt. He taps my leg and I get off, then wait as he dismounts and undoes the padlock on a rustic gate.

"Where are we?" Looking around, I see no fresh tire tracks on the ground, nothing to suggest that someone is waiting for us.

For a reply, he pushes his bike through the gate then waves me to join him. He closes the wood barrier behind him, failing, I notice, to reapply the lock, then gets back onto the bike and turns expectantly in my direction. I shrug. Well, I've come this far, might as well continue onto the end. Storing up the knowledge that if Chaz intends to betray me, it's a visitor I need to prepare for.

I stay quiet as he continues up a track that's barely suitable for a bike, and after a couple of minutes, the headlight reveals a cabin in the middle of the woods.

Okkayy. Another sign he might have brought me here to kill me—sure would be a good place to hide a body.

Without waiting for him to tell me, as he kills the engine, I'm already off the bike, standing with my hands on my hips and peering through the gloom at the building in front of me.

Exchanging the headlight for a flashlight, Chaz steps up beside me, and takes hold of my elbow.

"Watch yourself. It's a bit uneven."

"Where the fuck are we?" This time I ask, I get his attention, having whipped his own gun from his belt and now have it pointed at the back of his head.

Unfazed, he chuckles softly as he holds his hands out to his sides. "It's a cabin I own."

I suppose it's something I've not been brought to someone else's home, but I'm not even sure I believe him.

"And why have you brought me here?"

"Woman, I'm trying to fuckin' help you." Exasperation sounds in his voice. "You needed some place to hide off the grid, and that's what I'm giving to you." He shakes his head, and I swear he adds a murmured, "Fuck knows why."

Fuck knows why indeed. I certainly don't. I've no idea why he made sure his brothers couldn't follow him, or why he's brought me nowhere obviously near the state line. He's done nothing to make me trust him.

Warily, I examine what I can see of the cabin. It looks deserted from the outside, no other vehicle unless it's hidden, and no sign there's anyone else here. I've learned to have eyes in the back of my head, to be aware of threats before I can see them. As all my senses are on high alert, my ears pick up the sound of an engine. And, while it's still a distance away, I quickly realise, in this isolated place, there's only one place it could be heading.

"Fuck you!" I scream, jabbing my gun painfully into his scalp. "You've given me away. I'm going to fucking kill you!"

CHAPTER FOURTEEN

CHAZ

I*'ve lost my fucking mind.*

From the moment I heard Slugger talking about selling out Queenie for money, all I saw was red, and from that point on, I'd acted purely on instinct and hadn't stopped to think.

If Slugger hadn't been there, I'd have whipped the brothers into church and educated them about a few things. I'd have knocked their heads together and tried to convince them to come around to my way of thinking. Legend would have been on my side, StoryTeller, too, I think. Maybe I'd have gotten enough ayes to keep her breathing. But though normally, as prez, I'd have the casting vote on any course of action, with the national prez in the house, all of us would be expected to defer to him. Especially when he was endorsing what clearly a lot of them were thinking. As it was, Slugger had already gotten them riled up, their mindset like a group of piranhas heading in for the kill. I had a vision of Helo descending the stairs and her being torn to pieces, though that wouldn't have happened without her taking a few lumps out of my men. One thing I know for certain, she wouldn't have gone easily.

I couldn't risk it. Everything inside me had screamed, *get her away.* No time to stop and argue a battle I feared Slugger had already won. Getting her away would at least give me space to see if there's another route I could take to sort this mess out.

My overriding compulsion was that I didn't want Helo to end up dead.

It was only when I got some miles from the clubhouse, I'd realised how badly I'd fucked up. Even then, though, however I looked at it, if I wanted to save Helo, I couldn't see any alternative solution. With her affliction, I couldn't have simply handed her the keys to my bike.

But I can't minimise what I've done. I'm not just a member of the Wretched Soulz MC, I'm their president. I've turned on my club. I've taken away their chance of becoming two million dollars richer, and all for a bitch who stole from us. If I'm lucky, I'll be out bad. If I'm not, I'll, too, have a price on my head, and the first Soul to see me will have orders to shoot first and ask questions after.

And fuck me, but I'd had no chance to explain, and now I'm risking that bullet in my skull not from one of my brothers, but from the woman who doesn't yet know she owes me her life. Ironic doesn't begin to cover it. She's misinterpreted what I've done to keep her safe. Even if she doesn't kill me, I'm going to have a fucking bruise from how hard she just bashed the barrel of the gun into my head.

"Calm the fuck down," I rasp out. "It's not what you think." Belatedly I realise that telling a woman to calm down may not be the smartest thing.

It's not, as that gun rammed into my skull once again

proves. "You know about the bounty and you're going to sell me out."

Rolling my eyes, I refute, "Yes, I know you've got a fuckin' big price on your head, but I'm not selling you out. I'm protecting you, woman." While I'm irate at the situation, I try to keep my voice level, unsure how trigger-happy she is.

The car's engine noise grows louder, showing it's getting close, then dies as it comes to a halt. The gun moves from my head and now is jammed into my back as she shoves me toward the door of the cabin.

"Open it," she demands.

I do, then she sidles around me, wrenching me around, so I'm framed in the doorway and in between my expected visitor and her. As the car pulls up, I only hope Jacinta looks innocent enough that Helo won't pull the trigger.

"It's someone bringing us supplies," I say in an even tone, hoping the ancient bright pink sprayed Kia Soul will persuade her it's no one intent on doing her harm. No self-respecting man, let alone someone with a grudge, would be seen driving such a car.

Another prod in my back. "Put your hands up."

I do. Jacinta extracts a couple of bags from the car, then turns to face me. When she sees I'm clearly being held at gunpoint, she gasps loudly and the shopping drops from her hands.

"*Madre de Dios, ¿qué está pasando*?" Copying me, she puts her hands in the air. "Chaz?"

"Who are you?" Helo demands. The gun still held steady shows she hasn't yet dismissed our visitor as a threat.

"Jacinta's the woman who takes care of the cabin for me." I speak soothingly, but fast, seeing Jacinta looks like she might faint any second now. She doesn't know I'm the prez of an outlaw MC. As far as she's concerned, I'm just a city man who appears from time to time for a bit of R and R in the mountains. I doubt she ever expected I'd bring trouble to her door. I'm annoyed as good help is hard to find and I hope Helo hasn't scared her off. Though, I suppose, in the scheme of things, losing the caretaker for the cabin is the least of the disruption she's brought to my life. And it's only a loss I'll suffer if I stay alive.

"Open the back door," Helo nods toward the car and demands. Luckily, Jacinta's English is good enough to react to her command.

I wait as Helo analyses the situation. The trunk is open, only shopping bags have come out, and it's obvious there's no one in the car hiding. Jacinta couldn't look more innocent if she tried. Though she hadn't been issued with the instruction, she, too, has again lifted her hands high.

"Back up," Helo states, applying pressure to my shoulder. I take a step back out of the way of the door. When she's got us where she wants us, she calls out, "Bring the bags inside."

Jacinta looks dubious, but I give her a reassuring dip and rise of my head. I wouldn't put it past Helo to kill me, but I doubt she'd hurt an innocent woman. Bags in hand, Jacinta obeys, scurrying in quickly, dumping the bags, then turning to escape.

But she stops by me, and her work ethic clearly tops her fear as she asks shakily, "You want me to make bed?"

"I think we can handle that ourselves," I tell her.

Helo quickly glances down at what Jacinta's brought inside. Seeing just groceries, she says, "Just leave."

Jacinta's eyes narrow as she looks at me. "*Mujer loca,*" she decides. I have to agree Helo does indeed seem like a crazy woman. "*¿Necesitas ayuda*? Help? You need?"

As much as a man held at gunpoint can, I attempt a reassuring smile. "Nah, I'm fine, sweetheart. I'll call if I need anything else."

"Go," Helo directs as Jacinta seems to still be summing up whether I need rescuing or not.

It's when I add another sharp nod, Jacinta throws up her hands, and with one last "*Mujer loco,*" mumbled half under her breath, she goes back to her car and opens the door.

"Padlock the gate," I call out to her, and the up and down dip of her head shows me she's heard and understood.

She slides into the seat, starts the car, and performs a complicated and unnecessary five-point-turn manoeuvre to get pointed the right way. Helo stands still as a stone behind me as Jacinta disappears down the track.

While she's distracted, making sure our visitor leaves, I decide it's time for me to take control back. Swinging around fast to take her by surprise, I grab the gun, wrenching it from her fingers. Now it's me pointing the weapon.

"It's time we had a fuckin' talk." As, at last, I'm now in charge, I can allow myself to be angry.

But does my tone of voice faze her? Not one fucking bit. Her eyes narrow as she glances at the gun in my hand, then, as if assessing she's in no real danger, she turns her back. Stepping over to the table, she peers into the bags Jacinta had left. Extracting a package, she lifts it out, bringing it to her nose and breathing in deeply.

"Mmm. Coffee."

Ignoring that the sound goes straight to my dick, I jerk my head. "Kitchen's that way if you want to get some brewing."

My stomach rumbles, reminding me we need other sustenance as well. As she disappears in the direction I indicated, I take the risk of putting my gun back in the waistband of my pants, then pick up the rest of the groceries to check. One of the contents should be a frozen pizza that won't take long to prepare.

In the small kitchen area, she glances as I approach, but seeing a flat box has replaced the weapon, quickly resumes the task she's begun. For a few moments we work together in silence. Once I've a hot coffee in my hand and the pizza emitting tantalising smells from the heated oven, I sit at the table and kick out the second chair, then jerk my chin toward her, then toward the seat.

I watch, analysing her as she takes a moment before accepting the invitation. She's not uptight, but also not relaxed, and hasn't yet put down her guard. Wise, as she knows I'm the one with the weapon. Then I realise she doesn't seem particularly bothered about the inequality, leading me to have my suspicions.

"You're armed?"

Her eyes meet mine across the table, and one side of her mouth turns up. Guess she's answered that. Ankle holster, I'd bet.

We both know where we are, an uneasy truce. Who's going to survive the encounter may depend on who can draw first. I must need my head examined as the thought of meeting my match turns me the fuck on, meaning I subtly have to adjust myself to avoid the imprint of my zipper on my cock. That part of me thinks finding out whether she'd be just as feisty in bed is the most important thing to discover.

I can't hope to think other than she's worth it. Right now I'm a wanted man by my club. *What the fuck have I done?* But however I try to reason with myself, I can't see how I could have done anything else. Queenie deserves a chance, and hopefully, as I'm the one who's giving it to her, I'll get my reward.

Luckily it appears she reads nothing of my thoughts as she

cups her hands around her drink, then lets out a deep sigh. She grimaces slightly, and her brow furrows as though she's perplexed. When she speaks, her tone is far from combative. "What the fuck is going on, Chaz? Why am I here? Why didn't you just drop me somewhere and leave me?"

Good questions which I'm not sure I've got answers to, or none that she'll want to hear. Sure, I needed to get her away safe, but why did I come with her? I doubt she wants to know how much she intrigues my cock, or all the very dirty things I want to do to her. Or, actually, it's more than that. How much I want this amazing woman to be mine. Whatever, I'm a fucking grown man, a president with responsibilities. I shouldn't be led by my dick. I take a couple of sips of coffee, then begin to let her into my thoughts.

"I've fucked up royally by taking you," I admit, accepting what I've done today has been totally out of character.

If she wanted to hear I had a plan, I've clearly disappointed her. Puzzled eyes stare into mine for a moment, then she raises her chin. "I'd rather you were straight with me, Chaz. Are you going to betray me?"

I know she's intelligent enough to understand that if I was, I'd hardly be telling her. But as I see her waiting for my response, I notice her concentration, analysing my features for the tiniest tell. But I'm going to tell her the honest truth. It's up to her what she does with it.

I snort but with no amusement. "I worked for my patch, Helo, gave blood, sweat and tears to the club. Got the trust of my brothers. Carried on doing my bit, was made sergeant-at-arms. The brothers recognised my club meant everything to me, and when there was a vacancy, put me forward to be prez. Every day since, I've tried to be worthy of it."

Her eyes narrow and she shrugs.

I raise my chin, waiting until I can see her watching me,

hoping she'll understand the seriousness of what I'm going to say. Inhaling sharply, I admit, "Bringing you here might, nah, will most probably mean, me losing my patch." Which, before meeting her, was the most important thing in my life. I stare down into the coffee for a moment, then again raise my eyes to meet her face. In a solemn tone I voice the worst outcome. "I might be facing a death sentence."

For a second she stops breathing completely. When she moves again, it's to put her coffee cup down and to lean forward, elbows on the table, hands clasped. "What exactly are you saying?"

My shoulders rise then drop down. "I knew the size of the price on your head while we were still at the shop." I watch her face remain expressionless as if she expected nothing less. "I decided to keep that info to myself, and Legend, who'd found that little tidbit out had his own reasons for not betraying a Night Stalker. But my other brothers? Two million dollars could prove one hell of a temptation, and you," I point a finger toward her, "stole from us. Hell, most thought you intended to take off with the bike."

She winces, conceding the point. "But you weren't able to keep it quiet."

Brushing my hands over my face, I grimace. "It wasn't that. My tech guy is good, but your records are redacted. He got some help from another member of the club, one who's in another charter. He was the one who couldn't keep his mouth shut, and Slugger got wind of it."

She's gone tense as she asks, "Slugger?"

I meet her eyes. "Some call him the national prez of the Wretched Soulz."

"Some?"

I give a twisted grin. "It's not confirmed. Officially, each charter of the Soulz is a law unto themselves."

"So this Slugger holds some sway over your club." She's not stupid, but then I didn't expect her to be.

I raise my chin, then lower it. "While you were sleeping, he arrived. Spouted about the bounty and got my brothers riled up about it." My mouth quirks. "They'd all but gotten the Harley brochure out and were already ordering from it."

She stands and walks over to the window, her hands forming fists. She doesn't have to speak to let me know how upset she is that to my club her life's worth no more than a few new motorcycles.

"I didn't stop to think," I tell her, again rubbing my hands across my face. "Some of the men would have been with me, but I think the rest would have seen no reason for not giving you up."

"Because I stole from you."

That's it, exactly. Helo's hardly some innocent looking for protection from us.

She stares at the trees outside. "You took the payday away from your club."

Put so starkly, it sounds bad. "I've bought us some time." I'm hoping I'll be able to explain why and what I've done. Difficult when even I don't understand my precipitous decision that I had to get her away. If she asked me for an explanation, I don't know what I'd say. I just feel in my bones she's someone who deserves to be saved. Maybe not just my bones, my cock had a lot to say about it.

"I don't understand why," she says flatly. "You owe nothing to me. You don't know anything about me except I'm an ex vet." She does that little shrug again. "I know some people are grateful to those who've served, but it has to be more than that."

It's hard for me to put what I don't understand into words. "You're fuckin' brave, intelligent. You've probably faced death in the face a thousand times. To be a woman in the Night Stalkers you must have been a fuckin' demon in the sky. A life like that doesn't deserve to be snuffed out for whatever amount of dollars."

"You know nothing about me at all," she refutes, staring me down. "You surmise I'm a hero, yet you know little more than my name and rank. If I was a man, would you still be protecting me?"

I know enough about myself to know I would not. "A man could look after himself," I say, immediately knowing that was unwise. As a literal hiss comes out of her mouth, I hasten to rectify my error. "So shoot me," I start fast. "I noticed you were a fuckin' woman." I raise my hand to pre-empt her interruption. "I know you can protect yourself, but I didn't want you to have to. I wanted to help you."

"At the expense of losing your club?" Her words are spat out as if she doesn't believe me.

I have to give her more. I have to lay all my cards on the table. Running my hands over my skull, I prepare to bare my soul. "Never wanted an old lady. If I want sex, I've any number of volunteers. Never saw a woman as my equal, as a companion or confidant." I risk a glance up and see she's listening avidly. "Until you, Helo. Suddenly you appeared in my world and turned it upside down." I huff a mirthless laugh. "Here I am, spilling my cards, when even I can't understand my reaction to you. And hell, I don't even know how you look at me in return. I'm older than you—"

There's a ping from the oven timer. I stand and take out the pizza. Without me having to ask, she's by my side and taking down a couple of plates. As if by mutual agreement, we suspend conversation as we both sate our appetites.

I've bared my soul, and now she's going to reject me. Well, I deserve it. There I was, thinking I was some hotshot who had a chance with a superwoman who must be ten years off my age. The only reason she hasn't immediately shot me down is she's trying to be diplomatic about it. She is, after all, isolated in a cabin far away from any town, with no means of transport. And she doesn't know me from Adam. I could have a suppressed anger inside me that won't take well to any rejection.

I'm a fucking fool. I deserve to eat my own bullet.

Accepting I've probably already crashed and burned as far as any exploration of a relationship between us is concerned, like an addict grasping one last final fix before rehab, I can't seem to take my eyes off her.

She eats with economical movements, as if putting fuel into her body means little more than me pumping gas into my bike. As she chews and swallows mechanically, she doesn't once glance up, seeming to analyse every piece before eating. I decide she's buying time, expecting to have to walk out of here and sensibly taking the chance to fill her stomach first.

When she swallows a final time, then rubs her lips with the back of her hand, she emits a heavy sigh. As I brace myself for rejection, she leans back and a clouded look comes into her eyes.

"I stole from your club as I didn't think it was really theft if it belonged to criminals."

After her opening statement, she glances up. I don't know whether to laugh or be offended at her explanation, but as I can't deny we pride ourselves on being a one-percenter club living outside society's rules, I'm on thin ice if I deny the handle, even if I don't like it.

Still, I do defend myself, even if the same can't be said for a number of my brothers. "I've never been to prison in my life."

There's a slight upturn to her lips as she retorts, "Luck that you haven't been caught?"

That about sums it up. Though I'd exchange the word luck with one that represented my intelligence, and my ability to stay one step ahead of the law. For an answer, I raise my shoulders, then after a second, lower them down.

Her mouth purses, and any sign of amusement is gone as though it was never there. "I should have known better than to mess with your club, but it was a challenge. My career—my old career—I had to do whatever was needed to get the job done, pushing my Black Hawk to its limits, using all the weapons at my teams' disposal. Making decisions in a split moment, manoeuvring to give the gunners the best shots. Analysing masses of disparate data for hours, never letting my concentration falter. Missions were exciting, adrenaline filled. There wasn't a second that you could relax. I'm used to burning energy, using my wits and judgement, balancing risks and benefits, changing a plan at the last second to accommodate new threats or information based on weather conditions or updated intelligence." She pauses and glances toward me.

I lift my chin, showing I understand what she's saying. Then, in case she doesn't see my comprehension tell her, "Civilian life is boring."

She snorts at my adequate summation. But hell, I don't need that explanation. I, too, served, and while much was routine, shit came at you out of the blue and you had to react to situations. Had to cope with people being shot and injured —or worse—around you, and without pause take over their position, putting your feelings on hold until later. The military life is not for the faint-hearted, and it's why so many veterans return unable to cope with everyday life. It's why I joined the MC rather than seeking another occupation. I, too, understand the need for adrenaline, and to feel you're in control of your own fate and eventual destination. Of course, in both circumstances, it's not one big blast. In both the MC and the military, the majority of time is spent hanging around, trying to stay occupied while waiting for something to happen, then when it does, it's all-hands-on-deck while the shit goes down. The down time can hang heavy, trying to find something to occupy your mind and your hands. Knowing this about her makes it less strange she took the risk of breaking into our shop. It was a challenge she couldn't resist.

Helo's just like me and my brothers. We may not make old bones, but what we do while we're alive is make life worth living.

And fuck me, but her rationalisation has done nothing more than emphasise how she'd make an amazing old lady.

"You're fuckin' perfect," I breathe out, not realising I'm speaking my thoughts aloud. "Perfect for me." Sharp eyes meet mine. "I've never met anyone like you." I indicate myself, knowing I'm overreaching, but unable not to try. "From the moment I met you, you intrigued me. You're beautiful, sexy, but more than that, your soul calls to mine. Fuck, I'm messing this up royally. You probably wouldn't even look twice at me. I'm too old—"

"Not perfect. Far from it," she interrupts. Bowing her head, her body shudders. As if it's an effort to summon the words, her voices catches as she starts, "I was held captive for six months."

I open my mouth to tell her I already know that, when she shakes her head, a silent plea with her eyes for me to listen.

It's not long after she starts speaking that I, a hardened MC prez, am not sure I'm strong enough to want to hear the full story, let alone understand how she could have lived it. But instead of cutting her short and telling her I get the picture, I continue to listen.

I'm just glad we've already eaten.

CHAPTER FIFTEEN

HELO

I'd suspected part of the reason Chaz was helping me was because he'd like a sexual relationship. Old news, many men are attracted to me. Maybe it's the way I'm put together, but often, as a strong independent woman, I imagine they think it would be a challenge to tame me. Sometimes I'd say yes, other times I'd say no.

From the time I'd met Chaz, he intrigued me. On the physical front, he's got the strong, brooding looks, a muscular body that would attract me, and I've found nothing to dislike about his personality. While unable to admit it to myself, part of the reason I returned to the shop was to see him again. It's been a long time since any man has stirred my interest. But just because I find him good-looking doesn't mean I need to do more than admire him from a distance.

While we've had our ups and downs in such a short time period, I think I'm beginning to understand him. Like me, he's a leader, and in that I consider him my equal. And strange for a man, I believe he regards me as a partner, not a possession. If it had been *before,* maybe I'd give it a shot. It would have been fine if my attraction to him had been one-sided.

But apparently it's not. For some crazy reason, this man has put me in front of his club, and now I've got to throw a bucket of cold water over him. Whatever's in his head about a me and him has to stop. He's possibly given up so much, he deserves to know the reason.

But God knows, this is hard as fuck. I'm about to tell him things only disclosed before to my counsellor, and even that didn't help. I'm laying myself bare, stepping back into my nightmare, and taking him along for the ride.

Drawing in an unsteady breath, I prepare to enlighten him. "Though I was captured along with the men, I was soon separated from them."

He leans his elbows on the table, resting his chin on his hands, giving me all his attention.

"They had particular ways of torturing women, treating them very different from those with dicks." Whether it's the tremor in my voice or the way my hands shake, his eyes widen in understanding, and I'm happy I don't have to spell it out. "Their torture of me wasn't to get information. They didn't expect a woman would know secrets worth knowing. They just saw me as a toy, something they had no trouble using."

My hands clench and my leg starts bouncing. "They were clever. They didn't bruise my face or anywhere visible, and they paraded me in front of the men, taunting them that I was cooperating. Mocking I preferred them to American men."

He wipes a hand over his face. "Didn't you correct them? And fuck, didn't the other soldiers know they had to be lying?"

"It was made clear, if I said a word in my defence, they'd kill one of the men. The threat kept me quiet." I shrug. "At first I think they didn't believe our captors, but torture does funny things to a person. They killed anyway, and my lack of visible injuries, lack of protestation, well, I could see their attitude changing." I swallow a couple of times to get saliva into my mouth as my brain conjures up the images in full technicolour. "They stripped me of my uniform, dressed me in their female's clothes, and forced me to attend the executions, the beheadings. Parading me as a traitor was just one more cruelty for me and them. "

Jesus. Fuck. He breathes out the words, but I still hear them. I rub at my temples, trying to clear my head, which is intent on showing me the sights, sounds and smells, throwing me back to that time. Of meeting the accusing eyes of the man about to be killed as he'd been told I'd helped them choose the next victim.

Their torture wasn't just physical, it was mental as well. What could I have done? Protesting my innocence, screaming that, while not visible, I was being hurt as much as them, would only have resulted in more death. It wasn't mine I was worried about, but I know playing with their captives' psyche and emotions was an enjoyable game to them. If I'd stopped it, I might have escalated the end of everyone.

If hating me kept them alive, then that was the way it would have to be.

Chaz is waiting. I know I have to use the words to explain. "To the men held captive, I was being kept in luxury. I'd sold them out, was fed and clothed because I gave the terrorists what they wanted." My hands fist, and my eyes shutter. "My brothers-in-arms thinking that was bad enough, but they had no idea what I was actually going through. I was a toy, and it wasn't just their cocks they tortured me with." Pausing, I can't stop the whole-body shudder as I finally admit the consequences of how I was treated. "They may not have taken my life, but they took my present as well as my future. I can't fly, and due to their *tender* ministrations, they damaged me so badly I had to have a hysterectomy when I returned. I will never be able to have children."

Unable to stand receiving sympathy that would just sanction my self-pity, I fully close my eyes, resting my head in my hands. The cabin isn't cold, yet my body is racked with shivers. Now I'm guilty I hadn't explained how broken I was when we'd first met. He'd never have made the sacrifices he has if he knew I wasn't worth saving.

As he stays silent, I feel the moments tick by. Eventually I stand and go stare out of the window, trying to focus on something that will take my mind away from the scenes that keep replaying in my head. As I feel the air change around me, I'm alerted that Chaz has stepped into my space.

His deep voice sounds from behind me. "These fainting episodes you have. They're PTSD?"

That's safer ground than going back through the things that were done to me. "Vasovagal Syncope is the official name. When something triggers me, my heart rate and blood pressure drop."

"What are your triggers?" he asks, then quickly surmises for himself. "Let me guess, a man behaving in a threatening way, or children."

That's two of them. But there's more. "The way the air moves. A certain scent on the breeze. A sound, a word. Practically anything can have that effect on me."

"Is there any treatment?"

"Avoiding triggers?" I half-turn, letting him see that while they are so numerous and can come out of nowhere, that's hardly something that I can achieve. "Oh, they suggest not getting dehydrated or stressed, and, of course, trying to stay in safe places so you don't hurt yourself when the inevitable happens."

"Like lying on a beam, shooting at members of an outlaw MC."

"That's not my definition of stressful," I retort.

He chuckles loudly, then says, "I so want to give you a hug." His hands lift, but they remain still in the air, a physical as well as verbal offer. Just one move on my part would take me into his arms. Human comfort that I haven't felt for what seems like years.

Again, a shuddering sigh leaves my body. "I like you, Chaz. I appreciate everything you've done for me, but I can't repay you." I give a sad shake of my head. "I suspect a major trigger would be a man trying to touch me." And that had already been proven, the prominence of his enlarged cock had ended our fight.

"I can understand you not wanting a man to fuck you," he states bluntly, his eyes narrowing. "I just think you've been on your own so long, you'd like someone on your side. A hug is all I'm offering." He breaks off, harrumphs, then grins. "I've too much respect for my balls to push you too far."

My body wavers toward him. Something about what he's offering calls viscerally to me. He's right. I've been alone far too long, all my life if I'm honest. I feel drained from my confessions, and the idea of leaning on someone if only for a short time is something I'm loathe to turn down.

But I need to warn him. I have no clue what my traitorous body is likely to do. "I might..."

"I've got you. I won't let you fall." With that statement, he takes the decision out of my hands, placing his lightly on my arms and pulling me to him. His hold is so gentle there's no way to feel entrapped, and with his palm on my head as encouragement, I place my cheek on his chest. He feels solid. He's all muscle and no flab, and even though he's not wearing his cut, the scent of leather still pervades as though it's ingrained into his skin. I don't feel trapped, nor afraid. For a while, he holds me without moving, then slowly he starts to stroke my hair.

His non-threatening, non-sexual caress calms me, and rather than the rate of my heart dropping, its beat seems to sync with his. There's no telltale ringing in my ears, no dizziness, no signs I'm going to pass out. The longer he holds me, the more of my weight I give him, and the more I relax.

It's a few minutes before his chest rumbles. "You think the person after you is one of those who survived?" I start to tense, and he continues his caress. "Or maybe a relative of one who died?

"I got a medal," I whisper. "One I didn't deserve."

"You fuckin' deserved it," he snarls. If his words hadn't been in my defence, the intensity of his tone might have frightened me. "You didn't do anything wrong," he continues. "You probably saved lives doing your best to get the helicopter down, and then did what you had to in order to survive. You sacrificed for your country in ways men could never understand."

I might not be a girly girl, but like most women, I thought one day I might get married and start a family. Or, at least, that I would have that option. Of course, not every woman can conceive, but few have the opportunity taken away. I suppose it's human nature to want something when it's no longer a possibility.

"Way I see it is you're the same as someone who's lost a limb though there's no visible injury."

"Being without an arm or a leg would be worse," I disagree.

"But probably just as hard to come to terms with."

His arms are too comforting, so much so I make myself pull away. I can't get attached to anyone, not given the way I'm currently forced to live. I also don't want to feel I owe anyone anything, and Chaz has risked everything to get me away.

Turning toward the window again, I wrap my arms around my body. It's no substitute for his, but it's far safer. I speak over my shoulder.

"How did you get Jacinta here when you threw your phone away?"

"I always carry a couple of burners in my saddlebags."

Of course he does. But I'm glad he's got a way to communicate. "Ring your brothers and go back to them. It might not be too late to mend your fences."

"Darlin', I sealed my fate when I took you away. The only recompense I could make is taking you back with me and that's the price I'm not going to pay."

"I don't understand." I've told this man he can have no expectations, no hopes of a future with me.

"Would it help if I say neither do I?" He comes up behind me, resting his fingers lightly on my shoulders. "I've got no fuckin' idea what made me do such a crazy thing. I just knew I couldn't let whoever that bastard is get his hands on you."

"I'm no one to you."

"For some reason, you are," he contradicts. "At the very least I want a chance to get to know you and I couldn't do that if I gave you up or if you disappeared halfway across the country." His fingers squeeze gently. "Let me help you, darlin'."

Still addressing my comments to the world outside, I speak softly, "I was released from the hospital, came back and started to rebuild my life. Not that I knew where to start. There wasn't much call for a pilot who could no longer fly, or even a mechanic who couldn't drive. I was trying to work out what to do to survive when the threatening letters began to arrive." I pause, thinking back to how it all began. "I didn't think anything of them until they became more detailed and revealed shit that wasn't in the public domain. Then..." Automatically my shoulders shrug as the remembered pain comes back to me. "I was actually coming back from a job interview when two masked men chased me." I pause, wondering how much I need to say. Then decide my injury speaks for itself and that there's no necessity to go into the horrors of that day. "They thought the pain would be enough to disable me, but they were wrong. I got away. But it was obvious from then on, I needed to take the threats seriously. They knew my address, so I moved. More letters arrived. They were tracking me in some way. So I packed a bag, ditched my phone and took out as much cash as I could before stowing my cards away. I've lived off the grid since."

"Did you go to the police?" When I'm slow in answering, he prompts, "Well?"

Slowly I dip my head up and down. "I did." For all the good it had done. "They weren't interested."

His eyes narrow. "Not fuckin' interested? Surely you showed them your shoulder?"

I had, but it hadn't helped. "There was a photo of a Marine on the detective's desk." My eyes glaze as I remember.

"My son relies on pilots like you to get him out, not to crash." He'd sneered as though I'd done it on purpose. "You're accusing men who are either dead or returned half the men that they were."

He was right. One had lost a foot, another half his arm.

"And here you're sitting in front of me, nothing the fuck wrong with you and making up stories about real heroes. At worst, you're attention seeking. At best, you're suffering PTSD, probably because you spent six months without being allowed to put makeup on."

I hadn't realised I'd repeated what the detective had told me out loud until Chaz swears violently, and follows his exclamation by telling me, "PTSD is a given. No one could have escaped without that." He brushes his hands across his head.

"Being captured was bad for everyone, but the men weren't tortured all the time. You were. You were kept away from your fellow soldiers and isolated. You were made to put on a show so they wouldn't be killed in front of you. Losing a limb is fuckin' hard, not denying that, but it can be compensated for. No one's ever going to be able to give back what you lost, or for you to forget what you're carrying around in here." He taps my forehead as he finishes his monologue.

I suppose this part is hard to explain. "I knew I'd made a mistake trying to involve the authorities. I couldn't tell them anything to explain." I hold up my hand to pre-empt him asking why. "I knew it was all connected to my last mission, and who was on it and why was classified."

"Surely you could have reported it to someone in your unit?"

"It seemed easier to run."

"What about friends, family?"

"Most of my friends were people I served with. As for family, I've none." He must remember the explanation of how I got my name, how no one wanted me from the start.

After what had happened to me, I hadn't connected with any of the people I'd known previously when I returned. How could I admit I'd been raped repeatedly? How could I try to pretend to be normal when suddenly I might fall unconscious at their feet? It had been easier to make a new start, to have to think about nothing other than surviving day to day. Trying to cope in a world without a safety net of my savings or a bed of my own on which to lay my head kept me focused on moving forward.

"So you've never considered making a stand?"

Pulling out of his arms, I take a step back and glare. "Against what? Someone I don't know who's coming for me?"

He shrugs. "I didn't take you for a coward."

I've never been called a coward in my life. My muscles tense as I take a step forward and growl, "I'm no fucking coward."

"Walks like a duck..."

I swing for him. Anticipating my move, he blocks my fist, grabbing hold of it, using my momentum to turn me and entrap me with my back to his front. When I go to use a move that will release me from my hold, he roars out.

"Listen to me. If you had the balls to fight the right people instead of the one that's trying to help you, maybe you wouldn't be such a mess. I'm not your fuckin' enemy."

He doesn't remind me he walked out on his club to be with me, though he could easily take that advantage. If he had used those words, I would have ranted and reminded him I never asked to be rescued. But that he keeps the part he played in keeping me safe quiet somehow emphasises the importance of words he's not saying more than those that he does, and instead of fighting him, I start thinking.

I don't even know what I'm doing to myself. I'm a warrior, yet I've run from this situation. Maybe there was more I could have done, more help I could have requested, but instead, getting away seemed easier than facing my literal demons.

Because I have enough dealing with the ones in my head. That's what I'm trying to run from, and yet they always keep up.

I'm a fucking mess.

"You shouldn't have brought me here." Suddenly the weight of what he's done seems too heavy a load to carry, added on top of everything else.

CHAPTER SIXTEEN
CHAZ

There was no need for her to tell me I shouldn't have brought her here, I've been reminding myself ever since I left the compound. I still don't know what made me take such precipitous action—action which could quite possibly see me killed or has probably lost me the most important thing in my life, my club.

And now it seems it's all been for a woman who I'm unlikely ever to get into my bed.

But I'm fucked to hell and back because even that thought doesn't make me regret what I've done. I respect her, like her, and, if I have to look at her like one of my brothers, well damn, that's going to be hard, but it doesn't stop me wanting to help her.

Although she's made it clear that it can only be platonic between us, my brain screams that Helo is mine and can't be touched by anyone else. And being mine, I'm not going to countenance letting my club betray her or anyone hurt her.

She let me hug her, so maybe not all hope in the physical arena is lost. I'll just have to take things slowly. Deep inside that I'll want her even after her trouble is sorted. Which means I'm seriously considering having an old lady. What would it be like? StoryTeller seems to have done alright. Sure, Sheri gives him flack as she's more than capable of sticking up for herself, but he's not been emasculated. He still rides, fights, and knows how to have a good time. On top of that, he always seems to be content and smiling. That wasn't the case before Sheri tied him down. Back then I thought I'd never get him to stick in one place and give up being a nomad. He quite regularly admits finding her was the best thing that ever happened to him in his life, and he values her and his kid over his bike.

I smile briefly as I think of the forthcoming addition to his family he told me about, then frown. While I've only barely faced that I may be wanting to make Helo my old lady if there's any possibility at all that I could persuade her to see me that way, I'll never have what StoryTeller has. Even if I can get her into the sack, as a result of the abuse she'd suffered, she'll never be able to carry my, our, her, baby.

Rage sweeps through me at what she's already lost.

Since I called her a coward, and after her comment about the mistake she thinks I've made, she's become closed off. Though her posture is stiff, her hands keep moving, clenching and unclenching as if it's hard for her to keep still. I guess she wants to be moving, and on her own, not having to deal with me.

She didn't seem to make much effort seeking help to deal with the threats. It's as if she's accepting her nomadic existence as punishment for surviving, as if she doesn't deserve to live. *Survivor's guilt.* This wouldn't be the first time I've seen it. It's the only answer I have for why she's run instead of what I now think she'd have done before she'd been taken captive—stand and fight.

She's a fucking hero and she deserves to have everything

good. If my sacrifice is going to be for anything, I'll do my damndest to give that to her. But first I've got to work out how to achieve that objective, which means I'll have to get her enemies off her back.

I walk to the cupboard where I keep the good stuff, pulling down a bottle of Jack and a couple of glasses. Pouring two shots, I take one over to her. The small raise of her chin accepts my offer as a truce.

I allow her a few seconds to appreciate the mellow liquor.

"What we've got to do now is come up with a plan."

She rolls her eyes and opens her mouth, but before she can get out a word, I'm making shushing motions with my hand, putting down my drink and turning in disbelief to look out the window. A distant roar of multiple motorcycle engines has reached my ears. I stop breathing to hear better, but I'm not mistaken. They're headed in this direction, which means I immediately know who they have to be. But fuck knows how they found me, or how fast.

Helo's not deaf or stupid. Her eyes are wild. "It's your club."

"I swear I didn't call them." I know she's going to go straight there, and doubt she's going to believe me. All the steps forward I thought we'd made have been lost.

But it seems our conversation hasn't been for nothing. As she picks up her pack, swings it over her shoulder and walks to the door, she calls out, "If you want to help me, cover my back."

For once in my life, no quick decision comes to me. I don't want her to leave, but I don't want my brothers to sell her out. Realising I don't care what happens to me just emphasises how important she's become. But being the prez of my club also means I know the members, and that announcing their arrival isn't the normal way of how we'd do things. Which means...

As Helo opens the door, she's looking down the barrel of a gun, as simultaneously an ominous click sounds at the back of my head, and a hand takes my weapon from my waistband. Risking tilting my head to one side, I see it's fucking Fire, an ex-Navy SEAL who's lighter on his feet than any six-foot man should be.

It's Iron who's got Helo in his sights. I can see her tensing as though working out whether she's able to go for her ankle holster, when Weasel, also apparently having entered from the back, walks, like Fire, silently around me. Some sixth sense of Helo's must warn her of his approach as, ignoring the threat in front of her, she swings around.

I'm trying to process everything at once, like how my brothers arrived so quickly when I thought they hadn't known about the cabin, and had assumed we'd be safe. The hate I feel for myself in underestimating them comes only second to the devastation in Helo's eyes that suggests though she might not think I'd summoned them here, she blames me for leading her into a trap.

She might not yet, or ever, be my old lady, but I know some things about her as well as I know myself. She's going to try to fight her way out even though the odds show it's helpless. She'd rather die than be taken.

I'm opening my mouth to issue a warning, but the delay is I'm not certain who I want to caution first, Helo, who I've met so recently or the men to whom I've pledged allegiance to for years. Her actions are faster than I can get any words out, as Weasel's disarmed and pulled in front of her as a shield in a flash. *Oh shit,* I think to myself when in the next second, Weasel's a whir of movement and somehow turns the tables on her. Luckily the weapon flies out of both of their reaches and skims across the floor.

I try to move but Claw butts his gun into my head and

growls. Worse, Bull appears, wrenches my hands behind my back and zip ties my wrists together. All I can do is watch the bodies writhing on the floor, fearing for Helo but not being able to do anything to help her. If she breaks Weasel's neck, then she'll join him in death.

My heart pounds, my breath saws through my lungs, but I can do nothing. Then, another man saunters in through the doorway, slowly removing his gloves, placing them in his pocket, then raising his sunglasses to perch on top of his head. He looks only mildly interested in what's going on.

It's Slugger. After his eyes adapt to the gloom, he glances toward me, giving me a chin lift as though nothing was out of the normal and I was not bound and held prisoner by one of my own men. He starts to move toward me, having to jump out of the way as the brawling pair barrel into him. He kicks out, luckily hitting Weasel, not Helo, and growls, "Watch the fuck what you're doing." Then he continues over in my direction. He's got one of his annoying smirks on his face. While he's pretending to be oblivious, it's easy to tell he's loving the situation. Mind you, I've seen the man grinning as he happily burns off a rogue member's tattoo.

"You're a fuckin' idiot," he tells me once he's close. Obviously I can't argue with his summation so I ignore him. "You think you'd get away with running from your club?"

Again, I deign not to answer. Instead, my eyes find Legend who's just entering. I narrow a glare toward my computer expert. "How the fuck did you find me?"

"That was me," Iron answers. "I'm the fuckin' sergeant-at-arms and you're my prez."

"Was," Slugger interrupts. His grin, if anything, is even wider.

Iron ignores him as well. "Knew you were prone to go off

on your own, so put a tracker on your bike so I knew where to find you."

Helo has somehow gotten Weasel pinned underneath her, and shows she can multi-task, eavesdropping as well as subduing my brother. "You fuckin' what?" She glares first at Iron, then at me, and adds a hint of accusation in my direction.

It's wrong, but I'm proud as hell of my girl. *My girl?* As Weasel bucks and tries every trick in the book to turn the tables on her, she remains one step ahead. From the smirk on her face, some part of her is actually enjoying this.

Then Iron's words filter through my brain and I don't know whether I should be pleased that he was looking out for my safety or furious that he'd done it without telling me. In the circumstances, I'm angry that he was able to find us.

I've no idea how to get out of our predicament. Strangely, I'm not worried about myself. Outlaw MC life is always dangerous and for me to have lived to the ripe old age of forty-five is nothing short of miraculous. I've always lived with the company of death walking by my side, and it's easy to come to terms with the short time I've probably got left. My only regret is not having time to explore whatever kind of relationship I could have had with Helo, and my concern is that if only one of us can make it out alive, then I'd want it to be her.

At the moment, while she's got the upper hand with Weasel, there are too many of my brothers standing in line. Weasel's no slouch and knows how to fight, so it's a good sign she can take him on, but it's just one-on-one. Soon, someone's going to get bored and step in to help him.

Slugger seems be getting some amusement from the spectacle, but I can see by a twitch in his eye that he's losing what little patience he's not known to have. Restrained tight, I know there's no way I'm getting loose from my captors, so all I can do is draw in a deep breath when I see him going for his gun.

Instead of shooting at or indeed threatening the combatants, he fires a shot up into the rafters. Fuck knows what ammunition he's using, some kind of dum-dum bullet I suspect, as flakes of whatever the ceiling's made of start to flutter down, and a large patch of sunlight that wasn't there before illuminates a spot on the floorboards.

The extra loud boom also startles Helo enough for Skunk and StoryTeller to jump in and pull her off their brother. The rest of us are stunned from the damage done by one single shot.

"My bad," Slugger states, looking up. "Lucky this place isn't yours."

"It's fuckin' mine," I growl. "Inherited it from an uncle a short while ago." And up to today, the roof was sound.

"Oh well." He shrugs, looking unrepentant. "I'd offer to pay for repairs, but where you're going means you won't need to worry about making this place watertight."

Bringing my eyes back down and to the real danger I'm in, I move my line of sight to focus on Helo and Weasel. While StoryTeller's still got his hand wrapped around her arm, it's not a tight hold, and I can tell she's not trying to get away.

Weasel has stood and dusted himself off, and now gives his attention to the woman who'd recently bested him. I hold my breath, hoping he doesn't try to get revenge for having his ass handed to him by a woman, when surprisingly, he reaches out his hand, and she takes it with her free one.

"Impressive, Army," he says to her.

"Marine?" she asks. As his eyes narrow, and then he nods, she continues, "Ranger training. We were taught how to beat jarheads."

He chuckles, showing he's not taken offence. It's almost friendly the way members of the different services enjoy a good jibe at each other. And, of course, he can hardly refute her statement. She had been ahead of him all the way.

Then Helo turns my way and I suck in air, only just noticing she's bleeding from a cut over her eye. Seeing her blood does something to me and I roar, and, surprising my captors, almost manage to pull away.

Irrationally I call out, "You're going to fuckin' pay for hurting her."

As Weasel looks around and I see one eye already closed, and a swelling on his jaw line, he looks at me incredulously.

Slugger barks a loud laugh as he analyses the situation. "Fuck, Chaz, you've got it bad. Fight like a man, you're going to get treated like one. You going to ask Weasel if he needs a band-aid for his boo boo?" He turns an assessing eye on Helo, his gaze lingering on her for a moment, before giving her a respectful raise of his chin.

CHAPTER SEVENTEEN

HELO

Flying a mission is never simply following a plan. A pilot wouldn't survive if they didn't learn how to react, adapting to changing situations and being prepared for the unexpected at all times. The enemy can't be relied on to follow any rule book. A pilot unable to take alternative action in a split second is one who'll not remain alive long.

Even intelligence gained can be faulty, and the lack of it lethal. That was the very thing that took me down.

I wouldn't have become a Night Stalker if I wasn't able to analyse information at the speed of light, read every slight nuance and react accordingly, preparing for danger rather than expecting safety.

I'd thought Chaz had betrayed me, but now it's clear he's as innocent as I am in giving away our location. I can also see he's burning with anger and indignation. Indignant on my behalf rather than his, but I've heard the conversations and know he isn't to blame. It's not his fault. He got me clean away as far as he was concerned. It's just down to pure luck that his overprotective sergeant-at-arms wanted to know where he was at all times.

The man who fired the shot is obviously in charge, even over Chaz. The president over the whole of the Wretched Soulz that Chaz had told me about. Their national leadership which they normally deny. Not hard to understand, if one charter gets caught then if there's no acknowledged affiliation, the whole club wouldn't go down. But that makes him, to me, a very dangerous man. Every man here will do his, not Chaz's, bidding.

His chin raise just now, that was not the gesture of a man who senses victory, more like a sign of respect from a comrade-in-arms. Forcing my fight-or-flight mode down, I use my brain to re-analyse the situation. I'm used to reading people, those under my command and those whose orders I've had to obey. I read faces and attitudes just as well as I read the lay of the land when I'm flying. Something about this man suggests to me that Chaz, his adrenaline running high, is getting him wrong. He's making threats but I sense no actual urgency to carry them through.

"Slugger," Chaz calls out, sounding desperate, and the man I've been examining turns around. When he gets his attention, he states in a pleading tone, "I don't give a rat's ass what you do to me, but let Helo go."

Slugger's still got a smirk on his face, the one he's had almost since he arrived. I glance at the bikers standing around. While a couple look serious, others seem like they're trying to keep grins off their faces. They in no way look like a tribe about to make a sacrifice. They've got no loyalty to me, but I sense they've still got a lot for Chaz.

"Let me go!" Chaz roars, trying to escape from the men who are holding him. "You don't want to do this, Brothers." His eyes flick around his men.

From the numbers surrounding us, I suspect the whole club is here. Bull, his VP, I've met before, same as the bald-headed sergeant-at-arms. Both look serious with expressions that are difficult to read. Legend, a thoughtful-looking man, has a half-smile on his face. A man with a beard down to his waist seems to have difficulty standing still, but there are no worry lines on his forehead. There's a distinct smell of weed coming from the man standing close to me, and on the other side, one whose odour is not quite so pleasant. My nose wrinkles as I get an overwhelming whiff of stale sweat. Then there's a redheaded biker who's got his hand over his mouth. When he catches me looking at him, he turns away and I'd swear he was hiding a grin.

When the flight system screams a warning that an RPG is heading straight for the helicopter, a pilot cannot afford to have a second's panic. Their brain works in milliseconds, analysing the threat and taking evasive action. I'm pissed that if Chaz hasn't betrayed me, then it's the rest of his club. But like when I'm flying, I don't let emotion rule my head. I consider the threat and examine what exactly I'm seeing. And what all my senses are telling me is that this group of men are not getting ready to send me to my death.

They're fucking with Chaz. Interestingly, he's being too emotional to see. Is his judgement being clouded by me?

When Chaz's plea is ignored, he redoubles his efforts to get free, somehow managing to get an arm loose and send a vicious right hook, but his captors recover immediately. Chaz's own grunt of pain informs me retaliation has been made.

Unless something is done to break this impasse, someone's going to get seriously hurt.

My life, and that of my crew, often requires reading between the lines. Taking orders at face value then dissecting them to look for hidden agendas and threats, and knowing when things don't quite add up, is definitely the case here.

The hold on my arm seems looser than it was before. Testing it, I step forward, my movement unimpeded. Seeing Chaz starting to go ballistic, I know someone needs to deescalate the situation.

I step in front of Chaz. "They're not going to hurt us." It shouldn't be me who can interpret their intention better than the man they've followed for years, but I suspect Chaz is blinded both as he's not in control and because he wants to protect me. I park what that makes me feel inside to ruminate on later—I've never before had anyone to stand up for me. "Look at them," I demand. "They're fucking with you."

From behind me, Slugger snorts. "And you'd know that... how?"

"Years of military service and dealing with assholes," I snap back, turning to face him.

Someone barks a loud laugh and quickly turns it into a cough.

Fixing his eyes on me and raising an eyebrow, Slugger slowly lets a grin cover his face. "You're pretty opinionated for someone in your position." And as if I might be in any doubt, he adds, "Unarmed and surrounded."

Oh, honey, if only you knew. He's underestimating me, no doubt about it. But he's also trying to provoke me, and the more he does, the more I'm sure of my ground.

Instead of acting on impulse, on focusing on the need to escape or get to safety, I put myself in the position of thinking like them. Two million dollars is a good payday, and probably very useful to their club. But you can tell a lot about a team from the man who leads them. I know from the first moment he knew about the bounty, Chaz never had plans to sell me out.

So what would I do in their position? It's not hard to come up with a plausible idea, and, as long as they've thought through all the pros and cons, it's one that could benefit both me and the MC. The question is, do I stop running and stand my ground?

Of course it wasn't pleasant having my tat burned off, and I'd hoped that punishment would have been the end of it. I could understand why somebody would think I don't deserve to wear the Night Stalker insignia anymore, or how that would appear to them. How could a man know how a woman could be tortured without leaving visible marks? The terrorists had made me out to be a traitor, and I wasn't even able to open my mouth to defend myself. It's not fair, but how much in life is?

But that wasn't the finale. It was the start. They weren't giving up. I've been forced to leave what passed as home behind and have then been hounded across the country. Do my perceived crimes really merit such a penalty? No one deserved to be tortured or killed in that faraway country, to have their dignity and life stripped away. I doubt I'm the only survivor unable to understand why me, or find life hard to endure knowing it was only the throw of the dice that kept me living. I have no family, no one to mourn me. Maybe it would have been better to have been me rather than them.

Self-preservation keeps me running. I might think I don't much care whether I live or die, but there's something inside me that's intent on staying alive. Maybe it's simply because I endured so much and survived. Maybe it's because I owe it to the others who didn't make it out, to not throw away the gift given to me.

Why should my life be worth less than anyone else's? Or be sacrificed in place of someone who didn't make it?

There's only one way to end this. Either I die, or the person who wants me that way is taken out of the picture. I've no illusion that there'll be any benefit in arguing my case. The bounty on my head, for me to be captured preferably alive, or dead if needs be suggests there's no room for negotiation. Only my demise will satisfy the person who thinks they've been so badly injured by my survival.

I've been running as I don't want to be responsible for anyone's death.

As the thoughts go through my head, I risk a glance at Chaz who's still distraught and futilely struggling. *He* thinks I'm worth fighting for. It's the first time I've had someone who seems to care. To give up would disappoint him. While I know whatever's between us is likely only to be fleeting, I know I owe him. Never before has anyone offered to give up so much to keep me breathing.

I don't know these men standing around, but it's not unlike being introduced into a new flight team. I've knocked disparate groups of people into something resembling a cohesive group before.

Mentally girding my loins with the captain's rank that I'd earned, I straighten my back, ignore Chaz, and turn to Slugger, him being the man currently in charge. "Tell me the plan."

It's the tone of voice that I use, one to which even commanding officers listened, that makes his eyes widen. I can see him mentally take a step back, and his brain's gymnastics that take place as he seeks an answer that would put me, a woman, in what he sees as my place. Conversations around us have ceased as the bikers look on with interest. I reckon if any of them started a pot most of the betting would be on him.

As he recovers, the smirk returns to his face. "The plan? We're going to let the fucker who wants you know where you are and pick up the two million bucks." Breaking off, he shrugs. "Bit much for a whore as far as I'm concerned, but hey, what do I know?"

"You fuckin' bastard," Chaz roars.

Turning swiftly, I shoot him a look that would have made any member of my crew stand down. He interprets it correctly, but doesn't look happy about it.

Swinging back to Slugger, I breathe in air and let it out on a sigh. "When you're done showing me what a big dick you are, maybe we can get down to discussing business?" My stance lets him know I'm not buying what he's trying to put down.

"Oooh, I like her." The biker with the red hair sighs.

Like everyone, I ignore him. Deciding to take charge, I cast my eyes around until they land on Legend. "You," I say sharply, pointing his way. "Get yourself on the dark web and let them know you know where I am, and that you're willing to trade."

Their computer guy almost snaps to attention at my tone, but after a split second considering my request, shakes his head. "Someone's already been assigned the contract to find you and take you down."

But not them, I surmise. "Who?"

The man who could do with some lessons in personal hygiene literally spits out, "Fuckin' Dominators."

Fascinated, my eyes follow the globule of saliva as it lands on the ground. The gesture showing me just what they think of the group that have stepped in to find, then trade me for cash. I've heard of them, of course. Rivals to the Wretched Soulz MC. Rumours are they're just as bad as each other.

Chaz makes a startled sound, then calls out, "Fuckin' figures. Slugger, man, we're not in the skin trade—"

Again, I wave him down, and again turn back to Legend, wondering how he could find that out. And, if he's got that knowledge, does he know more? "You know who's behind putting a price on my head?"

Again, his head moves side to side. "No."

I like a man who doesn't waste words even though I might

not like his answer. Frowning, I change my instruction. “Make contact and tell them you’ve got me. A bird in hand, etc.” All these Dominators have is a wide network to keep an eye out for me. But wide it certainly is. They’ve got chapters in all of the US.

I hear Chaz roaring again, and take the couple of steps to put me in front of him. “You trust me, Chaz?” It’s a strange thing to ask as half the short time I’ve known this man I’ve been fighting against him. Why should he put his faith in me when I haven’t demonstrated I’ve the same in him?

“I trust you,” he blurts out, then raising his chin and circling his head, he adds, “But I don’t trust them.” At the hisses sounding all around me, an expression forms on Chaz’s face that makes even me want to take a step back. “I did,” he states, addressing his brothers. “But I can’t believe you’d put new bikes in front of a human’s life.”

A couple of men step forward, their hands on their guns, while others look like their prez has gone totally mad.

The funny thing is, I seem to be better able to get a handle on the mood in the room, and I trust the men who it seems Chaz now doesn’t. He’s been blindsided by their arrival, still focused on the words he’d overheard to make him escape with me, and, for some unfathomable reason, fully consumed by his desire to protect me.

“It’s your fault.” I point my finger firmly at Slugger who’s come up to stand right in front of Chaz, hands clenched at his sides. Pushing my way in between the two men, I again use my commander’s voice. “Now enough of this. We’ve got planning to do.” Having made sure they’re not coming to blows, I turn my back on them both and seek out another man. “Legend? You going to make that contact?”

“Helo!” Chaz roars. “What the fuck are you doing?”

Multiple pairs of eyes come my way, and brows are raised

in interest waiting for my response. I shrug. "Well, with the help of the Wretched Soulz, I'm going to get rid of whoever's after me once and for all, and ensure the club will end up two million richer."

"Well, fuck. Now that's what I'm talking about," the man with the long beard calls out.

CHAPTER EIGHTEEN
CHAZ

At first, I didn't hear Helo's suggestion. I was too torn up asking myself *what were those words that had just come out of my mouth?* Had I really said I trusted a woman I'd only just met more than the brothers I'd ridden with for years? In hindsight, it was a terrible thing to say, and I'm not sure when, or even if, my brothers will ever forgive me.

But as Helo starts to explain her plan, her words begin to filter in. I feel Claw's hold on me relax as he, and everyone else, become impressed with not only what she's saying, but her confident delivery. She's obviously got some bold ideas which, while I'd admire them coming from anyone else, I'm scared to death of her putting herself in danger. What she's proposing is risky with several huge fucking holes which we'd need to smooth out. But as she continues speaking, my brothers are entranced, and start making themselves comfortable—some sitting on the couch, some on the table that groans under their combined weight, and the others propping themselves against walls or sitting cross-legged on the floor. All seem completely engrossed as they listen to the woman speaking. Even Slugger is hearing her out without making a comment.

It's not often someone of the female sex can enthrall the members of an all-male MC. I can sense the mood in the house is one of respect, and I can't help but feel pride in her, though her words fill me with dread. Helo's not asking for help. She's determined to carry out the key role herself, standing right there on the firing line for, I admit, the not inconsiderable benefit of being able to go on with her life. She'd obviously given some thought to this. While she hadn't been able to face her enemies head-on alone, with the Wretched Soulz behind her, she could take them on. The only part where my brothers were dubious was when she explained that she couldn't afford to engage our services for payment. But it was Beard who pointed out, if all went well, we'd be richer by two million dollars.

Only Legit points out they could fill their coffers easier by simply turning her in, but he was only voicing the obvious. At least the dismissive waves and a couple of voiced protestations show me, even if he had been serious, he wouldn't have gotten much support.

My pride, a moment ago vested in Helo, now switches to my brothers. We're in an MC, we live life on the edge, and if there's a chance to stick our finger up to the man, we'll take it. Handing her over would be too simple, too much like a citizen turning a criminal into the law. By doing this Helo's way, we get action and fulfilment as well as the reward.

Helo's stopped talking, and is now taking questions, and it seems whatever they throw at her, she's got answers. Eventually Claw gets caught up in the discussion and he's not even pretending to hold me anymore.

"How do you know this will work?" I move forward as soon

as his arms drop away. "Helo, there's a shit load of things that could go wrong."

She turns thoughtful eyes on me. "What's the alternative? If I leave here today, I'm worse off than I've ever been. Up to now I thought perhaps I had one, maybe a couple of people trying to find me, now I know it's the whole membership of the Dominators. Their wide reach means they're bound, sooner or later, to catch up with me. This is the only way I'll ever be free from my past."

"I like the idea of sticking it to the Doms," Bull states with a large grin. "They'll be pissed as hell at losing those dollars."

"Especially when it's in our coffers instead." Beard chortles.

Helo's in her element, and I can easily see how she got to the rank that she had. Though she's decisive, she listens to everyone's suggestions, pulling some into the plan that's taking shape while dismissing many of the others, but in a way that doesn't cause offence. She even appears to give consideration to some of the inane ones which would have had me slapping the person offering it around the head. Gradually she's pulling them all onto her side, and I can see looks of admiration on more than one face.

The prospects arrive carrying crates of beer and boxes of pizza and everyone perks up, stands or pushes away from their perches and for a moment, no one is looking my way. No one appears to be bothered when I approach Helo. Having previously escaped the zip ties, I take hold of her elbow and lead her away to the kitchen. As I do, I notice I've caught Slugger's attention. He's got his eye on me, but he doesn't make a move our way. He knows I'm not going to try to make a break for it out the back door, there are too many brothers with guns, and obviously, I'm weaponless.

"What the fuck do you think you're doing?" I give her a little shake.

"Getting us both on the right side of your club," she hisses in return.

"I'm sorry." I've been thinking about it. "This is my fault. If I hadn't gotten Legend to look into you—"

"Now stop right there." When a woman stares at you with her hands on her hips, and especially when she's also an ace pilot, you'd be crazy not to take it as a sign that you better shut up. "You might have given whoever's looking for me a head start, but without your club, I wouldn't know who I was up against. Hell, Chaz. The fucking Dominators? Sure, I underestimated an MC when I stole those parts, but it's not a mistake I'll make again. Look at the way your club managed to find us? If the Dominators are half as resourceful, I wouldn't have lasted long. You've given me a way to end this. And..." she pauses, bites her lip, looks down, then, after a moment, looks back up, pointing her finger at my chest so I can make no mistake, "You. You've given me a reason to want to."

Me? Again, I'm stunned. And again, I stay quiet, not wanting the wrong assumption to come out of my mouth.

As I hoped, she fills the silence. "I never wanted another man's hands on me. I never wanted to get close to anyone. But I allowed you to hold me." Her eyes fill with emotion. "You know how damaged I am?" She's told me, so I simply blink slowly to show I understand. "I thought they were going to kill you."

"They still might."

"Which would be a waste of a very good man." I open my mouth to tell her I'm far from being an angel, but she goes and steals my breath. "For a moment, I thought I'd lost my chance. I don't want to waste what we might have, Chaz." Her voice drops to a whisper. "With you I feel like I want to try."

"A relationship?" I almost hesitate to ask.

She bites her lip. "If I can and if you want to."

I'm stunned, acknowledging what she's gifted me. No guarantees, no quick fixes. But I'll be fucked if I don't want to take that chance. A vision of her as my old lady flits through my mind, then reality sinks back in. There are more obstacles than her mental and physical injuries. "Then why put your fuckin' life on the line?" I growl, not understanding. "Wretched Soulz are always ready to take the Dominators on. You don't need to play a part in this." I'm thinking fast. "If I made you my ol' lady, that brings you under the club's protection." *If I remain a member, that is.* I ignore that small complication. At least now we know where to start to track down her enemy. The Dominators have to know who they're working for. "Let us fight your battle, let me protect you—"

"I don't need a man to protect me. I can do that well enough myself." She brushes a hand over her short hair and looks frustrated. "And I can't live always looking over my shoulder. Chaz, someone thinks I've betrayed them somehow, and I've got to put that right. Even if the Soulz got rid of the Dominator threat, someone else may come along."

"We'll get to the man at the top."

"That's my plan. Weren't you listening?" She seems frustrated, but tries to console me. "I never leave the fighting to anyone else, Chaz. I've got to play my part. And, once we're over this hurdle, I can concentrate on a future. With you, perhaps?" There's a little plea of hope in her last three words.

And those hit me right in the feels. I'll give her a future if that's what she wants. Fuck, if she asked, I'd try to give her the stars. Even if my club never forgives me, if I manage to stay alive, I'd be happy to start anew with someone like Helo by my side. It's what comes in between that and now that scares the shit out of me.

Slugger pokes his head around the doorway, rapping the doorframe as if his appearance hasn't been enough to get our attention. "Church," he rasps. "Now." As I start turning to Helo, he snorts. "She's included."

"Well fuck me." She grins as he walks away. "You religious?"

"Hell no," I respond. "He means he wants a meeting."

Her resulting chuckle suggests she was just yanking my chain and realised that anyway. Still, we walk out together. The rest of the club have already taken their spaces in a makeshift oval with Slugger seated at the head. There's a seat on the couch next to Skunk, but Helo ignores it, making me suspect she's already clocked his issues. Poor guy, there's no deodorant made to counteract his body odour. Fuck knows we've all tried giving him different brands. He doesn't give a shit, making out it's his pheromones. Personally, I think he'd do well to become more familiar with the shower.

Clasping Helo's hand, I lean against the wall, pulling her in beside me. My body is tense, suspecting I won't like their discussion at all. She squeezes my fingers, emphatically knowing I need the support.

Slugger's an ass, everyone knows it, but somehow he made it to the topmost position in the club. It's only times like this when he puts his serious cap on that the reason he made it to that spot shows. Gone is the asshole personality, and in comes the professional, willing to make the hard choices.

Banging the heel of his knife on the table, Slugger gets everyone's attention. He glances around, then catches my eye and holds it. "First order of business. What's to be done with Chaz? Brothers? You want him in, out bad, or six feet underground?"

I swallow hard, feeling my Adam's apple bob. While I knew it was coming, I didn't expect Slugger to table it so fast. I'd hoped we'd get Helo's business sorted before my fate was decided.

"For running out on the club? Taking our payday away?" Pothead raises a joint to his lips and takes a deep puff. Blue intoxicating smoke wafts out, making Legit, who's seated beside him, waft it away with his hand.

"Strong shit that," he chides him.

Pothead looks uncontrite. "Good fuckin' shit," he answers him. "Want to try?"

It seems Legit does and Slugger raps his knife on the wood again. Once he's got his attention, he points to the joint-smoking man. "Betrayal of loyalty to the Soulz, yeah. That's what we're talking about. Most serious fuckin' crime."

I keep my mouth shut, having nothing with which to defend myself. If things were the other way round and I was in the top seat questioning the behaviour of a brother who'd made the choice I had, I'd have gone for the toughest penalty.

StoryTeller sits forward. "There once was a man who couldn't understand how a brother would want an ol' lady in his life." There's a slight quirk to his lips reminding me of the times I've yanked his chain about his relationship with Sheri. "Then, one stormy night—well, it was probably clear and dry, but hell, my way makes a better story—" He breaks off to allow people to laugh. "A damsel in distress entered his life and it was like a bullet shot straight to his jaded heart."

Helo jerks beside me, but I place my hand on her arm. It's best not to interrupt StoryTeller when he's in the middle of a story, and I want to hear how this plays out. It at least sounds like he's on my side.

StoryTeller resumes, "The fearless, ferocious leader was cut off at the knees when the damsel cast her magic spell over him. From that moment on she weaved her magic, and he was gone, becoming a slave to her beauty, and unable to think of anything else. All previous loyalties fled as she'd stolen his soul and his heart."

"What the fuck?"

"Shush," I chide Helo.

Iron rubs a hand over his bald head as he sits forward. "So you're saying Prez is bewitched and not in control of his actions? Maybe what he needs is an exorcism."

"So now it looks like we've four options," Weasel says seriously, while Slugger lets out a weary sigh.

Giving one of his customary sniffs, Skunk wipes his nose with the back of his hand, then states, "Can't fault a man for falling in love."

"Nah. Just like I'm in love with the idea of a new bike," Fire retorts.

Helo pushes away from my side, goes to the table and plants her hands there palms down. "And you'll get your new fucking bike. Instead of moaning like old ladies and discussing Chaz, why don't we get on with planning how we're going to accomplish that?"

"Lady's got a point." Bull nods appreciatingly.

"So you're going to let Chaz's behaviour stand?" Slugger asks.

"Yeah." StoryTeller looks me straight in the eye. "Can't fault a man in love."

I'm not in love. Am I? Oh fuck it, he's right. Else why would I want her as my old lady, or explain my desire to keep her breathing. Maybe StoryTeller's right and she's cast a spell on me.

Helo stays in position, but slowly casts her eyes around. "What would have happened had he not taken me away? Would any of you assholes have given me up?"

Claw shrugs. "Thought about it."

"We don't know you, lady," Legit says. "We don't know if you might deserve what you've got coming to you."

Helo shakes her head and gives an incredulous huff. "No, you don't know me. But it seems Chaz knows you. If he hadn't taken me away, someone could have acted impetuously and betrayed where I was without giving us a chance to look through the options."

"Still don't know you," the redheaded Fire insists.

"But your prez does." She fixes him with a stare that I'm sure has made many a man crap his pants. "Seems trust and loyalty work both ways. Chaz knows my story, and has decided the rights and wrongs of it for himself. Seems like you, his brothers, ought to give him some credit for that."

"Oh for fuck's sake." Slugger kicks back his chair and turns to me with a glare. "Come sit the fuck down, Brother."

"What?" Skunk's eyes open wide. "We're not going to kick him out?"

Walking over to take the offered seat next to Slugger, I take the opportunity to slap Skunk around the head. "Not getting rid of me that fuckin' easily." I say the words, but inside, I'm full of relief that I've still got my place.

Helo pushes away from the table and starts to return to her previous place against the wall. As I sit my ass down, it's to Iron's roar of, "What the hell?" and I helplessly watch him leap from his chair, but he's too late to catch her before she hits the ground.

It's pandemonium for a few seconds. I'm on my feet again, then drop to my knees, pulling her into my arms, checking whether she might have any injuries. From what I can see, she's sound. Skunk vacates the couch, allowing me to lay her down, and Slugger stands, shaking his head in bewilderment.

"She just went out like a fuckin' light," Slugger observes.

He pinches the brow of his nose, then asks, "What was the fucking trigger?"

That's something I'd like to know, but unless it was the release of tension when my club didn't show me the door, I'll be fucked if I know. All I can tell him is, "PTSD. She can have these attacks out of the blue which bring her down."

"Poof!" Legend demonstrates with his hand crashing to the floor, having seen it happen before. "She goes out like a fuckin' light."

Slugger sighs, his eyes fixed on the woman in my arms. As I check her out, willing her to start stirring, each time I've seen this I worry that she won't come around. Just when I'm relieved to see her eyelids fluttering, he speaks. "Well, that's that then. Any idea of her taking point in a plan to give herself up voluntarily is bust." He even looks sad about it.

I understand what he's saying, how dangerous it could be if she just collapsed, but... *hang on one damn minute.* He's not thinking about going back to plan A and turning her in for the money without giving her a chance, is he? Once I've thought it, that takes foremost theory in my mind and suddenly I'm laying Queenie down, then standing, growling and throwing myself at him.

"You're not fuckin' betraying her!"

I've arms around me holding me back before my fist can make contact, and a gun pointed in my face being held firmly in Slugger's hand.

He thrusts it forward, barrel to my forehead and uses it to push me back. I, myself, am still unarmed, else I wouldn't be letting him get away with it.

"You and I. Outside. Now."

As I start backing up, a voice calls out, "You need me, Slugger?"

Damn StoryTeller. Is it now I'm going to find out I can't

trust the man? I remember he acted as escort and enforcer to Slugger many times when he was a nomad. Is his loyalty to the Alpha and not myself?

"I can handle him," Slugger replies, brave man that he is with a weapon held securely. My fists might be good, but they can't do fuck all against a bullet.

As I walk backward, I find someone has helpfully opened the door, and, unlike StoryTeller, who offered to stand up for Slugger, my enforcer remains in the room with the rest of my so-called brothers.

What if this is my execution?

"Put that fuckin' gun down and face me like a man," I snarl as soon as we've privacy with the door closed behind us.

"I'd take you on—and win—anytime, Chaz," he sneers back. "But beating you with my fists ain't gonna solve anything."

"You can't have her." I wave my hand toward the cabin behind me. "They're good men in there. Once they understand what you're planning on doing—"

His face glows so red it looks like it's going to catch fire. "And what exactly the fuck am I planning?"

I wave my hands. "You're going to take an innocent woman and—"

"Innocent?" he interrupts me again. "No one's fuckin' innocent from the moment they've escaped the womb." Before I can counter that, he continues, "I've had it up to here," he indicates his neck, "with you, Chaz. You're so wrapped up in that bitch you can't see straight—"

It's my turn for an interruption. "I'm not wrapped up in her." I say the words even though I know Helo's got to me, so deep, any thought of harm coming to her hurts my soul. "I can't have you give up a woman who should be revered and respected for what she's done and what she's lost for the sake of money to buy a few new Harleys."

A sly grin comes to his face. "Who said anything about Harleys? Might fancy myself an Indian—"

Ignoring the gun, I launch at him. He fires a shot that luckily goes over my head but the loud gunfire has the result of at least stopping me. *Won't be much use to Helo dead.*

Now, again, he's got the weapon pointed clearly at me. Gone is the joker. Gone is the man intent on messing with my mind. Instead, in front of me, is the man who clawed his way up to be the Wretched Soulz head.

"Now you're going to fuckin' listen to me." He beckons with his hand not holding the gun and indicates a low wall. "Shut the fuck up and go sit over there."

I don't immediately obey, which gets the gun cocked more firmly my way. Unsure if he'd really shoot me, I do read that Slugger's losing what little patience he has.

Still trying to retain, or regain, the upper hand, I take the indicated seat, then demand, "Okay. I'm listening. What have you got to say?"

"You're a fuckin' idiot."

As a starting point, it's direct, and I can't argue he's wrong. I've never acted so much out of character. But I'm not about to show I agree with him, so I just let my eyes rest quizzically on his.

"How long you been prez of your charter?" After asking the question, he shakes his head. "Nah, don't answer that. Obviously too long and not fuckin' long enough."

This time the rise of my brow shows my confusion.

Suddenly his fist bangs down on the picnic table so hard it makes the thing bounce. He's certainly got my intention when he states, "You're a fuckin' moron. You misread your men. You misread me. At no fuckin' point were we going to turn that woman in."

CHAPTER NINETEEN
CHAZ

My jaw drops to the ground, then closes, then my mouth opens shaping the first letter of the word, *but.* At Slugger's furious glare, I slam it shut, and take a moment to rearrange what I'd heard in the clubhouse and my, admittedly hasty, interpretation of the facts.

It doesn't take long for me to come to the same conclusion that he has. *Christ, I've been an ass.* Sure, I'd heard the brothers talking about the windfall to come, but should have given them credit. Men I've lived and ridden beside for the past decade and more would never let *me* down, and whatever perceived wrong Helo had done to the club didn't merit giving her up. Of course my brothers would want to have their cake and eat it too. Particularly if, as we now know, it means snatching the prize out of the hands of our archenemies.

Then I could be partially excused. My brothers were one thing, but I'd had Slugger to add to the mix. And he was unpredictable. Doesn't exonerate me though. I should have waited, talked, listened, and maybe have better thought things through.

“You come to your senses?” Slugger asks. When he sees the shrugging movement of my shoulders, his gun magically disappears. “Are you ready to start actually planning how we’re going to keep your ol’ lady safe, and get that money into the club?”

“I’m going in.”

Both of us swing around at Helo’s quiet, but insistent tone. Eyeing her carefully, I look for signs of whether she’s recovered from her recent episode. Her face is drawn, her eyes don’t look completely clear. To my mind, she looks like she needs some down time and not to be involved in a serious discussion about how to save her life.

Slugger gets there before me. “There’s no fuckin’ way you’re getting involved.” His voice leaves no room for doubt or argument. Or, at least, wouldn’t for any members of the MC.

Helo, of course, is a different animal. Dazed as she still must be, she takes on a stance that screams *who the fuck do you think you’re talking to?* She doesn’t even need to say a word.

It’s only for a split second but I wish I had my phone out at that exact moment to take a picture of the expression on Slugger’s face. It’s like he’s never been faced with such female derision. It puts him on the backfoot and shows as he all but stammers, then quickly recovers himself.

“You… back there…” his hand waves at the door of the cabin. “You fuckin’ passed out.” His voice strengthens as he gets himself back on firm ground. “There’s no fuckin’ way you can take point on any mission, let alone go in by yourself.”

She doesn’t seem to give any weight to what he says, as she replies, “The Dominators won’t get the money until they pass me off to whoever is behind all this. It’s got to be me. They won’t be interested in anyone else. The objective is not getting rid of a nest of one-percenters, it’s getting the two million dollars.”

Slugger's raised eyebrow shows she's made a good point. He crosses his arms over his chest and regards her for a moment. "And how do you suggest we do that?"

I don't like her grin one little bit. "They could kill me on sight, so I need to give them an incentive to keep me alive." A chilling chuckle, then she adds, "I go in as a literal bomb."

Her first words are bad enough, but I'm one hundred percent certain that when I do hear the rest of her proposal, I'm not going to like it. My lips momentarily press together, then I ask, my words coming out in a controlled monotone, "Would you care to expand on that?"

With total oblivion as to my feelings she says in a completely matter-of-fact way, "I go in wearing a suicide vest."

"And the trigger?" Slugger asks, his voice menacingly low.

"Pressure switch on a remote control that I'll be holding."

"Fuck no!" I exclaim. "You pass out and you'll blow yourself up."

"Dummy switch?" Slugger asks, almost hopefully, making me feel a wave of relief that he has to be right.

But Helo shakes her head. "No. It's got to be believable. *I've* got to be believable, if I'm going to get the information from the Dominators and get them to disclose the name of the fucker who's after me, so we can take them down."

"Then no," Slugger states firmly. "You need our help to get the explosives unless you've got a supplier on speed dial?" He pauses, raises a brow, then continues when she ruefully shakes her head. "Admire your bravery, girl, but ain't gonna help you commit suicide." The next time she makes her short hair fly side to side at her dismissal of his comment, he softens his features. "Not questioning your abilities, but back in there?" He waves his hand toward the cabin. "You went down for no fuckin' reason. I'm not risking that on my watch." He shoots a crafty look my way. "And that's just me being gentlemanly. I'm not even enamoured with you like our friend Chaz."

A statement I couldn't deny even if I wanted to waste my breath.

It's a stalemate. Helo is right. We need to get information from the Dominators and it's hardly unlikely they'd just give it to us. As soon as they get their hands on her, then all they'll see is a payday. As far as we know, they may still get one whether she's dead or alive.

There must be another way. Our clubs are evenly matched, animosity shared. Any direct attack will end in a bloodbath, and not without loss of life. Of course, there's the option to take one prisoner and find what we want to know by torture, but will that info be known to everyone in the club? My brothers, for example, wouldn't necessarily know all the details. It's more likely their prez, VP, or maybe their treasurer will be the ones that we want. But cutting them from the herd will take some planning.

Helo's on the right lines. We need to do something spectacular to get their attention. But sending in a woman who's liable to pass out and accidentally blow herself, and anyone in the vicinity into smithereens is not an option.

Yeah. I can see the merits of her proposal. "I'll do it." Both pairs of eyes swing to me, both exhibiting identical expressions of surprise. Knowing I have to convince them, I start to tick the plus points off. "Firstly, they will know who they're dealing with, a Wretched Soulz prez who wouldn't fuck around, whereas Helo's an unknown female. Secondly, I've already set the play in action. Let there be a rumour that I've been ousted from the club. It will make it more believable that I want a part of their payment. I'll walk in with Helo as if I'm ready to auction her off. I'll be the one wearing the vest and in control of the detonator."

Slugger's face undertakes a transformation as his mouth widens. "I like that plan better."

"Well I don't." Helo's hands again go to her hips. "It sucks."

"For what reason?" I challenge her.

Her expression hardens. "The Dominators would be able to tell I would be prepared to let that damn bomb go off—"

"Which is more rationale why you're not fuckin' doing it," I snarl. My stance is similar to hers, both facing each other in a standoff.

There must be something in the tone of my voice or our posture that alerts Slugger. "I think the two of you have things to hash out." Uncharacteristically, he turns as if to leave us alone. Normally he likes to be up in all brothers' business. But he doesn't go without imparting one final bit of advice. "I think the two of you should work out exactly what this relationship between you is, and exactly how far either of you are prepared to go."

He turns and disappears back into the cabin.

Helo stares after him. "What did he mean by that?"

I close the space between us. Tentatively, I hold out my hand. After a pause, she takes it. As I wrap my fingers around hers, I make sure just to hold them loosely. "Walk with me?"

At the dip of her head, I lead her around the path that takes us to the back of the cabin. There's a track that leads up to the mountains from there, a pretty path, dappled with dancing sunlight coming through the breeze driven leaves of the trees. As well as the lighting show, nature helpfully provides the shelter from the harshest rays of the hot Arizona sun. As we progress upward, the sounds of my brothers fade, and soon all we hear are the squawking of birds, presumably warning of intruders invading their space.

I've not had the cabin long, but have previously explored, finding solace in the peace. I follow the track, which is overgrown in parts, and lead her to a flat boulder. To one side there's a fair drop, with water glistening below. I lean back against the rock, automatically spreading my legs. To my surprise, Helo steps in between them, and cups her hands around my face.

After gazing into my eyes for a moment, she gently leans forward and brushes her mouth against my lips. Hers are just as soft as I expected they'd be. So surprised she's initiated this intimacy, I hardly dare breathe as I wait to see what she's going to do next. After pulling away, she examines my face, before once again moving in and melding her lips to mine. This time, she closes her eyes and gives a small sigh.

When her tongue flicks at my lips, I take a chance, open my mouth, and she takes the invitation, advancing inside. As if she's a wild animal I could so easily frighten away, I make no sudden moves, don't chance putting my arms around her, and leave her in control.

The kiss becomes more heated. I groan as she moans. With everything that's happened to her, while I want to take this further, if she pulls back now, even if she leaves me with blue balls, I won't think she's a tease. I'll be quite happy if this is as far as she thinks she can go.

I try to lock my hands into place, but the impulse to touch her is almost overwhelming. Before I can lose my senses, she eases away, resting her forehead against mine in a gesture of such intimacy I feel it right through to my bones.

When she straightens, I open my eyes and see that she's staring, and unfortunately, straight down to my groin where there's nothing I can do to hide the bulge that's formed, and with her in such close proximity, there's no way it's going away.

"I'm sorry."

"It's okay," she replies softly.

But I feel the need for more explanation. "It's not okay, but it's automatic when I'm around you."

Her response can be read a number of ways. "I know it's a normal male reaction."

Yeah. She knows only too well. I grimace as I remember. "It's a reaction that led you to passing out—"

Her gaze snaps up to meet mine. "I didn't know you then, Chaz. All I knew was that there was a very aroused male on top of me, and my mind shot me back into the past." She pauses, then waves her hand downward, drawing my attention to that part of me embarrassingly standing to attention. "I don't think you'd ever force me or hurt me."

"Too fuckin' right," I growl. "I'd cut off my fuckin' dick before I put it somewhere it wasn't wanted."

She sighs deeply. "You've got to let me take point with the Dominators, Chaz. I need it. I've been fighting for my life because it's an automatic reaction, while wondering why the hell I'm trying to stay alive." Her face twists. "Those bastards took more than the obvious from me." Before I can give a consoling and probably meaningless reply, she continues, enlightening me as to her true meaning. "I was a woman in a man's world. I had to be better, work harder, prove myself, not only that I could do the job, but that I deserved to be there. Respect isn't given, it's earned, and I'll be damned if I didn't give my all to achieve that." She doesn't have to explain how female Night Stalkers are a rarity, and I have no problem believing her, so when she raises her eyes to mine, I lift my chin to show my understanding. "I became a person where what I have or didn't have between my legs wasn't important. It was my skill that was in demand. And by fuck if I didn't prove myself time after time." Her mouth quirks. "I'd like to say I wasn't reckless, but I sure skirted the edge of danger. But if soldiers wanted to be rescued, they wanted Helo flying their way." She shrugs, letting me know it's no idle boast. "Not that I was any better than any other Night Stalker, but I was their equal, not their worst."

A rustle in the undergrowth gets her attention for a moment, her reaction as fast as any soldier who's served. She turns, tenses, then just as fast relaxes as a bird hops off, searching for food. As her back is now turned toward me, I pull her to rest against my front.

"I couldn't show any sign of weakness." As she speaks, her chest vibrates against my arms holding her close. "I couldn't be any different, so when we had down time, I drank, and fucked—never another Night Stalker, but there were other servicemen, other ranks. I was as hotblooded of a woman as any male soldier."

I squeeze her slightly, knowing I'm just the same. I've no right to judge her as I'm certainly no monk, and women have needs just like men. Especially when living on the edge when surviving another day isn't a given.

"I was in control of my life, strong, capable. Right up until I wasn't."

"You were captured," I remind her.

"But *they* didn't treat me like one of the men." She pulls against me and I let my arms drop immediately, thankful when she nears me again, turning to voluntarily rest her cheek against my chest. "They stripped me mentally and physically. At first, I'd fight them, but then realised to them it was a game." Her hands curl into my shirt. "They made me nothing more than a weak, defenceless woman. They fucked with everything in my head." She raises her eyes to mine and now gets to the point of this conversation. "Let me go into the Dominators' club, Chaz. Let me take that risk. It doesn't matter what happens to me. Helo is already dead."

If she'd punched me, I couldn't have reeled more. How can

this beautiful person in front of me think she's been reduced to nothing worth living for? I try to put myself in her place. What if I was stripped of my rank and my club? What if I'd been tortured and kept as a prisoner? I've known brothers who served who've come back under such circumstances and were never again right in the head. While my immediate inclination is a rebuttal of everything she's said, I know I have to choose my words very carefully.

"You're right. You're not Helo the Night Stalker anymore." Even though she was the one to say it, she tenses as if she was expecting me to say the reverse. "You're not someone less, nor someone better. You're just someone who's been transformed." As she goes to speak, I shake my head. "Let me tell you about Queenie, the woman I've met. She's brave, fearless, transcends her difficulties."

"I—"

"My turn," I remind her, waiting for her acquiescent nod. "I understand more than you know about not having space for a relationship in my life. I may not have had to fight because of my gender, but I've had to be the best, to deserve to be this club's president and ensure I give all to the club every day." Though I'd been at risk of throwing that all away. I still find it unbelievable how little that matters. "Our pasts shape us, they don't define us. You deserve to be the person you've become, and not be burdened by your past, but stronger for it."

Queenie—yeah, she should leave all prior labels behind her now, she's my queen, or hopefully will be—stares into my face. Her mouth works, but for a moment she doesn't know what to say. Instead of words, her fist comes out and punches me lightly in the chest, then she does it again.

"I don't know what you've done to me, Chaz," she finally begins. "You don't scare me, and I want to be close to you. I want you to touch me... I'm just so fucking scared that I won't be able to..."

"Hey." I cup my hand under her chin as her voice trails off, forcing her to look into my eyes. "That I'm aroused doesn't mean I need to do anything about it. I can wait until you're ready." I swallow hard. "I can wait a lifetime for you."

"But what if I don't want to wait?" As I raise a querying eyebrow, she continues, "You don't want me to walk into that den of vipers alone, and I'm not going to stand by and let you take the risk instead of me. Whatever we do, the chances are that one or the other of us aren't going to come out of this alive. Before I die, I want to again have sex on my own terms, to remind myself what it should be like."

She's not going to die, I vow. But if I take her place, I might. It's a big temptation to take what she's offering while we can. I don't like thinking of the men who took advantage of her, but I don't even want to consider any men she had before she was captured. I know she's got a past, just like I have, but if we do this, if we actually go there, then there are two things I'm sure of. "When I finally get inside you, I won't be evoking memories," I growl. "You give yourself to me and I'll take you to places you've never dreamed of." I pause, make sure I've got her full attention, then add, "But it would be no fuckin' goodbye. This is the start of something. If you give yourself to me, it's for fuckin' life. I'll want you to be my ol' lady, maybe even my wife."

I might have surprised both of us with that statement, but know immediately as the words leave my mouth, every single fucking word is true. I'm not going to let Queenie slip through my fingers. For that, I'm going to need her to stay very much alive.

"And," I continue, watching as her jaw drops to the floor,

"it will be no quickie out here in the wild. It will be in my bed, and it won't be fucking. It will be making love."

CHAPTER TWENTY
HELO

Chaz wants me? I knew he wanted me sexually, no woman could miss the signs. But to think of a permanent relationship? I don't know how to begin to process that. And making love? Sex has always been a function for me, a transaction between two consenting partners at best, a lack of consent and control at the worst. I haven't any expectations, just hopeful of just being able to get a pleasurable release. I've never known tenderness after doing the deed. Sometimes a perfunctory thank you was all I got. But on my part, I'd never needed anything more. I didn't need distractions. So focused on my career, nothing was going to divert me from that.

But Chaz? Something drew me to him from the first moment we met. In the beginning it was because I wanted to get something over on the smirking MC prez, but though I fought it, there's no denying I'd felt the growing attraction between us.

What would a man like Chaz want from a relationship? While I don't know his exact age, I'd put him in his early forties, half a dozen, maybe ten or so years older than me. If he hasn't yet found someone to spend his life with, why should he want to change now?

I know my plan for getting information from the Dominators is risky, particularly due to the affliction that affects me. But up to now I hadn't considered I had very much to live for, even if I could come out of hiding and stop always looking behind me. Those fucking terrorists had destroyed the woman I was. And if my demise results in me taking a den of Dominators along with me, well, personally, I can't see much wrong with that. When you serve you, however much you might put it out of your mind, there's always a risk you could die. The odds so great you need to make a will to leave behind you. My desire for life has taken a large hit. Without being able to fly, what the fuck do I do now?

And here's Chaz, offering me a future, a glimpse of something I'd considered out of my reach. While, before him, I could never imagine allowing a man to touch me again, let alone wanting him to, my body has already started to crave his. It's still debatable whether my mind will allow things to proceed, but there's starting to be a part of me that says I don't want to die without at least giving it a try. Hence my push for Chaz to just take me.

That's not playing to his plan. He wants to ensure we both survive, holding that tantalising image of sex with him as a bribe.

I don't want him coming into the Dominator's club with me. There's so much that could go wrong. With or without me, Chas has got a life worth living, and a family of sorts behind him.

Since his intense declaration, I've stood still as a stone while my thoughts have been racing. Obviously Chaz has come to the conclusion he's stunned me.

He sends a wary glance my way. "Too much too soon?"

"Too much," I tell him. But before he can take that as a complete rejection, I carry on, "I've never thought about slowing down and simply living, enjoying life. Never had a chance before. First, I had to get out of the fucked-up childhood I had, then I soon learned being a soldier wasn't enough. As a female, I had to continually fight to wear the uniform, and then that became habit and I never stopped. Before I could even near the pinnacle of what I could achieve, that was taken away. Now, I'm Stateside, with a destroyed career, but I still can't fucking stop. Not with some bastard trying to kill me." I pause, collecting my thoughts, wanting to find the right words to put forward what I'm thinking. "I've never had the time to take something for myself, or to try what you're describing as a relationship."

He offers a wry shrug. "You've never been loved. Truth is, I've never found that myself. Or not until I met you."

"You think you love me?"

His eyes close and his brow creases as he thinks for a few seconds. Then his startlingly dark pupils are regarding me again. "I've never wanted someone riding behind me. Nor thought that my life would be better for having you in it. I love my club, yet I almost gave that up because of you. Now I value my life much less than yours. Is that love?"

What is love? I answer him honestly. "I've never been drawn to someone as much as you. As it's out of my experience, I can't say more than I'd like to explore it. And I can't with that asshole at my back."

Chaz's eyes harden, then he pulls me into him. Rather than feeling trapped by his steel embrace, I allow myself to feel cherished. "We're going to get rid of the fucker and not by you blowing yourself up."

"Last resort," I murmur against his chest.

It's him who initiates the kiss this time. Our lips touch, our tongues explore, our hands caress. My heart rate and breathing speed up, only to be matched by his. His hardness pushing at my groin makes me aware of a throbbing inside me. I'm about one breath away from saying *fuck this making love shit, just fuck me now* when he pulls away. He rests his forehead against mine.

"Now we've both got a good fucking reason to go get your shit squared away." His eyes hold mine. "And without either of us dying."

Without giving me a chance to object, he takes a firm hold of my hand and starts leading me back down the track. For the first few steps my thighs make my core ache as they rub together, but seeing as he's stepping extra wide paces, I know he's affected the same way.

As we descend though, our breaths even out and our posture gets back to normal as thoughts of a sexy time put in abeyance are replaced by the seriousness of what we do next. I'll never have a chance to find out what Chaz can offer with a price on my head.

"Do you mind me calling you Queenie?" he asks when we're about halfway down.

His expression shows me it's been on his mind. Handles that come by honestly are to be proud of, and I always thought I'd hang on to mine. But he'd put it in a different perspective. Helo is my past. Maybe being Queenie would help me leave that baggage behind. But there are limits.

"Only you, Chaz."

"Fair."

We take another couple of steps. "Why haven't you got a road name?"

He snorts. "I have, babe."

I stop him. "You're not Chaz?"

"Until I joined the MC, I was Charlie. I preferred that." A wide grin appears, and he chuckles. "Made a rookie mistake as a prospect when a full member shortened it to Chaz, and I corrected him." He pauses at my confusion and shrugs. "You've met Shitface? Prospects can't complain, whatever we call them."

"So it stuck?" I smile.

"Yeah, it stuck. When I got patched in, the same member pushed for me keeping the road name."

"Charlie." I try it on for size, not sure whether it suits the man I've become so used to calling Chaz.

But I make a mental note to remember it when he rewards me with a wide smile. "Like my name on your lips."

"You fucked and got shit sorted?" Slugger roars out, letting me know we've neared the cabin once more.

Slugger, along with some of the other men, are out smoking by their bikes. Others not partaking in the same habit are stamping their feet or showing other symptoms of being ready to get on the move.

It seems neither of us are the type to kiss and tell—not that there's anything to say—as neither Chaz nor I deign to answer his question.

"Thank fuck you don't last long," their road captain states as he swaggers out of the cabin, pointedly holding his bike key in his hand.

"Shut it, Weasel," Chaz growls, then approaches Slugger. "You got a plan?"

"Yeah." Slugger smirks. "While you two have been coming to your fuckin' senses, we've planned how it will all go down. You," he points a finger at Chaz, then shoots his thumb sideways at me, "and her will play your parts just as we decided."

"What fucking parts?"

"Now, now, Chaz. You going to give us reason to think you don't trust your brothers?"

Chaz shoots a suspicious look around the assembled group who refuse to meet his eye or shrug as if they've no clue what anyone's talking about.

"Prez," Bull states. "We're gonna go back to the clubhouse and get things in motion."

"Yeah, like building a bomb for her for a start," the man who doesn't seem to have a clue about body odour states, then laughs.

Chaz swings around but before he can get a word out of his mouth, Slugger shouts out, "Mount up. Now."

Whatever Chaz had been about to say is lost in the roar of motorcycles. Slugger positions himself at the front, then Weasel gives his prez a pointed look and then jerks his head toward his bike.

"Fuck it," the man with his arm around me growls, then leads me to the bike I'd ridden here on only the day before. I get on behind but before he starts the engine, he turns his head. "We'll sort this out back at the clubhouse. There's no fuckin' way you're going to be a human bomb."

Frowning at his back, I wonder if he had all this planned. I'd steeled myself to have a quick fuck, something to try to get him out of my mind. Been there, done that, move on. But the fact that he'd denied me only seems to make me want him more. Now, *damn it,* instead of accepting the inevitable, I'm working on how to get out of this alive so I can take him up on all that he promised.

A new life. Sure, I wouldn't be Helo, Night Stalker anymore. But somehow I know Chaz and his club would be able to give me a life worth living for.

Fuck the man. I grin into his back.

CHAPTER TWENTY-ONE
CHAZ

It's clear as soon as we arrive back at the clubhouse that in the time Helo and I had been making out like a pair of teenagers back at the rock, Slugger and my brothers had come up with a plan. I soon found that there was no room for me to have any input, or at least not without going against something that all my top officers had endorsed.

While I voiced, and not for the first time, my preference that Helo should play no active part, I was firmly shot down. Their reasoning was sound. Without her, the Dominators would not fall in with any part of our agreed strategy. They had, however, agreed that taking account of her affliction, they'd monitor her role carefully.

There were certainly parts of their tactics which I didn't like, but I steeled myself as more of the starring role fell on me, the less danger she'd be in. Or so I believed.

Since meeting Helo, there's been a lot of shit happening that I never expected to find on any bingo card. I hadn't dreamt of being unceremoniously dropped off at the Dominators compound with my hands and feet bound.

Especially when a Slugger I don't recognise, his hair covered by a flat cap, leans out of the van and shouts, "He's all yours."

I wouldn't be normal if I didn't have a bad feeling in the back of my mind, a question about whether I'd been filled in on all elements of the plan. Having hit the ground hard, at this precise moment if asked, I'm not sure whether I could swear that I trust my brothers. Some part of me questions whether this is their retribution for putting my woman first.

I recognise Ogre, their prez, as he approaches. Equally, even though I've already been divested of my cut and colours, there's no mistaking who I am, causing Ogre to regard me suspiciously, and for that I can't blame him.

Wretched Soulz and Dominators have never gotten on. The truth of whatever started the enmity between us is lost in the depths of time, though urban legends abound. But that doesn't mean it's water under the bridge and forgotten. No, we'll be enemies for all our lives.

Slugger, the engine of the truck still running, remains looking on, as if expecting to be asked questions, while I'm trussed like a pig and completely at my foe's mercy. Clearly suspecting me as a Trojan horse, Ogre steps over me carefully, refraining from issuing the kick in the ribs that I'd prepared for.

Approaching the truck with his sergeant-at-arms and enforcer either side of him, Ogre contemplates Slugger for a while. His eyes narrow. "I know you, don't I?"

Slugger shrugs. "Unlikely. But you know him, and that's all that matters."

"Get out," Ogre demands, his gun pointing unwaveringly into the truck.

Fuck, that man's got balls, I think, as the elusive head of the Wretched Soulz obeys the prez of the Dominators. Ogre has no idea of the prize he almost holds in his hand. But what he notes is a non-descript, grey-haired man whose shoulders are bent over and the back of the cut that he's put on, having exited the cage.

"So why have you," he turns, his gaze resting on me momentarily before again facing to the front, "given me Chaz, Prez of the Arizona Charter of the Wretched Souls MC?"

Slugger's eyes darken. Even from my prone position I notice both that, and the vein that throbs at his temples. He must be one hell of an actor to pull that off. "He's not Prez." Slugger emphasises his disgust by spitting saliva into the dust. "He's a fuckin' traitor. Pissed on his club."

Again Ogre swings his head and regards me thoughtfully. I try to keep my expression blank. Once again his attention returns to the man who'd been driving the truck. "I repeat. So why have you given him to me? Surely the Soulz have their own methods of punishment."

Slugger obliges with an explanation. "He'll probably tell you himself if you give him sufficient incentive." He manages a sideways look at me, and I mouth a response. *Fuck you, Slugger. Their torture won't need encouragement.* His face twists as though he's suppressing a grin, and then he continues, "Soulz fuckin' got hold of a girl with a high bounty on her head, and this bastard here, well, he let her go. Helped her get out of the state..."

"You what?" Ogre rounds, and this time doesn't hold back as he kicks me in the ribs. "Where the fuck is she now?"

Sucking in air as the man has steel-capped boots, I wait for the wave of pain to pass before I answer him, then with a wide smirk respond, "I've no fuckin' idea. Just gave her the money and the means to get clear." The first part at least, isn't a lie. The second I wish was true.

"Thought you'd appreciate the chance to get even as that bastard stole from you as well as us."

Still not accepting things at face value, Ogre sneers, "And you want me to believe all this and yet your club left him still breathing?"

"Bunch of pussies," Slugger remarks in an agreeable tone. "Vote was taken, but he's got allies. So he was dethroned and defrocked rather than receiving the death penalty."

"And you brought him here?" Ogre raises a brow.

"I was supposed to drop him off someplace else, but I thought he deserved more punishment."

Ogre regards him carefully. "Fuckin' old to be a prospect, ain't cha?" He indicates the cut Slugger's wearing.

"Served my fuckin' time." Slugger spits at the ground. "He blocked my way at every turn."

A loud laugh comes from Ogre. "Biker's should be able to fuckin' fight, not look like they're already halfway to the grave. You even able to hold up a bike?" He eyes him and sneers. "Reckon in this, I side with your prez. What the fuck are you doing trying to join an MC, man?"

I want to snort at how much he's underestimating Slugger. But then, strip away the years of experience, not see the covered-up muscles and tats, and maybe you're left only viewing a shell of a man.

"It's what I fuckin' want. And might get. With him out of the way."

Ogre takes a moment to respond. Part of me is screaming out for him to see through the ruse and have me slung back into the truck for Slugger to take away. But were the positions reversed and I had him at my mercy? I think I'd be sorely tempted by the chance to score points off my enemy. I know Ogre's not going to let me go.

Now my concern is for Slugger. He has to be crazy as hell to even think of delivering me himself. But Ogre remains oblivious to his true identity, and Slugger's clearly getting his kicks from staying in role. Still, I'm anxious about the outcome, until, instead of shooting the man on the spot, Ogre waves his hand impatiently, instructing, "Get out of my sight, old man."

Slugger wastes no time getting back into the truck, and zooming away with tyres screeching.

It's not hard to see how Ogre got his name. He's a tall fucker, ugly as hell, and covered in tats. His muscles are so pronounced I'd be hard put to believe he spends all the necessary time in the gym, and think it's more likely his physique comes from steroids out of a can. But whether earned honestly or not, it wouldn't do to underestimate the man. Though I don't suffer from a lack of confidence, in a fair fight, I'm not sure I'd come out the winner. And anything fair is far removed from the current situation, being trussed as I am. The helpless state I'm in is confirmed as Ogre waves his hand and two equally brawny men start to drag me into the clubhouse.

Wretched Soulz are an outlaw MC, but in most charters, we respect our women. Even the sweet butts are allowed to say no from time to time. We look after them and protect them, and in return they work with the prospects to keep the place tidy and relatively clean. I already knew the reputation of the Dominators. They look on women as only good for one thing, and the absence of a woman's touch is clear from the interior. It stinks of stale beer, cigarettes, and grosser things I try not to distinguish. *Could someone really have taken a dump and just left it there?* I dismiss the thought, thinking that blocked heads are hopefully more likely.

The best of Ogre's men seem to be the ones who've dragged me in. Looking at the others, I honestly start to wonder why he was so dismissive of the persona Slugger showed to him. A number milling around regarding me with interest have paunches, showing they spend no time at all exercising, and most of their hours by the bar drinking. A waft of something far stronger than nicotine greets me, familiar as it's also common in my own clubhouse. But the sight of members openly snorting cocaine is something I wouldn't tolerate. Doped-up men are sloppy, and withdrawal can make them do the craziest things. An addicted man can't be trusted. Ogre, though, apparently runs a far looser ship to my own.

But that just makes my predicament all the more dangerous.

We'll get you inside, Chaz. Just play it by ear once you're there. That had been Slugger's passing comment. I can't recall him confiding how he was going to get me out again. That part had been deliberately left vague. If I don't know the plan, I can't unintentionally give away any part of it.

I'd had his assurance that Queenie wouldn't be put in danger. *I had, hadn't I?* Or was Slugger again being obtuse?

For a second, I wonder whether there could be any truth in what he'd told Ogre, that my brothers had voted me out. Surely not? No. Fuck no. Not a chance. But I wouldn't be human if I didn't harbour some doubts about it. Especially as Ogre approaches me with a look of glee on his face.

"You're going to tell me where to find the woman."

I grin at him. I'll be telling him shit. It's the truth that I don't know exactly where she currently is. I'd give anything to know she's tucked in my bed back at the clubhouse.

The Dominator prez doesn't like my non-response, as his steel-capped boot in my ribs would suggest. I swallow the oomph while keeping the corners of my mouth turned up. Slugger's got something planned, and all I've got to do is survive until he and my brothers turn up.

I am starting to doubt the merits of Slugger's initiative though. Does he think giving me to Ogre will make him take his eye off the ball and leave his clubhouse undefended? I begin to wish I'd demanded more details, but that ship has now sailed. I'd been only too happy that Helo wasn't going to be walking into this den of vipers. I'd have agreed to anything other than that at the time.

Ogre spits down at my face, a globule of saliva landing on my cheek. It feels like it's burning my skin as, with my hands tied, I've no way to remove it.

"Cocky fuckin' bastard, ain't cha?" he remarks, then grins broadly. "I don't think you're going to hold out against our interrogation methods." He cups his hand under his chin. "One chance. Tell me all you know about Ms. Queenie May, and I'll kill you fast."

I'm telling him fuck all. He can hack me into pieces before I say a word that could cause any harm to one hair of her head. She's a fucking hero while me? Well, I'm a jaded MC prez. Anyway, while he might be proud of what he can dole out, it will pale into insignificance against the months of horror my woman experienced. For her I'll endure anything I have to. I just hope Slugger doesn't take too long and I'm still left with most of my body parts.

"Hatchett. Screw. Take our visitor down to the basement."

As the two burly men who'd carried me in approach in order to take hold of me once again, there's a roar of a motorcycle engine coming up fast to the club. Nothing unusual, except that I recognise the sound of that exhaust. *It's my fucking bike.* My bound hands clench into fists. It's one thing for Slugger to use me as bait, but my ride? No fucking way. I'm going to kill whoever the fucker is who's riding it.

But when the door opens and a vision appears, my anger escalates into fury. My fingernails bite into my palms, drawing blood as I suppress the urge to scream *get out of here.* Doing so would alert Ogre to my strength of feeling for her, and right now, I'm not only unsure how this is going to play out, but no one has even hinted at the game play.

I thought I was the Trojan horse armed with bugs, banking on Ogre not diligently searching a trussed and bound man, and one his club obviously wanted to get rid of.

As my face fills with horror, I notice Ogre's fills with delight. Or, at least, before he gets close to her.

"That's near enough."

Seeing what I saw seconds ago stops Ogre in his tracks. She's let the sides of her light jacket open to reveal the suicide vest underneath. It's then I see that her hand is clenched around the trigger. All that goes through my mind on repeat is *don't faint. For fuck's sake, don't faint.*

Recovering fast, Ogre gives an evil chuckle and sneers. "You want me to believe that's real?"

"It's real," Helo responds in a soulless tone. Her eyes are so cold and devoid of emotion it makes me shiver inside. On Ogre it appears to have a lesser effect, but there's still a miniscule straightening of his back.

After considering for a moment, the Dominator prez scoffs. "Nah, you're not going to blow yourself up, honey." His dismissal of any concern makes his men who'd all stiffened, relax and laugh.

"Aren't I?" Once again she uses that cold, dead voice. "What do you know about me except that I've got a bounty on my head?" It's her turn to sound scornful. "You'd be quite happy to give me to someone who wants me dead, but have difficulty believing I'd rather go out on my terms instead?" She eyes Ogre for a few seconds, then shrugs. "Either you do what I ask, or you'll have no clubhouse left. I'm carrying enough C4 to erase it out of existence." She gives a chuckle that makes goosebumps rise on my skin. “Of course, that includes you and everyone inside.”

“And him.” Ogre jerks his head over his shoulder toward me.

“And him,” she confirms, emotionlessly, leaving no one in any doubt that she’s ready to do whatever she needs. “And in case you didn’t know, the bomb will explode if this trigger,” she raises her right hand, “is released. There’s a limit to how long I can hold this before my hand cramps.”

Or she faints. I swallow fast.

Ogre contemplates her for a moment. “Okay. Assuming I’ll buy that you’re really wearing a death trap and are prepared to set it off—” His tone is sneering as if he still doesn’t believe she’d commit suicide.

“She’s got nothing to fuckin’ lose,” I interrupt with a shout, wanting him to know she’s serious.

He turns momentarily to spare me a scornful look, then starts speaking again. “Right. So what would make you take that fuckin’ bomb off?”

“Chaz set free for a start.” Her eyes rise in challenge.

Ogre snorts. “You came here to rescue him?”

Helo shakes her head. “I came here to find out who put the contract out on me.” She gives me a cold glance. “Him being here has nothing to do with me. If the bomb explodes, he’s collateral damage.”

It’s only because I know her so well that I know she’s lying through her teeth. Helo might not give a fuck about her life, but she cares about me. As long as she stays upright, I’ve got a chance to get out of this unscathed. Slugger? Well, I’m already planning his painful death after sending her in, knowing the risks.

Helo widens her stance. “Who posted the contract?”

"You don't know?" Ogre's eyes open wide. "You destroy a family and don't know who they are?"

Hatchett gives her a sneer of his own. "Probably fucked up too many lives to remember one in particular. Bitch." The last word he sneers, accompanied by a splat of his spittle hitting the ground.

CHAPTER TWENTY-TWO

HELO

My teeth grind together. Of course I didn't fucking know. If I did, maybe I could have done something about it. An enemy you can identify and track down is far less dangerous than the unknown. My hands fist and as my eyes catch Chaz's, I see he's looking at me with concern.

Could dealing with assholes be one of my triggers? Fuck knows. I'm starting to hope Slugger gets a move on with the rest of his plan as there's a strong possibility I'll be unintentionally blowing us all to hell. That thought makes me check I've a firm hold on the trigger.

"I haven't destroyed anyone's lives," I point out as calmly as I can once I've regained control.

Ogre snorts. "So you didn't unemotionally sit by watching others lose their lives while protecting your own?"

"What else was she to fuckin' do?" Chaz growls, thrashing against his bonds.

The sight of him struggling reminds me of my number one

goal. "Untie him." I punctuate my demand while raising my hand, bringing the detonator into full sight.

Ogre glares. "You wouldn't fuckin' dare."

"Try me."

It's a standoff, but Ogre's not willing to take the chance. He gestures to Hatchett who swears loudly, then goes to untie my man. Once his hands are freed, I deign to explain myself.

"I was pointedly told if I raised one finger or said one word in an attempt to save any man, then they'd kill another as well."

Ogre raises a disbelieving brow while Chaz, who's now freed, comes to stand by my side.

"She hid how much they were hurting her," Chaz starts to defend me. "That the men believed she was helping the insurgents meant they didn't make things harder for themselves trying to protect her." He gives me a glance full of despair. "She was literally taking it for the team."

"She was probably taking it alright." Leers and jeers come from Ogre's team.

"Fuckin' assholes!" Chaz yells. "Shut the fuck up. You have no fuckin' idea what she went through."

Ogre's loud voice joins his, "And you've no fuckin' right to give orders in my clubhouse!"

I've lost control of the situation, but I'm still holding all the cards. All I have to do is remind them of the threat that I am. I try to move forward, putting myself between the two prezes who are eyeing each other, just one step away from coming to blows.

"Stop!" But my commander's voice seems weak.

I shake my head, but that doesn't rid me of the telltale pricking at my temples nor the cold shiver running down my spine. My vision starts blurring...

No, for everything that's holy, no. Not now. No...

CHAPTER TWENTY-THREE
CHAZ

As I face Ogre, I flick my eyes toward Helo, just in time to see her eyes roll back. With no time to consciously think about my actions, I throw myself in her direction, my fist closing around her hand, the one that's holding the detonator. I've faced a myriad of fucked-up situations which could have ended in my death, but I don't think there's ever been a time when my heart's felt so much like it was going to leap out of my chest.

For a second, I just hold my fingers tightly around hers, my chest heaving as if I've run a record-breaking mile. When my blood pressure starts to lower to a measure more reasonable, gently I lower her unconscious body to the ground, kneeling beside her, then prise the detonator out of her hand. It's only then I feel I can breathe normally once again.

Closing my eyes briefly, I send up thanks to any possible but unlikely deity that's been looking out for me. When I open them again, it's to see Ogre's completely blood-drained face staring down.

He swallows once, then twice. “She wasn’t fuckin’ kidding, was she?”

“She never fuckin’ kids,” I respond with a growl.

“What the fuck’s wrong with her?”

“What those fuckin’ bastards put her through left her with PTSD. You know, the shit you were just laughing about? It makes her pass out.” I sneer at him. Gently I stroke my hand over her head, pulling her into my chest, knowing my heart is still beating too fast. It’s not about how close I came to death—she could have died. Something tells me that Queenie “Helo” May still has a mark to make on the world.

He gives me an incredulous stare, then sinks to his haunches, his hands coming far too close to my woman.

“What the fuck do you think you’re doing?” I snarl. “Get the fuck back or I set this thing off now.”

Scrambling backward so fast that he falls on his ass, Ogre raises his hands. “I was just trying to get the vest off her.” He narrows his eyes. “What the fuck? You’d blow yourself up and her?”

I shrug. “She’s got the right to a life, but one which is worth living. She’d rather die on her terms than anyone else’s, and where she goes, so do I.”

My explanation doesn’t make colour come into Ogre’s face. In fact, he seems to pale more. “You’re both as fuckin’ mad as each other.”

He’s probably right. But I don’t want to live without Helo, and she, in true hero style, would only go taking the bad guys with her.

As normal, after one of her blackouts, it isn’t long before Helo starts to stir. At first, it’s with a soft groan and a touch to her forehead, then she pulls down that same now-empty hand and stares at it in horror. Anticipating her reaction, I hold the detonator in front of her eyes. I don’t need to use words for her to understand how close we all came to losing our lives. The way her throat works as she swallows fast shows me how much she comprehends.

Ogre gets back onto his feet and holds up his hands as if trying to ward off madmen. “You let an unstable woman come into my clubhouse with a bomb strapped to her chest? What the fuck do you think you’re doing?”

“It wasn’t me.” I narrow my eyes at Helo, knowing she knows as well as myself that had I been listened to, I’d have forbidden this course of action. As it is, it came too close to mutual destruction for my liking.

Ogre seems torn whether to believe me or not. He’s confused and I don’t blame him. “If not you, then who the fuck was the lunatic who decided this was okay?”

A gruff voice announces loudly, “That would be me.”

All eyes swing around to the man who’s just entered. But it’s not only him who’s arrived. All around, Dominators are reluctantly surrendering their guns. Having been so embroiled in watching the drama in front of them, they hadn’t noticed my brothers invading their clubhouse.

Slugger doesn’t resemble the cowed man who’d dropped me off, but Ogre recognises him anyway. He also realises the now hatless, strong, confident man with his back ramrod straight, with the voice oozing with confidence, bears a strong likeness to someone else. It doesn’t take the prez of the Dominators long to recognise the mistake he’d earlier made in letting him drive away. *This* man is no prospect.

“Travis ‘Slugger’ Winslow,” Ogre spits out.

Slugger shrugs, clearly not devastated by being recognised. He gives Ogre only a cursory glance before turning to me. “You can let go of that now.” He nods to the device I’m holding in my hand.

Instead, I tighten my fist. *Has he gone completely mad?*

Helo, now fully back to herself, has fire spitting from her eyes. "Is this vest a dummy?"

The Dominators seem to breathe a collective sigh of relief and some start flexing their muscles at the idea of there being no immediate threat. But Slugger disavows them of that hope in just a second.

"The vest is carrying enough C4 to blow everyone here to hell," he replies to her casually. "That detonator though, that's not the real one. I have that here." He frees his hand from his pocket and reveals a device almost identical to the one I hold in my hand.

I couldn't define exactly what I'm feeling right now. Rage, sure, but at what? If I'd known the plan all along, I wouldn't have reacted the same. Both Helo and I had been taken in, which in turn meant the Dominators believed the ploy, giving my club the chance to infiltrate their clubhouse. But I could also, surprisingly, hug Slugger for not actually putting her in the situation I thought he had. In my head I'd been cursing him for being a bastard from the moment Helo had appeared. Now though, I realise that it's this devious thought process that has made him into the man for whom all clubs have a healthy respect.

Ogre appears to be on my wavelength. "Fuck it," he yells, his fingers brushing back through his hair before he lowers his hand to point an accusing finger at Slugger. "You're a conniving fucker." For a second, he lets admiration shine through, before regret covers his face. "You let us think you'd thrown Chaz out bad, and her?" He spares a second to glare at Queenie. "Why would she have any connection to you?" He slams one fist down onto the other, making an audible thud. "We didn't think to watch our backs, believing all the danger was inside..."

"Letting me and my crew, well, Chaz's," Slugger corrects

with a nod my way, "to walk in undetected." He doesn't even allow Ogre to react before continuing, "And now we're here, why don't we put the dick measuring aside and concentrate on what matters?" Being who he is, he doesn't wait to be invited, and just kicks out a chair and sits.

Ogre must be in a quandary. His men disarmed, he's at the disadvantage. What choice has he got? After a moment's pause, he copies Slugger and draws up a seat, indicating for what's presumably his inner circle to come closer. In turn, I grab two chairs, and Queenie and I join the group. After looking around and reading the room, Ogre indicates that his prospects should get the beer flowing.

While people are distracted, I lean into Helo. "Why don't you take that fuckin' vest off now? We've got the Dominators under control."

"What?" she asks, her brow furrowing. "They've no hidden weapons on them, are you totally sure of that? And this is *their* clubhouse. They could have all manners of shit at hand."

I just hate seeing her wearing it. I don't think I'll ever forget the terror I'd felt watching her going down, and only just having a second to take the detonator from her hand. *Dummy detonator,* I remind myself. But I can't even be thankful for that. My heart had all but stopped as I dove to reach her in time.

"Then just take it off." I glance around, my eyes spying Shitface. "I'll get the prospect to hold it."

"Chaz," she says, in a remonstrating tone. "I'd rather I was at ground zero if this thing goes off. Poof, gone, not surviving as a bloody mess with body parts missing." Her brows, rise in challenge, and the curve to her lips shows she's part yanking my chain, but mostly fucking serious.

I turn and eye Slugger who seems to be overly casual with the remote device capable of mass destruction, noticing Story-Teller's helping him to get the button taped down for now. But it seems all too much is depending on a small patch of sticky tape.

"Let me wear the vest." I wouldn't want to live without her.

Her smile broadens as she whispers into my ear, "Promise you this, Chaz. If it looks like Slugger's about to lose control, I'll give you a hug."

Give me a hug? I snort when realisation dawns. Mutual destruction, as in she'd take me with her. Fuck, this woman. Even in a situation like this, she can make me laugh.

The sound of caps being popped off beer bottles has ceased, and the liquid is being downed. But even with liquid refreshments, the air is far from relaxed. My brothers are still holding the disarmed Dominators at gunpoint, and trust is the one element that's nowhere to be found. I'm only too conscious that the only thing keeping tempers from flaring is the bomb worn by the woman at my side. I hope like hell that Slugger has a plan.

Before he starts speaking, Slugger rubs at his temples. His eyes then rise and focus on the prez sitting opposite him. He shakes his head slowly. "Already know it's pointless asking you for information about who wants Helo taken down."

A skeletal-like grin spreads across Ogre's face. "You've already threatened to blow up our clubhouse. Reckon we're dead men whether or not we open our mouths." His shoulders rise and lower. "Rather take secrets to our grave knowing that she," he jerks his head in Helo's direction, "will eventually be taken down."

Asshole. I cast an eye around Ogre's men, showing not all are comfortable with the death sentence uttered by their prez. Enough, though, seem as equally determined that so be it if that is the only way out.

It's an impasse. Before Slugger can speak again, Helo suddenly rises from her chair, takes the couple of steps that bring her face to face with Ogre, then leans forward, her hands resting on the arms of his seat and her nose so close to his I suspect he can feel the warmth of her breath.

"You and me? We're so fucking alike, it's a joke."

Ogre rears back at her strange announcement, and, clearly uncomfortable with her proximity, uses his hands to push her back. A growl comes from my throat at his audacity to touch her, but a major part of me is too interested in knowing where she's going with this, that I force myself to stay otherwise silent.

The Dominator prez stands, and now it's him leaning into *her* face. "Ain't nothing like you, bitch."

Again I'm tempted to intervene, but also intrigued to see where this will go.

Helo throws her head back and belly laughs at his words. Straightening again, standing tall, back like a ramrod, it almost puts her eye to eye with his squat figure. Slowly her smile slips from her face. "Both of us are prepared to die." Ogre's eyes widen. Her hands open in a casual gesture. "When I signed up, I was made to write a will. I accepted then I might not return. Every time I was deployed, every time I took the helicopter controls, I knew it might be my last." She shrugs. "Couldn't let that worry me. Couldn't be controlled by fear. Instead, I used the edge to do my job better."

Ogre sneers. "And that makes us the same, how?"

She points to his vest. "You wear that patch. You knew when you put that cut on—"

Without waiting for her to finish, he interrupts, "That my life might be a short one?" He snorts. "Better that than a slow death preceded by illness and having to have someone else wipe your ass."

"You're prepared to give your life to protect your brothers and the life that you know." Helo stares him straight in the eye.

"I'm the same. Before it was my country, now it's my friends who have my back." She shoots me a glance which I interpret means me and the other Soulz. "But ask me to make that sacrifice just to satisfy someone else's insane desire for revenge, or whatever the reason is, then I refuse to comply. I know what I did. I also know there were a hundred different ways things could have played out. Don't you think I've been over and over it again in my head?" Her eyes appear unfocused as for a few seconds she seems lost in the past. "But the delay to the helicopter taking off wasn't my fault. Any decision to risk the storm and we'd never have made the extraction site. The Black Hawk could have been downed and all of us would have died. When we lost comms with the team we were heading to rescue, there was no way of knowing why other than the best guess that their batteries had run out. I had to balance the precautions I should take to prevent risk to my crew's life with the wellbeing of those we were sent to save." Her voice falters slightly. "It was nothing different to anything I'd done before. Only, this time, we fell for the ploy. When captured, I did all I could to prevent further loss of life, even though it killed me to keep my composure as I was forced to watch men die. I felt their misdirected hatred, their misassumptions that I was leading a cushy life while they were suffering. I refused to play into my captors hands—"

"Helo," I say sharply, then when that fails to bring her back from the past, snap, "Queenie!" When dazed eyes meet mine, she closes her eyes briefly, then when she reopens them, gives me a slight nod, giving me the assurance she's back with us now. I glance at Ogre to see if her emotionless recount of her situation had any effect on him, having to remind myself he probably knows nothing of her past, or only what the person or people after her have told him. To my surprise, he's now watching her with new regard in his eyes.

For a moment, I'm not certain he's going to speak, and when he does, the two words surprise the fuck out of me.

"Chet Netherton."

As a wave of what can only be described as pure hatred floods over Helo's face, I can only think to myself, *huh?*

CHAPTER TWENTY-FOUR

HELO

Chet Netherton? After being shocked into momentary silence, I look around the room. No one else seems to be reacting to the name that fills all those who serve with horror and derision. Even Ogre doesn't appear to understand the impact his announcement has had.

Perplexed, I raise my eyes to meet those of Chaz. "Chet Netherton?" I ask, as if me repeating it would form some connection in his brain. When that doesn't work, I offer his title. "*Senator* Netherton?" A slight frown and a quick shake of his head shows there's no recognition.

"Don't have much truck with government," Bull enlightens me. "Citizens might get tied up in politics but what matters to us is our club, our rules."

It seems like a lesson is needed. Taking a breath, I proceed to educate them. "Netherton is a minor senator who holds extremist views on how the military should be run. He might not have much power, but he can hold up or delay procedural votes with his outdated views."

When I pause, Iron prompts, "Like?"

"Like no woman should be on the front line or in command, and only serve in administrative roles. He still holds out that only card-bearing heterosexuals should be allowed to join up, and heaven help anyone who's trans."

"Bit like us," Claw states, closing his mouth quickly when Chaz shoots him a frown.

Ignoring him and raising an eyebrow, I address myself to Ogre. "Surely just me being female isn't enough for him to want me underground?"

The prez of the Dominators shrugs. "Didn't stop to ask him the whys and wherefores, just accepted the contract that would make us two million richer."

"Delivering me dead or alive." I scoff. "Is there anything you won't do for money?"

"He'd sell his own mother if he thought he could make bank," Slugger helpfully explains.

Again Ogre's shoulders raise and lower as if he's not disputing that fact.

Shaking my head, I turn away from him and start to pace, tuning out the murmuring behind me and try to focus. I know the who, suspect the why, but surely just because I was a serving female isn't enough for a senator, albeit one with extreme views on women, to want me dead.

My steps cease as I near Legend. "Can you check the names of the people who died on the Night Hawk, and also the personnel on the ground?"

"You're looking for a connection?" He catches on fast, while wasting no time extracting his ever-present laptop from the rucksack he'd brought in. He spends a second finding a table where he can sit and get to work.

Once he's planted himself in the best he can find that would fit the description of a quiet corner, I leave him to it after putting in another request that he finds the location of the man who so clearly hates me. Then I hear Ogre shouting out for the prospects to bring in another round of beers as well as some shots, but I correct him, using my best commanding officer voice.

"Coffee."

Ogre snorts. "What the fuck? You don't get to demand anything."

A few strides takes me right up in front of him, and my finger comes out, only just stopping short of prodding his chest. "I intend to ride to confront the man who's put a price on my head. I suggest if you want any chance of getting your payment, you prepare to ride with me." I glance around. "And that's best done sober unless you want to lose any of your men on the way." To me it wouldn't be any great loss, but my hastily evolving plan involves flummoxing old Chet with my own brand of army.

Holding his belly, Ogre bursts out laughing. "You're signing your death warrant. Or how the fuck else are we getting two million? You, me, in the vicinity of Chet? Only one outcome, sweetheart."

Moving faster than I thought was possible for a man of his bulk, Slugger is facing him before I can blink.

"The only ones getting money out of this are fuckin' Soulz," he growls in an admirably menacing voice.

The two face up to each other, but I get between them. As my hands hold them apart, I speak fast. "There's more than one way out of this, and one which means I don't forfeit my life. And," I add quickly in appeasement, "I reckon Netherton will pay quite a lot to keep whatever his part is in this quiet." I let the sides of my mouth turn up. "I think four million would just about cover it."

"Knew there was a reason I liked you," Slugger imparts, while I muse I've not had reason to feel that vibe from him.

I've clearly caught his interest, but am unsure about the other man.

"Four million?" Ogre probes cautiously.

I spell it out. "Two million for each club."

Ogre's eyes widen, he takes a moment, then barks another laugh. "Coffee it is then. And brothers?" His eyes rise and trace the room. "Got to be ready to ride."

Although his men are unarmed and are standing with guns trained on them, there are shuffling sounds as they straighten their backs as if preparing themselves for action.

Slugger shakes his head, shoots a sad look Ogre's way, and corrects, "Not so fast. First, we plan."

Ah yes. Planning. The undeclared head of the Wretched Soulz goes up in my estimation. He's speaking my language now. *Fail to plan, plan to fail.*

We don't even know where to find Netherton yet. Raising my head up and down, I direct my words to Legend. "We need to know where Netherton lives. Then we'll need a schematic of Netherton's house and grounds, and..."

"Fuckin' simmer down," Slugger barks loudly. "Chaz? Get that vest off your woman and take her out."

What? Bristling, I turn to shoot him down, but Chaz is beside me. "Just take the vest off, Helo." Before I have a chance, he's unbuckling it himself, handing it to Slugger, who places it carefully down on a chair that's beside him.

"Come outside with me. I need to talk to you."

"But..."

"Please?"

It's that word and the soft expression in his eyes that has me agreeing. Promising myself I won't be long and will be back to monitor whatever scheme they come up with, I follow him to the door.

Outside the air feels refreshing, suggesting I needed this

break from the odour of masculine sweat inside. With the members of two clubs in the small clubhouse, the air had become stifling. But the sun mercilessly blazing down has Chaz leading me over to some welcome shade. Still taking deep breaths to refresh my lungs, I gladly accompany him.

He props himself against a wall and takes both of my hands. For a moment, he holds them lightly as I stare at where our fingers are joined. Then he squeezes them so firmly I raise my eyes. The fierce expression in his face takes me by surprise, and my gasp gets him talking.

"Fuck, Queenie. The bomb... I thought I was going to lose you."

"I—"

"Stop!" he commands, his eyes locking onto mine. "It was a fuckin' risk you had no business taking." Before I can talk, he pre-empts me. "I know what you were doing, trying to get Ogre's attention, and boy did it work. But Queenie..."

"I'm a fucking mess," I finish for him. "I could have—and I did—collapse at anytime. But it was worth it."

"In the end," he interrupts me. "You didn't know the detonator was a dud, did you?" As I shake my head, he continues, "Promise me, never, ever, will you do that again."

I stare at him earnestly. "I'd rather die than have you tortured, or land into the hands of my enemy. I can't promise you I'll be able to stay away from danger." It's me holding tight to his hands now. "I can't promise you I won't run into danger. That's not me, not how I live my life. All I can vow is that any risks I take will be calculated, and I'll do my best to keep both of us alive. But there are no guarantees in this life."

His head slowly moves side to side. "Fuck, woman. You have no idea how brave you are. Or..." he pauses and shudders slightly, then chuckles in a self-deprecating way. "Or how much you fuckin' turn me on." Pausing, his expression goes from mirth to a frown. "And how fuckin' wrong is that? How can I do that to you? But everything about you, how you took on the role as my protector, the way you stood up to Slugger, the way you took Ogre on. You make me so fucking hard all I want is to sink my cock so deep inside you, you forget anyone who's ever been there before."

After all that I've been through, his words should fill me with horror. Instead, he makes my muscles clench in anticipation and arousal shoot to my core. We're out here, in the open, a clubhouse full of men behind us. But they're engaged in coming up with a plan that will earn them millions and may, hopefully, save my life while doing so. Instead of being worried I'm not part of their planning, I feel myself becoming wet and lust floods through me. I should want gentle, I should want everything so far removed from my captors that Chaz's declaration should make me terrified. Instead, he arouses me so much I forget where I am, and all that's gone before him.

"What's stopping you?"

There are a hundred, a thousand reasons he could voice. But, thank God, he's on my wavelength. As if he can read my mind, he knows it has to be here and now. Before we confront Chet Netherton, in case all the best laid plans go to hell.

Chaz slams his lips down onto mine, and I open and welcome him in without hesitation, any thoughts of a slow seduction leaving both of our heads. I'd had no idea Slugger had had other plans. I'd taken a risk, knowing I could have passed out. That bomb could have signalled the end of both of our times, and our bodies know it.

It's not carefully choreographed as our bodies come together. He fumbles but has my zip pulled down fast. His fingers finding my pussy wet and ready only encourages him to shove my pants down. I don't care. I'm simultaneously undressing him, relishing when his bare, hard cock falls into my hands.

I couldn't say whether it's me positioning him, or he who's taking charge, as my back is suddenly against the tree and he's fully seated within me, causing me to audibly gasp.

My exclamation brings him back to reality.

"Fuck, I'm sorry..."

"Don't you dare stop!"

And, thank fuck, he doesn't.

There might have been no foreplay, no fondling, no attempt to prepare me. But in this moment, it's so totally right. I want to be fucked and he doesn't disappoint. He starts to move, swivelling his hips, managing to hit that spot inside me that I always thought was a myth. It feels so glorious and tension starts to build within me. Even before my capture and torture, no man inside me has ever felt like this. I want to hold out, want to prolong the moment, but God, he's so fucking good. His moves just right, the way he's holding me, pounding into me, I don't want it to end but am unable to stop the tsunami as my muscles contract, waves of pleasure flooding through me as my orgasm hits.

"Fuck, Queenie, I can't..."

His hips rotate, his pumps erratic. I'm still at the summit of my own peak when he stops, grunts, and releases inside me.

Aftershocks keep my muscles contracting rhythmically, as he keeps pumping gently. Then his forehead falls, touching mine. After a few seconds, he manoeuvres so our mouths are aligned. This time our kiss is controlled, not savage, and our tongues waltz instead of dancing a frantic tango.

Eventually he pulls his head from mine. His hands move, gently, but masterfully pulling up my pants and underwear while all the time his enlarged, satisfied pupils stare straight into my eyes. "I wanted us to have a bed. I wanted you to have the control. Queenie, when I brought you out here, this was the last thing on my mind."

Placing my fingers over his lips, I reassure him, "It was perfect." Then, returning the favour, I raise his jeans, tuck his now flaccid cock back inside, and carefully fasten his zipper, eliciting a boyish grin from this normally taciturn man.

I hadn't lied. It had been perfect. Just how I needed it. I hadn't wanted to think things through, hadn't wanted to go over everything in my mind. It had been uncontrolled, pure lust. Sex thoroughly wanted on both our parts. Our coupling so far from something being taken, that wasn't given willingly. For the first time since my captors took so much from me, he's given everything back. I'm not cured, I'll have flashbacks, even he might trigger an unwanted memory and subsequent reaction from me. But there's strength in knowing they haven't permanently damaged me. That I can respond to a man's desire and want him back.

"Prez?"

Bull's shout breaks the moment. We move apart guiltily, like teenagers being caught by our parents. I wince, feeling my wet panties clinging to me, dampening my pants.

Chaz notices my awkward shifting. "I'm sorry..." But as his voice trails off, he grins again. "Fuck, I can't deny how good it is to know that we'll go into whatever's facing us with you feeling me."

It's not the first time I've been left with a man's cum running down my legs. My captors didn't stop to use condoms. But it is the first time that I wouldn't change a thing. His release, inside me, might have no possibility of resulting in a baby, but it reminds me I'm alive, that *they* didn't kill that part of me.

As Bull spies us and approaches, I lean in and say quietly,

"With this no condom lark, when we're in that theoretical bed, you're sleeping in the wet spot."

"Fuckin' right I will," he barks.

"Prez. We need you inside." Breaking the moment, Bull approaches. He gives no indication that he might have ideas of what we've been doing though it must be pretty obvious.

Truthfully, I don't give a damn.

Chaz, though, as if he's staking a claim, puts his arm around me as he follows his VP into his rival's clubhouse, and doesn't let go of me once we're inside. Part of the reason I don't object is that during the past moments he's completely taken Chet Netherton off my mind.

But why we're here slams back into me with full force. And again, Chaz has given me reasons for wanting to stay alive. And it's not because I don't want Netherton to think that he's won.

So when I catch Slugger's appraising glance, I'm ready to raise my chin, silently conveying, *let's get on with this.*

I notice there's a different ambience in the room from that which was there before we had our tryst outside. Men are looking purposeful, and rather than being guards and captives, both clubs are mingling. In particular I notice the pairings of bikers wearing similar patches, sergeants-at-arms, enforcers, and road captains conversing seriously amongst themselves.

CHAPTER TWENTY-FIVE
CHAZ

As soon as I entered the room, I didn't need Slugger's discreet and clearly satisfied chin lift to let me know that a plan had been formed. It didn't settle easy I hadn't had any input, but given the choice between discovering, at last, what it felt like to be inside my woman and listening to a roomful of old fuckers blowing off steam, I wouldn't have chosen differently.

Now, though, it's back to business. I need to know what we'll be getting into, but as Ogre and Slugger simultaneously wave their hands and everyone starts heading out of the door, I realise that may not be in my cards.

"Bull, Iron, Claw," I call out, making sure my voice can be heard. When their heads turn my way, I beckon them to me.

Bull's first to approach, his eyes switching from me to the now re-armed Dominators fast disappearing. Without me having to ask, he starts to update me. "Netherton's close so we're taking advantage. Similar plan as before. We're—"

"Let's get the fuck out of here." Slugger's approach and loud voice interrupts Bull and doesn't allow him to say anymore, especially when he adds a precise instruction. "Get going." Accompanied by a deliberate jerk of his head, my officers obey him. I open my mouth to protest, but Slugger leans in. "You chose your ride, brother." Another pointed head jerk toward Queenie leaves me in no doubt what he's talking about.

"Don't like going in blind," I warn him, preparing to stand my ground.

He raises a brow. "You trust your brothers? You trust Legend?"

Of course I fucking do. My glare is enough to confirm it. Well, for a time I'd had doubts and almost paid a price for it. Can't afford to do that again now.

"Well we've got a fuckin' window, and pussying around, pandering to your whims to debate what's already been decided will see that closed down." Slugger turns as if he's going to broke no argument.

I grab hold of his arm. "Just tell me no harm will come to her."

"Her?" Slugger grins widely. "We are talking about the same woman, aren't we? I can't see her being taken down."

Is he forgetting how easily she can pass out? "Her affliction can take her at any time. Something you should have remembered, asshole. You fuckin' let her ride here on my bike."

Taking no umbrage, he snorts. "Give me some credit, Brother. *I* rode it here. She only took over for the last half-mile." *He rode my bike?* His answer doesn't stop my fist clenching, as I try to work out whether his explanation makes it better or worse. He shrugs. "Knew you'd recognise the pipes and know that help had arrived."

Fucking weak explanation in my eyes.

"It's a sweet ride."

I only just manage to stop myself swinging for him, but at that point notice Queenie has not only left my side but is in deep discussion with Screw. Tamping down the verge of jealousy that she's not only talking to another man, but one of the fucking enemy, I breathe deep, and instead notice the concentration in her eyes. Seems like at least one of us will know what we're doing. Her chin lifts. A quirk of her lips and the positive gesticulation of her hands shows me she's got no argument with what she's hearing.

Usually, the sound of engines roaring and the smell of exhaust fumes energises me. It's the sound of brothers heading out on a run. But normally I'm in pole position, leading the pack. Now without any other ride, Slugger once again has arrogantly headed for my bike, swinging his leg over the saddle while offering me a wide smirk, as I'm being ignominiously led to the crash truck with Shitface behind the wheel. Knowing I can't get into any arguments which would hold us up now, I bite my tongue. The saving grace is that Queenie is also heading the same way.

My eyes narrow again as I see Ogre accompanying her, and carrying something I immediately recognise.

I don't even wait for them to come close. "No fuckin' way."

Even Shitface doesn't look comfortable when he sees the cargo he'll be transporting. "Is that even safe?"

Laconically, Ogre replies, "Depends who's got the trigger."

"And who'll have that?" I growl.

To her credit, Queenie doesn't even bother to reach out her hand, but she jerks her head toward me. "Him. Or this is off."

The corners of Ogre's mouth turn up, revealing uneven yellow teeth. "Aw, shucks." He puts his hand over his heart. "It wounds me you don't trust me."

Trust him with a way to get rid of a rival prez? No fucking way in hell. I try to get Ogre to transport the C4 instead, but showing some intelligence, he refuses.

For once in my life, I'm out of control as I find while I've been arguing about the use of my woman as a human bomb once again—just as unpalatable as when I'd discovered it before—Slugger's already heading out with *my* men obediently following behind him. Ogre makes a hasty retreat before I can ask more, and soon his own crew are heading out after the Soulz.

Helo, my Queenie nowhere to be seen, lithely hops up into the truck, and taking the C4 from Shitface, carefully stores it. I glare at the detonator with the button still taped down as if it could bite me, not wanting the responsibility of carrying it, but neither wanting anyone else to have it in their control. Accepting the Catch 22 I'm in, gingerly holding it, I climb into the cab, realising I've been left in the ignominious position of having to ask my prospect where the fuck we are going.

The truck's already moving, catching up with the rear riders, before he answers with a quick glance my way, showing my lack of knowledge has taken him by surprise. "Tucson."

Tucson? "Netherton got a base there?" I ask, directing the question to the woman at my side. As far as I recall, he was a Wisconsin-based politician.

She shakes her head, and the slight frown shows she's as confused as I am. Narrowing my eyes, I subject the prospect to the full force of my stare.

After he shifts uncomfortably, I snap. "Spit it the fuck out, Prospect." There's a nervous twitch in his eye. "For fuck's sake, Shit." I know prospects are supposed to be deaf, dumb and blind, but I'm also very aware he's got a habit of being able to skulk around, something he learned in the Army, perhaps. He can walk silently, fade into the background, and only emerge when he wants to be heard. In the past, I've found it kind of annoying, but now I need him to be my spy. So I put it to him in the best way I know how. "You want your patch? Tell me what you fuckin' heard."

A quick glance as if to confirm his admission is the only way forward for him, he emits a deep sigh. “Overheard Ogre. He contacted this Netherton guy. Offered up Helo, but insisted that he comes here to collect. Said some bullshit about some of his assholes can’t travel across state lines.”

I doubt that’s a lie. I suspect some, if not most, will be on probation. Doesn’t surprise me. Soulz are better than Dominators at staying out of the cops’ eyes. Doesn’t mean we always toe the line, just that we’re more careful when we come to crossing it.

“If he’s coming here, why are we heading out?”

There’s more enthusiasm in Shitface’s voice now. “For some reason,” he grins widely, “he wasn’t keen on coming to the clubhouse. He offered to come to the state, but to meet us on territory he can control.” His voice drips with disdain at the thought any politician could get the better of us.

“And that’s Tucson?” Helo prompts.

“That’s Tucson.” Shitface glances around me to her. “Sorry, but he wants to combine his pleasures. He’s going to use a friend’s mansion that sits conveniently near a golf course so he can get in a few rounds while he’s here.”

Helo snorts. It would take more than that to upset her. Knowing my old lady, she’ll be thinking that Netherton’s got no chance of being able to use his irons on this occasion. Or ever again. His puttering days will be over.

I watch as Shitface carefully follows the bikes, keeping an even distance. Something occurs to me. The timeline is all wrong. “He teleporting or something?”

Shitface laughs. “Nah. He was a bit cagey about when he’d be able to arrive, but Legend’s been tracking his credit card. He’s booked a flight first thing tomorrow. First class, of course. Should be here late afternoon. Slugger thought we’d go and get into position before his security arrives.”

I'm wondering where the prospect had positioned himself to "overhear" the amount of information that he had gained. Apart from making a note to check on his whereabouts in the future, I'm in no position to chastise him. He's been far too valuable, and at least now I know what I'm heading into.

Or the guts of it, at least.

CHAPTER TWENTY-SIX

HELO

What does a man do when he arrives at a property late in the evening after a long dreary flight? The assumption was that maybe he'd have a drink in the luxurious lounge, but his most predictable destination was probably the bedroom. The master at that, it had obviously been prepared for him.

But it wasn't just guesswork that leads me to the here and now, which finds me lounging back on the California king-sized bed in the kind of luxury I've never enjoyed in my life. I'd been both amused and impressed to see the men from both clubs—once the insults and threats were pushed to one side—come together to work almost as well as any military special forces team I've ever been part of. I'd been worried about discipline, but with the burly sergeants-at-arms kicking their men into shape, and Claw and his counterpart enforcing their words, no man seemed to dare take a misstep.

Despite Slugger having had to take off to deal with something in one of the other Soulz charters, the men bonded against a shared enemy. Like a well-oiled machine, obviously taking advantage of the military experience within their ranks, the skeleton staff and minimal security manning the estate, vastly outnumbered, were taken down, and admirably, with minimum bloodshed. All are now securely detained in the basement, with some of the bikers making sure there's no way they can escape or otherwise raise an alarm. They'd been provided with cushions, blankets, and enough food and drink that they'd decided to co-operate. None seemed particularly loyal to either the owner or the guest who was about to arrive.

From our captives we'd learned that Netherton would be expecting a meet-and-greet man, a typical butler. It had taken a bit of debate, but in the end, it was Fire who was assigned the role. As it was agreed redheads never look "normal" in most people's eyes, they thought he could pass despite his shock of red hair and matching beard. In a borrowed suit hiding his tattoos, he looked almost respectable.

Legit, and one of Ogre's men, Squint, were chosen to act as security, believing their muscles would make them look the part, but they were also given strict instructions not to open their mouths.

The absence of the myriad of other staff it apparently takes to keep one man satisfied would be explained by them being off duty due to the lateness of his hour of arrival. The only unknown will be the number of men he'll bring with him, though Legend has checked the seats booked on the flight and there were no more in his name. There's no doubt a man like Netherton should be worried about dealing with a group of bikers. Surely, he must consider they could be about to scam him. We'd been on the lookout in the event he'd employed local security, but so far none have arrived.

Perhaps he's confident in the company of one percenters.

Scum does clump together. While I don't personally know the man, that he's been hounding me for months is enough to convict him, let alone that he'd go to such lengths to see a woman, who, to my knowledge had never personally harmed him, meet her death. In my mind, he's earned his place among the bottom dwellers.

"His plane's landed. He should be here in half an hour." Chaz looks concerned as he provides that information, his mood confirmed when he adds, "Are you alright?"

The man standing beside him takes a different stance. "She going to play her part?"

Chaz inhales sharply, and I jump in fast to stop the two fighting. "*She* is going to play her part admirably," I inform him, then remind him what they should be doing. "Shouldn't you be finding a place to hide?"

I was perfectly happy to be left alone to confront Netherton, but neither wanted me to face him without backup. Ogre, because he doesn't trust me, and Chaz out of some misguided sense of chivalry, and concern that something I learn could trigger me, causing me to pass out.

There would be an easy way to end this, a bullet in Netherton's head, but that wouldn't get the closure I'm after—the answer to the question of why it's so important to him that I'm dead. There's always the chance with him out of the way, others may come after me instead. And shooting him wouldn't achieve the bikers' primary objective, the money. Apart from Chaz, I know few are here because of their concern for my health.

So my role is to get the explanation I want, and to get Netherton to open his coffers. After that, I've no issue with what happens next, nor that Netherton is unlikely to leave in anything other than a coffin.

Minutes tick by. Chaz and Ogre check out possible positions. A closet with slatted doors seems the ideal place. When word finally reaches us that the unsuspecting senator has arrived on the estate, and, as predicted, is only stopping for an expensive tot of brandy before making his way up the stairs, the two bikers disappear as silently as a discreet fart in fresh air.

The door slams open, Netherton strides in, flicking the light switch and illuminating the scene. I brace but he doesn't even look my way as he shrugs off his jacket and throws it over the back of a chair. Next, he undoes presumably expensive cufflinks before pushing up his sleeves. He rolls his neck, and winces, and I feel a brief twinge of sympathy for the stiffness that comes from hours spent on a plane, although he was in first class with little to complain about. It's only then that he turns and spies the strange female lying under the covers.

His reaction is of surprise, but not one of regret. His first words are mumbled under his breath, and I have to strain to hear them.

"Hey, John boy. You certainly came through for me."

He starts moving in my direction, a smirk on his face, his tongue licking his lips. His obvious thoughts of depravity to come makes me swallow hard, as memories of when I last saw such expressions on men's faces threaten to shoot me back to the time when my captors knew they had it all their own way. A hard swallow, and a strict reminder that this time I hold all the cards enables me to, for the moment, play my part.

I smile sweetly at him, an expression I hadn't thought was in my physical vocabulary, and wait for him to get close.

"Well, you're pretty enough. I'll give him points for that. Could have done with putting a bit of makeup on though, honey." He chuckles softly. "Though practical I suppose, your tears would soon wipe that off."

From his reaction, I take having strange women procured for him is not abnormal in his world. But his reference to making me cry has me wondering just what he does to them. The realisation knocks a dent in my decision to hear him out, to decide whether he's got a case against me.

At my lack of response, he continues the initiative. "Well, take off the cover, sweetheart. Let me see what you're hiding under there."

I can't resist obeying his instruction seductively, lowering the covering one inch at a time. I see his gaze narrow when the straps of my tank top come into view. Naked was obviously his expectation.

I'm watching him carefully as I reveal the rest, and am rewarded with his loud gasp and the way he staggers back from the bed as I expose the explosive attached to my chest. I'm not worried when he races to the door, one of the bikers will have locked that already. And again, I enjoy his look of distress as he tries the handle, rattling it uselessly, before realising he's trapped and turning to face me.

"Who the fuck are you?"

I don't expect the visceral punch in the gut that that question causes. Sure, I already knew that he hadn't recognised me, but it suddenly hits me that this is the man who wants me dead and he *doesn't even know me.* I'd always imagined things like him sticking pins into a voodoo doll impression of me.

He must have given someone else the information to investigate me, and took no further interest himself.

Sitting up, I swing my legs off the bed. He pushes himself back against the door, hands splayed and the whites of his eyes showing.

"Who are you?" he asks again, his voice not quite as firm as before.

I stalk toward him. “You don’t know? Just how many women have you taken a hit out on?”

He looks like he’s just been kicked in the balls. His Adam’s apple works as he swallows a couple of times before he spits out my name. “Queenie May?”

Having no need to confirm it, I don’t. “You want me dead. I want to know the reason for that.”

“Take off that... thing,” he waves his hand toward my chest, “and we’ll talk.”

“It’s comfortable.” I shrug. I’m not lying. For all the time I’ve been wearing it, I’ve gotten used to the weight. “Just start talking.” My eyes narrow. “If you’ve got a good reason for wanting me dead, well, perhaps I can get on board with that.” Inwardly I wince, knowing Chaz will be hurt. But whatever he says, so many things could have been done differently that day, maybe more people left breathing. It might have not been my fault, but why is it me who survived? Why not someone more worthy? “If you don’t give me anything I can agree with, then this bomb explodes, taking us both with it.” My tone is flat. There’s no doubting my words.

His eyes have gone wide, and his chest is heaving as though he’s run a marathon.

My shoulders rise and lower once again. “Or maybe I’m just so fed up with everything, I’ll press the trigger anyway.” I show him a device I’ve been hiding in my hand. It’s the dummy switch, but he doesn’t know that.

His mouth opens. “You’re suicidal.”

“Maybe I am. Maybe I’m not. But I’m getting pretty fucking tired of not hearing any explanation.” My lids half close over my eyes, and I tilt my head. “Perhaps I should just forget it. I doubt there’s anything you can say that’s worth telling.”

That lights him up. “No?” He takes a threatening step forward, and I raise my hand in reminder and warning. “No?”

he shouts, but stops a few feet away from me. "You're a woman playing games in a man's world. You're the weaker sex. You shouldn't be anywhere near a uniform. And the result was just what I'd been cautioning people would happen. You got good men killed, and all for nothing."

"I did my job."

That my tone lacks emotion seems to incense him. "Your job? You're crazy. You flew into a sandstorm against expert advice. You crash landed, killed or got your crew captured. You should have stayed grounded, both you and your craft."

But that's not how it works. Pilots like me follow orders. Of course we've got leeway whether the conditions are too dangerous to fly, but you don't get medals for being too careful. Anyway, it wasn't the weather that proved our downfall, but Netherton isn't impressed when I tell him.

His hand slashes down through the air. "If you'd taken off when those SEALs still had radio reception, you'd have known they'd been captured."

He's right. No matter what duress they were under, any message they were forced to send would have included a coded warning. Then the rescuing part would have been planned accordingly.

I turn my back on him, knowing my senses would alert me if he went on the attack, and that even if the device I'm holding is a dummy, I've got backup nearby. But I can't face him while I get my thoughts in order.

The batteries died.

But the SEALs had already been captured.

Should I have taken the lack of radio contact as an indication all was not right? Fuck, I would have done, had the weather not delayed us.

Another thought hits me as I spin around again. "Who told you of the delay? Where did this expert advice come from?" All of our missions are top secret, and no details should have been leaked about them.

"I was on the committee."

God save me from politicians.

His voice goes hard. "I recommended my nephew for a posthumous commendation. But like they never listened to me about the dangers of having females serving on the front line, they refused to give it to him. They gave you the medal instead."

"Your nephew?" I frown at him, trying to think of any of my crew who had relatives in government. Or maybe it had been one of the unfortunate SEALs. I can well understand why there would be any number of reasons they'd want to keep their relationship with Netherton quiet.

He swallows hard. "Brendan Scott."

My eyebrows hit my hairline. "*Karen?*" Crews have more than enough time to share their backgrounds, and the information he'd shared was about how he'd grown up poor. Like so many, he'd joined the Army to escape going down the rabbit hole of crime. He was the unlikeliest man in my view to have a senator in his family. Surely not one who could fly first class and golf at expensive mansions.

"*Karen?*" Netherton repeats. "Even now you won't do him the courtesy of calling him by his name and insist on using that ridiculous and demeaning handle."

I don't bother answering. I don't know exactly when he'd gotten tagged, but it was before I knew him. None of us chose our call names, and some certainly didn't win that lottery. But once given, it stuck. I'd feel more disrespect if I called him a name that he hadn't earned, and one which had been used with affection.

"Brendan went over your head to your major, but he backed you instead. Told him to follow his chain of command,

and that any objection had been noted. And look how that ended." He sneers.

Back Stateside, Major Harper had been one of the many to take our debriefings after we were rescued. We'd hashed out every detail, and while there were future lessons to be learned, he hadn't apportioned blame to me. He'd recommended me for commendation instead.

There's so much I don't understand. Trying to keep my voice even, I give an explanation in order to prompt him. "People who serve know they might suffer physical injury up to, and including death when they sign up. Karen," I refuse to call him any other name, "knew that as well as any of us. He also knew we all follow orders." I brush my hair back with my free hand. "He was an excellent co-pilot, one I was proud to have by my side. But he didn't get promoted because of his doubt-saying. I took his advice on board that day, as normal, but the situation was urgent, and I knew when we'd be able to fly safely." As he snorts and his mouth opens to object, I add forcefully, "And it wasn't the weather that brought us down."

"You wouldn't have had that missile fired at you if you hadn't flown."

"Karen wanted a delay. Not a cancellation."

"When contact was lost with the SEALs, you should have aborted the mission."

"And left them to die?"

"Half of them did."

And he's on our defence committee? I speak my next words carefully, reading the expression on his face. "And if it had been me who died, would Karen be standing here being berated? Would he have a two-million-dollar price on his head?"

He doesn't need to confirm the negative answer that's the only one he can give. Instead, he again spits at me, "If the Army hadn't let women fly, then the decision would have been taken logically."

Thoughtfully, I keep my eyes on him. "It doesn't add up. Why are you so worried about your supposed nephew now? Where were you when he was alive, as I'm pretty damn sure you weren't in his life?"

CHAPTER TWENTY-SEVEN
CHAZ

I honestly thought dear old Chet was going to have a heart attack on the spot as I open the closet door and me and Ogre step out. His hand goes to his chest, his face goes red, and it's easy from here to see the increase in his breathing. He's staring at our cuts, even putting up his hands as if to ward us back. I stifle a laugh. He thinks we're the threat? Even without that fucking bomb strapped to her, with Helo he wouldn't have a chance.

Maybe I'll let him go one-to-one with her to prove that females have a place on the fighting line.

The woman herself is raising a querying brow toward me. True, she'd given no signal she needed help, nor had there been anything remarkable in the conversation that would have warranted our appearance. But little did she know it all rested on the last question she'd asked. *Those questions about his relationship with Karen.*

She'd go up in my estimation again if it was possible for her to rise higher. There's no remonstration, at my interruption, no *I'm handling this.* She's just interested to know why.

"I can answer that," I state, then realise a few seconds have passed so I add an explanation. "What Karen is to him." I wave my phone. "Legend's come up with some interesting details."

Netherton has made an effort to pull himself together. "Ogre, I presume?" he asks, addressing me, the wrong man. From my side Ogre huffs loudly, but doesn't bother to introduce himself. "Look, you've fulfilled our bargain. I've brought two million in cash..."

"The price is now four." Ogre grunts the new demand.

Now the senator's gaze settles on the man behind me, but before he can speak, I inform him, "You thought you'd get away with your little plan, but now the extra payment is for our silence." Though from what we know about him, there are secrets here that will be taken to the grave. His to be precise. I let my eyes find Helo. "See, Chet here is a lovely man. He might call Karen his nephew, but the relationship is closer than that. Twenty years back, when he was running for senator on a platform of being a family man, he had a second family waiting in the wings. A family that he was ashamed of. Karen was his son."

Ignoring the opening and closing of Netherton's mouth, I continue, "He'd been paying his mother off for years, buying her silence. Oh," I pre-empt her question, "Karen didn't know. His mother happily kept quiet, blaming some long runaway man. Maybe she knew Chet wouldn't be a good influence in his life." As an enraged snort sounds, I add, "I mean, a liar, cheat and sexual predator—oh, did I fail to mention Karen's mother was only sixteen at the time? — well, she rightly concluded that Karen was better off not knowing the man." Helo makes a gimme gesture, and I don't disappoint. "I don't really know why Karen was better off with his mom. Apparently she went crazy when he was killed, and the person she blamed was Chet for not looking after him and making sure he got only cushy jobs. I suppose that was part of the bargain for her not opening her mouth. That and the money."

Helo's chuckle is loud. "Then she really didn't know what he was doing. It was no fucking desk job."

"What he was doing was classified," Netherton snaps.

I don't let him add more. "Karen's mom was threatening to disclose their sordid affair, even get him charged with child rape as retribution. With Karen gone, there was no reason for her to keep quiet. But Chet found how to weasel his way out. He had to find someone else to blame, and promise to get revenge for her. He persuaded her Karen dying wasn't his fault, but was down to the person piloting the helo. The person who'd taken her precious son's promotion and job from him."

"Which she had—"

I wave Helo down when she righteously bristles. "Only in your warped mind."

Ogre speaks for the first time. "And she was happy with that? Helo's death would avenge her son and leave you free to do whatever the fuck you want to? Why not just off her instead?"

It's a valid question. Us two bikers look to him to respond, but it's Helo who supplies the answer. "Because he already hates me and all that I stand for. He tried to discredit me but that didn't go anywhere. He'll get more satisfaction taking me out, and honestly, who'd miss me? While his baby momma presumably has family who'd raise a fuss." She snorts. "He probably rubs one out to the thought of having taken out a female soldier. Outwitting me when he thought I'd survived without a scratch."

She might not have visible injuries, but those she has go bone deep.

She takes a step toward Netherton. "You know what? I felt guilty for what happened. I felt so much remorse for having survived when others died. But you? You regard life so cheaply. You wouldn't have blinked an eye that your son died if it hadn't been for the complications it could have caused you." A slight nod my way suggests that she might be on the way to healing.

I'd been worried if Chet had had a justifiable reason for landing all that had happened at her door, she'd have pulled the trigger on herself. But knowing she wasn't being chased as anything other than a scapegoat for his own misdemeanours might help restore balance within her. No one, except for this asshole, placed one ounce of blame on her. And I know I'm going to spend the rest of my life making sure she understands what an amazing woman she is, and how no one could have done more in the circumstances she was under. She's worth a thousand Chets.

I've heard enough. Helo deserves to live her life without fear, and Netherton doesn't deserve to live his at all. I call Legend up as he's necessary for the rest of the plan. As I thought, he'd been hovering close by, and soon he is seated at the desk with Ogre's gun pointed at Netherton's face to make sure he complies. Which he does, seemingly without hesitation. Does he still think there's a chance we're going to give Helo up? Nah, even he couldn't be that stupid. He must be trying to appease us in the hope it will save his life. Zero fucking chance of that. Even though there might not be tangible evidence, I can smell corruption on the politician which makes me suspect the whole country would be better off without his interference in our military. And, at the least, it would make serving in the armed forces more comfortable for people of Helo's sex.

Without knowing the details, another thing that makes me admire her more, the woman beside me looks on without questioning as Chet contacts his bank, arranges for a two-million-dollar transfer, and then obeys Legend as he sends it through various unidentifiable accounts, some overseas, and some dealing with bitcoin. I note Legend consulting his notes and am pleased he'd taken the advice of the financial wizard, Data, in Texas, who seems to know what he's talking about.

Surprisingly, it doesn't take long before the Dominators and Soulz have a million dollars in our bank accounts, and now it's just a matter of dividing up the remaining two million that Chet brought in cash. Ogre assigned two of his men and told me they were happy doing that task. Yeah, right, and I was born yesterday. Beard, as treasurer, has been appointed to make sure they can count.

My phone rings. I pull it out of my pocket, check caller display, and step out of the room.

"Slugger," I greet him.

"How's it going?"

"Almost finished. Time for the grand finale coming up."

"Good. Look, I've got to stay here for a while. Got a bit of a mess to sort out. Won't be making it back to AZ anytime soon." *Can he hear my sigh of relief? I hope not.* "Take care of your woman, Chaz. I like her."

Praise indeed from the man himself.

I grin, though no one's here to see it. "Ain't going to be cutting her loose."

He chuckles. "I rather thought not. But," his voice turns whimsical, "will she stay when there's no longer a price on her head?"

He's voicing a thought that had only recently occurred to me. It was easier to keep her when she couldn't go out and show her face. The world will be her oyster in just a few hours.

I decide not to answer him. "Ride safe, Slugger."

"You, too, Brother. You, too."

Taking the hint, he ends the call without pressing his last

point. Nevertheless, his mention of my own fear escalates it in my mind. *Can I keep her? Helo, Queen of the Skies? Why the fuck would she want to stay by my side? What have I got to offer her?* Except for my dick. As I recall, despite the rushed circumstances, she had enjoyed that ride.

"Ogre's ready." As if I conjured up an apparition, she appears at my side. "But as I wasn't let into that side of the plan, I don't know what they're planning." She sighs.

I do. Ogre and I had exchanged text messages and had quite the conversation when we were forced into close proximation in the closet and forced to keep quiet. While Queenie and I had been getting our rocks off, Slugger had suggested a course of action which Soulz and Dominators alike had agreed with. Okay, so sometimes the man does come in handy.

Yeah. Sometimes Slugger comes up with a good plan. What man doesn't enjoy some liquid indulgence after a long flight?

As if summoned, Weasel appears at the top of the stairs, and I can overhear his conversation clearly.

"Should be running a bath for you, fucker."

Even before he comes into sight, I can guess at his companion. Skunk. I grin. Yeah, Chet's last olfactory moments won't be exactly pleasant.

"What's going on?" Queenie asks casually, as two of Ogre's men follow behind mine.

"Come see." I risk taking her hand, and she allows it, even going so far as to squeeze my fingers. Her touch makes my dick pulse and I resolve that soon I'll be getting her horizontal and proving how much it's worth her staying in my life.

But once we re-enter the master bedroom, my attention rightfully returns to making sure this is done right. A murder but one which will leave no clues that it was anything other than an unfortunate accident.

Ogre raises his chin as we approach and nods toward the

whisky bottle and glasses he's already lined up. I lift a querying eyebrow when I expected just one. He grins as an answer.

Filling four glasses, he passes them out. One to me, one to Queenie, takes one for himself and offers the other to Chet who looks totally bemused at what's going on. There's a cockiness in his eyes as if he thinks that he's won.

He even clinks his tumbler with Ogre's when invited, and gleams. "You're going to fulfil the bargain, aren't you? Hey, man to man. You don't allow females into your clubs. You know where I'm coming from."

My head shakes in confusion. *Has he bonded with Ogre in the time I've been gone?* Nah, he couldn't have done. Helo was with them. It's more likely that Chet fully believes he is in a likewise-minded male world.

"Look, I'm no angel, but you know I have a point." Ignoring me, Chet appeals to Ogre, as if having given me up as a lost cause.

"Don't have much truck with bitches," Ogre agrees, topping Chet's now empty glass up. Chet doesn't notice the side-eye look he spares for us. I might not wear the same patch, but I understand him just fine. *Can you believe this dick?* he's asking without using words. I manage to suppress my laugh.

The three of us sip our drinks while Chet downs his, not appearing to notice his never-emptying glass. He swallows, licks his lips, and seems to enjoy watching Helo until something clicks in his rapidly befuddling mind. "Why's she not running?"

"Don't worry," Ogre says soothingly, tipping the whisky bottle again. "She knows there's no way out. There's more than enough of us to stop her."

I actually doubt that or not without a fuck of a lot of bloodshed. But I'm not telling him that.

"She's got a bomb," Chet suddenly remembers with a decided slur to his words.

"Dummy," Ogre reassures.

"No, no more," Chet finally protests. But Ogre pulls his hand away from the top of his glass and offers him more.

Chet starts to sway. I nod my head toward Weasel and Skunk that it's time for their part of the plan, the man now so far gone having consumed half a bottle of whisky fast, that he's unlikely to hear the running of the bath.

"Hey, Helo. Why don't you help the man out of his clothes?" Ogre's mouth splits his face from one side to another. I stiffen, but Helo cottons on fast.

She tightens her fingers around mine before letting me go and kneels in front of her tormentor. "You're a handsome man, Chet," she purrs. "How about one for the road?" Ogre produces a pair of rubber gloves from somewhere, and so gone, her victim doesn't notice her sliding them on.

"You're... deaf... Dead," he corrects, having difficulty forming words.

Looking totally unbothered, she replies, "Maybe I am, but how about some fun first. Let's get you out of these clothes."

He might hate her, but I can see that male gleam in his eyes showing he's not going to turn down any chance to get his dick wet. As eagerly as a drunken man can, he sits up and accepts her assistance to pull off his shirt. His paunch is flabby, and I have to give top marks for her acting skills as she doesn't let any disgust show.

"Now your pants."

"Undo me."

There's clearly a limit to how far Helo will go, but at the shake of her head, Chet's so eager that somehow, he manages to fumble and undo himself, and manages to raise his hips and kick his pants off, followed by his underwear. I'd laugh at his flaccid, unimpressive cock, if I thought that wouldn't spoil the show.

His eyes are all for Helo. I think he's forgotten his audience now. She takes the glass Ogre offers, and yet more whisky goes down the senator's mouth. His head rolls back as I notice a second bottle of whisky is half-empty.

Ogre produces more rubber gloves, and we both put them on, then haul Chet to his feet and half-guide, half-drag, him to his final ever bath. It takes a little manoeuvring to get him into the water, but we manage it. He even helps. Being so drunk, he slides under the water. Then, at first, little resistance as I apply pressure to his head, keeping it down.

His automatic sense of self-preservation kicks in and he makes a feeble attempt to fight for his life as water enters his lungs, but so drunk, it's ineffective, barely making a splash. It seems anti-climactic when he goes completely limp.

"I almost wish his final moments had been worse," Helo remarks softly.

"Dead is dead," I tell her, though I agree. What we'd done to him was nothing like the mental torture he'd put her through for months. "And now, you're free." I grimace as I voice the truth.

She's free. Will she still want anything to do with me?

What can I offer as a jaded MC prez when she can pick up the reins of her life?

CHAPTER TWENTY-EIGHT

HELO

While getting a story into the press used to involve the expertise of typesetters and a whole printing press, let alone the distribution network it then required, nowadays any news can have worldwide reach within minutes of the words being written.

We're still checking that we've left no trace of our appearance in this bedroom. Legend appears with his phone showing an article. All the sordid details about Senator Netherton have come out, about his statutory rape of a child, and the resulting son he'd ignored. It was the perfect excuse for his suicide.

Some of the cash received went to buying the silence of the staff who'd been treated well, albeit confined to the basement.

It's taken more than a minute for the words Chaz had uttered after Chet took his last breath to sink in. *You're free.* As I sit between Chaz and Shitface as we return to his clubhouse, that simple statement keeps going around my head and I'm not sure what it means. Free? But to do what?

I've no career to return to, my affliction isn't going away. I might no longer have a price on my head, but I've nowhere to stay. Except here, with the outlaw MC prez who's turned my head. As the roads pass by and my view in front is that of a long line of bikes, I realise this is where I want to be.

In the presence of the prospect, we don't talk much. We don't elaborate or examine Netherton's demise, nor what our future will be. But there are tactile indications that Chaz's thoughts are running on the same lines as mine. He's saying a multitude of things without using words, such as the pressure of his knee against my thigh, and the grasp of my hand when he takes it and holds it on his lap. Then, there are his little glances toward me. Questioning, as though he's not sure of me.

But still we don't speak. Not until the end of the two-hour drive, the truck's parked, Shitface has left us, and it's just him and me.

"What do you want to do now?" he asks, but he doesn't sound sure of himself.

I've been wearing the same clothes for the past few days, and he's in much the same predicament as me. "Shower." I grin. "Oh, and is there any chance of getting my stuff from Harold's? All my clean clothes are there."

"A shower sounds pretty good to me. And..." he raises his voice. "Shitface?"

When the prospect appears, he's given instructions to go to Harold's and not scare the shit out of the old man while getting what belongs to me.

I'm tired, exhausted. It's been two long days without sleep. Suddenly depleted of all energy, I use the banister to pull myself up the stairs as Chaz is delayed by a couple of brothers wanting a word. At the top, I pause, realising I'm making assumptions about heading straight for his room.

Does Chaz still want me? Was all that had been said been heat of the moment and both of us driven by the reminder of how fleeting our lives could be?

Before entering, I pause. *What do I want for me?*

It's a hard question to answer. As I open the door and step toward the bathroom, thoughts whirl around my head. After I was medically discharged, I'd already had no idea what to do with my life. Although a helicopter pilot might have found work in civilian life, I couldn't fly due to my medical condition. Then, before I'd come to terms with the little I had left, even that was taken away from me when I was forced to go on the run.

Being realistic, even before I signed up, I was fighting to survive, then in the Army, I'd follow the rules and direction that others laid out for me.

Now, what should be a huge weight off my shoulders suddenly feels like the whole world is weighing me down. Feeling I'm having the biggest adrenaline drop of my life, my legs feel unable to support me, and I sink to the ground, with my head in my hands.

Moments later, that's how Chaz finds me.

"Queenie?" I hear the sound of the door close, and then he's beside me. "Queenie—"

As his arms surround me, I reassure him, "It's okay. I haven't had one of my turns."

"You're shaking." He pulls me into his chest. "What's the matter? Talk to me."

I hate showing weakness. Rather than accepting the comfort he's giving me, I push him away. "I'm just tired."

His hand is there to help me get to my feet. "Let's take a shower and get to bed."

Not sure how much I want to shower with him, I mean, we've already been intimate, but showering together is a level of intimacy that I'm not quite sure I'm ready for next. "Can I go first?"

"Sure."

Without any argument, he lets me disappear alone into the small bathroom. I take a military shower, one that's quick, wasting little water, making sure some is left for whoever's coming after me, but it's enough to get rid of the grime and sweat that's had my clothes clinging to me for the last few hours. As follows, a bald man has no need for shampoo, so I make do with the soap, thankful it doesn't take much to wash my short hair. Only a couple of minutes have passed when I've finished and have wrapped his bath sheet around me.

It's then I realise I'm unprepared, having no clean clothes with me.

Bracing myself, I re-enter his room with a, luckily generous, towel wrapped around me. Instead of finding him waiting for me, he's stripped the bed, and is tucking the new sheets in. Not quite with military corners, but close.

Becoming aware of my presence, he points to a familiar duffle bag that's been dropped inside the door. Then, having replaced the pillows, with clean covers I notice, he picks up some of his clothes and enters the room I recently vacated.

Hurrying to what passes as my "go-bag", belongings I would need if I needed to leave town at any point, I extract some essentials—clean underwear and a t-shirt. Feeling self-conscious and strangely shy, I slide between the crisp and fresh sheets.

I've perfected the art of being able to sleep anywhere, so many times in my life I didn't have the luxury of a real bed. The soft, yet supportive mattress should feel like a luxury, but as I wait, I can't get comfortable. It's all because I don't know what Chaz expects from me, or perhaps more to the point, can I be all that he needs?

Our frenzied coupling driven by predicament and circumstances hadn't caused me distress, nor sent me back into my memories. Right now, though, I don't feel aroused at all.

How the hell my training failed me I can't say, but I don't know Chaz has finished the shower until I feel the sag of the bed. Opening my eyes, I see him looming over me.

"So fuckin' glad to see you in my bed." I can't help it. I tense. "Oh, babe." He sighs, cupping his hand around my face.

Swallowing hard, I admit. "I don't think I can do this."

He chuckles softly. "We've had hours of stress, nights with no sleep. Much as my dick wants inside you, Queenie, I'm content to just hold you while you sleep. Just knowing you're here with me..." he pauses to shake his head. "I have no idea what I've done to deserve this, to deserve you. And we've all the time in the world. We can go at your pace." His arm nudges at my shoulder, and automatically I raise my head, lying back, resting against his warm, shower-fresh flesh.

All the time in the world. His words repeat in my head. "You want me to stay?"

"Fuck, yes." He pushes up on his other elbow and looks into my face. "I thought you already knew that."

As he stares at me, a tear, one of those I never shed, leaks from my eye and rolls down my cheek. To my surprise, as well as to his, it's followed by another.

"Fuck, babe. I thought you wanted this. Thought you felt the same way."

I raise a hand and try to brush the tears away, but they keep coming, and I'm flummoxed when they're chased by a sob. "I do. I..." I swallow hard, and then decide to tell him the truth. "I don't know who I am anymore."

Now I'm in his arms, not imprisoned so I couldn't easily escape, but held gently in such a comforting way I find it impossible to resist. He rests his chin on the top of my head.

"You've got time to figure that out, darlin'. And maybe you'll come to discover that what comes next could be better than what you've lost. Different, for sure, there's nothing to say what you make won't be as good. I want you to stay with me, Queenie. I want you to make your place here. But if that's not what you want, if I can't give you enough, then there's nothing holding you here."

"I can't promise you anything."

"I'd promise you the world, but I don't deserve you."

He's so wrong. He's shown that he does in spades. No man, no person, has ever put themselves in a position where they were going to give up so much for me.

As if he can read my mind, he murmurs softly, "You owe me nothing. You don't ever need to do anything you don't want. Though it would kill me, I'd let you go. Fuck, some of that money belongs to you anyway, and that will get you started elsewhere."

"I don't want money. It's your payment for all that you've done."

He shakes his head.

"I don't... I don't know if I can be what you need." The tears, which had ceased, start flowing again.

Again, he's on the right wavelength. "You think I can't control my dick? Fuck, Queenie, just holding you, lying here, is enough for me. Can't deny I'm a fuckin' man, and I want you so bad, but we'll go at your pace." He yawns, betraying he's just as tired as me. "For now, why don't we just sleep?"

As they often are, his expression of tiredness is contagious, and I raise my hand to cover it as my own mouth gapes. He doesn't let go of me, his only movement is to place his lips to the top of my head, and then our breathing synchronises, our hearts in unison slowing their beats.

Maybe it's my extreme tiredness. Maybe it's being able to

let go of all the months of stress. Or, maybe, it's the arms holding me, but I fall into a deep, dreamless sleep.

CHAPTER TWENTY-NINE

CHAZ

She sleeps in my arms as if she's meant to be there. On my part, I've never felt more comfortable in my bed. It's taken forty-five years for me to find her, but now I know I want this woman in my life, and I'll do anything to keep her.

But she's not someone I can chain and control. She has to want to be here.

As her chest rises and falls, I listen to her breath inhaling and exhaling, and start to think of all the ways to convince her she can make a life here. But what the fuck can I offer her?

Eventually, still having found no answer, I join her in slumber.

When I awake, there's bright light coming in through the chink in the curtains, suggesting we've slept through a good part of the day. Consciously I keep my body still, my senses savouring her closeness. Her skin is so soft against my own, and when I breathe in, it's a scent of her own perfume combined with my soap. Her face is a vision for my eyes, and for a moment I soak it in, worried having her this close could be for the last time.

As she stirs, she rolls over, into me, not away. I'm all too conscious that the natural effects of the morning and her very presence had made my cock swell. I try to twist so it's not so obvious, but my slight movement makes her open her eyes.

"Good morning," she says softly, her lips curving into a cautious smile.

"Good morning," I answer, knowing I want this for the rest of my life.

"What time is it?"

"Who fuckin' cares?"

She chuckles at my answer. "Always the outlaw."

"Always," I confirm.

The tears that had taken me so much by surprise have dried. Instead, there's a new brightness in her eyes. As she stretches against me, I reluctantly release my hold, giving her space if she wants to get up and leave while my body screams how much I want to clamp her to me.

"I need the bathroom." Of course, she does. And then she'll dress, leave… "But I'll be right back." Her hand rests on my chest momentarily as if instructing me to wait here.

I'll wait as long as she fucking needs me to. Forever if necessary. I hardly dare breathe as she leaves the bed. I listen. The walls aren't thick so I hear a long tinkling, then the flush, then water running as she washes her hands. I'm near dying of asphyxiation when she returns, wondering what she's going to do next.

What she does surprises me. She strips her tee shirt over her head, baring those admittedly small but luscious tits to me. Then she strips out of her underwear. I feast my eyes for the first time on all her amazing glory, feeling my heart thump so hard it's about to jump out of my chest.

With a smirk, she yanks the sheet off me. Without speaking, her hands move to the waistband of my boxers, her intention clear. I'm certainly not averse to getting as naked as her.

My hands itch to touch her, but the gleam in her eyes tells me this is her show. I fight to suppress my natural dominance. I'm not going to stop her taking control.

My dick leaks precum just from the look in her eyes as she bends one leg and places it on the bed, following it with the other, then situating herself until she's kneeling over me, her hands resting on my chest.

"You've got a nice cock."

I snort. "Not sure I've been complimented before." I might have had praise for my performance, but not for its shape. I fist my hands to stop reaching for her, waiting to see what she's going to do next.

What I don't expect is for her to bend forward and for her tongue to lick the head of my dick. Nor for her mouth to fully widen and for her lips to enclose my girth.

Fuck, I've died and gone to heaven. Or maybe this is some wet dream. Whatever, I don't want her to stop. I've had blow jobs given by all manner of women, those who wanted to warm a president's bed, or club girls who knew what was expected of them. But never has it felt this good.

And fuck me, but Queenie seems to be enjoying giving me pleasure. I can tell by her expression it's not something she thinks she should be doing, but something she wants.

She raises her head briefly and chuckles, warm breath huffing over my overheated balls. "You like that, huh?"

"I like," I manage to stammer out, as again she takes me into that glorious mouth.

I allow her to play, to torture me for less time than I'd like before it becomes all too clear I'm not going to last. And I'm no longer a teenager. When I spill my load, I want it to be in her.

As I get far too close to the point of no return, I gasp, "Enough."

Chuckling again, that vibration alone damn near pushing me over the edge, she releases me, my dick reluctantly dropping out of those lush moist depths with a pop. I take a deep breath and a second to regain control, before my hands rest on her sides, guiding her onto her back.

Her face is full of expectation as our positions are reversed, and I'm determined not to disappoint her. If this is my chance to show her how pleasurable her life will be if she stays, I'm going to take every advantage and use everything in my repertoire.

Of course, I've gone down on women before, but her taste? Like no fucking other. Previously it might have just been tit for tat, but as soon as I get her flavour on my tongue, I know I could stay here forever. I try every trick I've ever learned, eliciting such sounds from her I know my ears will want to hear that music for ever.

Licking her clit gets her tensing, but in a good way. Her muscles clench, and her thighs squeeze my head, but it's when I put two fingers inside her and find that special spot she starts to thrash. I continue my assault, winding her up, and then bringing her down before she reaches her climax. She huffs at the denial, but doesn't beg me to stop, both of us knowing I'm just raising her higher and higher.

She doesn't scream when she finally goes over, just a loud exhale of my name. My true fucking name. *Charlie.*

Well, now she's getting no mercy. I bring her down then bring her up all over again. Her second orgasm is almost as strong as her first, her third a little weaker. Only when she starts to plead for mercy do I raise my head.

"I want you inside me," she gasps.

There's nothing I want better, but I tease her. "You want my cock?"

"God, yes."

"This *nice* cock?" As I repeat the adjective she'd used, I fist myself, pressing into the root, hoping I'm going to be able to last long enough to satisfy her.

"Your pretty damn amazing cock! In my cunt. Now."

Her dirty words thrown back at me almost do me in. I waste no time lifting her legs up and over my shoulders then guide myself in.

I've had her before, but not like this. It feels different now she's in my bed. I can let myself go, taking time to find out what arouses her best. I swivel my hips, this way then that, then complete a full roll. I slowly pull out then slam back in, and then again. She bucks against me, a full participant as I repeat my performance.

I want to savour this, want to make it last, but that's not going to happen. Taking hold of both of her hands and imprisoning them over her head, I feel her muscles contracting, pulsating against my dick. She's close, and she's going to take me with her.

"Open your eyes. Look at me," I demand, determined she's going to see who's doing this to her.

She obeys, and the sex-glazed expression of those amazing eyes are all it takes. My cock swells which in turn seems to do something to her. For a second the world's rotations seem to come to a halt as we both suck in air, then let it out in mutual groans.

Careful not to put my whole weight on her, I slip over onto my side, pulling her with me, my throbbing dick still inside her. While I hate all she'd been through and the reason that I can, I love that I can take her bare, love the feeling of our combined juices running out of her pussy and leaking onto the sheets. I have a fleeting feeling of sorrow knowing my seed will never take root inside her, but understand my grief for what can't be could never rival her loss. I vow then and there to always be enough for her.

As our heart rates begin to return to normal, and our breathing evens out, words spill out of me that I never thought I'd tell another.

"I love you, Queenie."

She doesn't say it right back, but that doesn't matter. Hopefully I've a whole lifetime to convince her.

She snuggles into my arms. "I could stay here all day."

Chuckling, I agree. "Can't see anything wrong with that. We've nowhere to be."

Except, it's then I hear a commotion from downstairs. Loud shouts, angry ones at that. And one of the voices reaching my ears is definitely not from a member of my club.

"You can't go up there." That's Bull's deep tone.

"Like fuck I can't. Where the fuck's Helo? What have you done with her?"

Then come heavy footsteps on the stairs and a banging at my door. "Prez? Think you ought to get down here. Can't get rid of the fucker unless you want us to shoot him."

"It's Harold." Queenie's already halfway out of bed.

I, too, had recognised MacPherson's voice. Quickly, I slide into my pants and, taking out a clean t-shirt for myself, take a second to throw it to her. "Put that on."

She regards my Wretched Soulz tee and barks a laugh. "Making a point, are you?" But nevertheless, she puts it on, and I waste a moment thinking just how good my shirt looks on her and wondering whether I should let my brothers just shoot the asshole to save us from having to go downstairs.

While I've been ruminating, she's finger-combed her short hair back, so it doesn't look quite such a mess, but can't hide the recently fucked look on her face. She shrugs, and grins, and puts on her pants and boots, then takes a deep breath and straightens her shoulders.

I hold her back, take time to ravish her lips, then open the door and let her walk down the hallway in front of me. I wouldn't be a man if I didn't take the opportunity to admire her tight ass.

There, waiting at the bottom of the stairs, is a MacPherson I never thought I'd see. He's not the broken man who came to beg us to restore his son's bike at the shop, nor the man who gave in and paid us off so easily. He's grown a backbone. He's standing ramrod straight, his eyes blazing as he shrugs off the hold of my sergeant-at-arms. He's a fucking warrior come to defend one of his own.

I knew I owed him for giving her sanctuary, and in a round-about way bringing her to me. But it's now I realise how much he, too, has fallen under her spell. And now he's here, wanting to protect her.

Kudos to the old man. I realise I want to repay him for all those months he was keeping her safe.

"What the fuck, Helo?" he yells as he spies her. "What the fuck have you been doing?"

Leaning over the banister, I call down to him, "She's been making sure you get that bike of yours fixed up." Instantly the words are out of my mouth, I realise they weren't best chosen. Not with her looking so obviously just fucked.

His face, which was already ruddy, goes a blazing red. He marches forward, putting himself right in front of my woman. "What the fuck have you done, girl?" He examines her from head to toe and comes up with the only conclusion he can. "You been whoring yourself out?" His hands gesture wildly. "If they've forced you, I'll kill the fucking lot."

Idle threats, as shown when the brothers who are in the

clubroom bark laughs. But instead of taking umbrage, like me, they seem happy enough to watch and see how this plays out.

Queenie, herself, is snorting with laughter. “I’m no whore,” she tells him. “But I do owe you an explanation.” Stepping closer, she slides her arm around MacPherson’s back and leads him to the bar. “There’s a lot to talk about, old man.”

“Less of the fuckin’ old,” MacPherson grumbles as, after only a moment’s hesitation, he allows her to lead him across the room.

CHAPTER THIRTY

HELO

I owe a lot to this old man, more than I can ever repay. It wouldn't be a simple monetary debt. He'd given me a place to stay and a reason to keep getting up every day. Sourcing parts for that bike had brought me into the path of the Wretched Soulz, and that, in turn, had led me to Chaz as well as vanquishing my enemy. If Harold hadn't rescued me out of the goodness of his heart that day, I may not be breathing now, and definitely not be able to consider a future.

I'm stunned he ventured into the clubhouse to come to my rescue. I obviously had grown on him more than I thought. Venturing into the Wretched Soulz clubhouse is something no one would do lightly. In truth, though, I'm not too sure how much effect one old, unarmed man would have had should there truly have been reason to save me.

"What the fuck are you doing here, Helo? With them. Him." He adds the last in a hiss, sending a sneering glance Chaz's way.

"Long story, old—" I bark a laugh. "It's a long story. Best heard with a beer in your hand."

At my words, Chaz signals to Shitface who's behind the bar. He reaches for a few bottles and starts to hand them out.

"I'd rather have one of those." Harold, challenging Chaz with a glare, points to the whisky that's hidden on the top shelf.

Chaz chuckles, but gestures agreement to the prospect, adding, "I'll have a shot myself."

Sticking with beer, I take a bottle in my hand, idly starting to pick at the label. Harold takes a sip of his whisky, then one more, before turning impatient eyes on me and raising a brow.

"It was Senator Netherton who was after me."

Harold slams his glass down. "Netherton? What the fuck?" His eyes become slits and deep furrows appear on his brow. "The senator was all over the news this morning. Seems he committed suicide last night."

"Ain't it funny how things work out?" I say casually, while being unable to suppress a grin.

His mouth opens and shuts. He turns to survey the room, but I'm certain while there may be a few faces showing amusement, no one will be giving anything away. His shrewd eyes narrow again once he's back looking at me. "So there isn't anyone after you anymore?"

"Nope." I pop the p. "I'm free."

He continues to look suspicious as he examines my face. "You owe a debt to the Soulz, girlie?"

I laugh, as Chaz states firmly. "No debts to be repaid, old man."

At his look of disbelief, I, too, reassure him, "Soulz and I are even, Harold. There's no need to worry. I'm totally here of my own volition."

"And him?" He shoots a wrathful glance at the man standing close to me.

Taking a moment to smile up at Chaz, I defuse the situation, putting it as plainly as I can. "I'm in his bed, willingly." And just to make sure there's no misunderstanding. "And his are the only sheets I'll be lying between."

For a second, Chaz rests his lips on the top of my head, his gentle, loving gesture, seems to speak volumes.

The tension visibly fades from Harold, and he drinks more of his whisky. "So you're free." He looks almost whimsical. "You can go anywhere you want now." At my nod, he asks, hopefully, "You going to be coming home with me?"

Placing my hand over his gnarly one, I know I'm going to be letting him down. While he was always moaning, he clearly appreciated the company. "No, I'm going to be staying here."

"With him?"

Smiling up at Chaz, I confirm, "With him."

Chaz indicates that Shitface should top off Harold's glass. Then he leans forward, placing his arm firmly around me.

"We're going to get that bike of yours fixed up like new, MacPherson," he states, while Harold's eyes widen in confusion.

His lips purse. "Why the fuck should you do that?"

Chaz grins. "Because Queenie here will need something to keep her occupied."

Harold frowns. I reach over and plant a kiss to his cheek. "I'll be staying around, Harold. This is not the last of me."

And it's not. Weasel and Claw waste no time loading up the frame, engine, together with the other bits and pieces onto the crash truck and transporting them to the shop, some admittedly, returning to their original home. Of course, they can't resist making snide remarks when I rummage to find parts.

I've now got the proper tools and access to source everything that I need. Harold's son's bike quickly starts taking shape. When it's discovered I made no idle boast when I said I could fix anything with an engine, the Soulz put me to work, and gradually I start taking some of the maintenance and servicing workload off, allowing them to concentrate on the customisations which they most enjoy, and which bring in the most dollars.

That first night after Netherton's demise, when I'd entered Chaz's bedroom, I wondered how this would work, how I could find a place here living alongside outlaw bikers. But fitting in hasn't been a chore. It seems to have happened naturally, with no real decisions being made. No surprise really given MCs are a draw to many discarded veterans, now I can certainly see why.

I'm Chaz's old lady, but I'm treated like one of the guys and give back just as hard. It doesn't take long for the members to become true friends, and in a short time, I know I wouldn't want to give up my new life.

I learn new things about the man I'm starting to hold in high regard, such as his love of old cars. While I'd give anything to be able to drive myself, I live for the moments when I'm flying down the road on the back of Chaz's bike, and get equal pleasure when we're in his 1960s Ford Mustang convertible.

Unfortunately, not everything's a fairy tale. When I finally finish Harold's son's bike it wasn't the miracle cure that he'd been hoping for. Only a day after he was able to tell his son it was ready to ride, he'd succumbed to his injuries, and without coming out of his coma, had died.

I'd known from the start it had been a crazy delusion, a fantasy with no basis in reality. But I'd bought into the dream, partly to have a reason for staying with Harold, but also there was a part of me that hoped there was something more in this world, a spirit that would reward Harold's efforts by bringing his son back to life.

Although Harold was obviously hit hard, the months spent restoring the bike had given him hope, a purpose, something to focus on and something to keep him alive. And after his initial foray into the clubhouse, impressed with his audacity and bravery, the brothers had invited him back, and respect had been earned on both sides.

When his son died, Harold found he wasn't alone anymore. On the news, Chaz had dragged him away from his farm and plied him with enough whisky until he'd passed out. He spent the days before the funeral at the clubhouse, with Beard handling the details when it got too much. And on the day, the bikers supplied a guard of honour for his son's coffin, respecting a kindred soul who'd lost his life on two wheels.

Of course, Harold, being the independent person he was, returned to the farm when he'd sobered up after the, admittedly, boisterous and drunken wake. But in the meantime, StoryTeller's daughter, Maria, had adopted him as an honorary grandpa, and the kid's sunny outlook had brought back his smile.

As he confided, one evening, on his now regular visit to the clubhouse, he might have lost one son, but he'd ended up with a club full of boys to keep in line. Or, at least, to try.

It's strange how the universe works. Harold is no longer lonely, and I, a Night Stalker, am living the dream of an outlaw life.

CHAPTER THIRTY-ONE
CHAZ

I rap the gavel, bringing, or attempting to bring, the rag taggle group of bikers to order. They're still full of excitement about the enrichment of our coffers, and full of ideas about buying new bikes. It's been a hard job convincing everyone that we can't just run out and spend our newfound riches, without drawing unwelcome attention of how we've suddenly been able to afford the better things in life.

Beard's been helping us make good investments, and spending the money that comes via that route and legitimately to us. We'd made the right choices. The Dominators, undisciplined group that they are, immediately started splashing their windfall around, drawing the attention of the FBI who are always watching one-percenter clubs in the chance they slip up. Last I heard Ogre was firmly under investigation and, unable to explain the origin of the cash, was heading for a RICO indictment. Couldn't happen to a better man in my book.

The thought makes the corners of my mouth automatically curve, but I bring myself back to the here and now as I see Claw trying to get my attention. I bang the table again to shut the assholes up so he can make himself heard.

Once there's glorious silence, he wastes no time. "I've been looking at new premises. It's in a better spot, gets a lot of foot-fall, should be able to expand the tattoo business. Maybe get another couple of ink slingers as well."

"Everyone in agreement?" This is the kind of idea I've been looking for. Using the money to future proof the club.

We discuss that, then other business. Then when I think I'm going to be able to bring down the gavel for a final time, Weasel raises his hand.

"There's that Soulz rally in California coming up." He waves down the jeers. He doesn't need to remind us, we're all looking forward to that. He waits for the noise to subside, then asks, "Will old ladies be coming along?"

StoryTeller chuckles. "Yeah. But Sheri will be riding in the crash truck. Not having her on my bike when she's pregnant."

Weasel shakes his head as if he's stating the obvious, and questions, "Helo?"

Not for the first time I note that while my woman's Queenie in private, the brothers still use her handle as a mark of respect. And respect is certainly what they have for her. She's probably the best mechanic we've ever had, being able to turn her hand to anything. For a moment I muse how she transformed Harold's son's bike. It's just a fucking shame it hadn't had the outcome we'd all ended up desiring. Her expertise, however, had made her a welcome, and permanent, fixture at the shop.

Realising I've zoned out, I pull my mind back to the here and now, and catch up on the conversation.

"...property rag, otherwise, she'll be fair game. Prez has got to get his name on her."

Pothead snorts. "My money's on Helo if someone from another charter dares touch her."

"That's my point." Legit bangs the table with his hand. "We'll be mopping up blood—theirs, not ours—if she goes without any kind of ownership on her."

Jesus. I stifle my laugh, realising the compliment they are paying to my woman. But it does make me think. I'd love to have my property patch on her, but Queenie's not someone you own. I'll never be good enough to deserve her, and I give thanks every day for whatever fates brought her my way.

"Okay," I enter the conversation. "Are you fuckers suggesting that, if Helo comes to San Diego, she needs a patch?"

"We going to patch her in?" Mac innocently asks.

There's a stunned silence. It had never crossed my mind to have a female member. Truthfully, if she had a dick, there'd be no question. She's got all the qualities we'd look for in a brother.

"No fuckin' way." Bull's the first to speak. "I have a fuck load of respect for her, but she ain't a brother. She's a bitch."

"We'd be a fuckin' laughingstock," Fire states.

For a fleeting moment, I'd had a vision of her riding up front with the brothers. But there's the rub. She can't ride. And she's not got the right equipment hanging between her legs. Two good reasons to exclude her. But hell, it fucking stinks. "She'll go as my old lady." I shut down this shit.

"So, she'll need a property patch." StoryTeller says through a laugh.

"Are you brave enough to tell her?" Claw directs the question to me with a smirk, miming slitting his throat.

"I want a front-row seat for that conversation." Iron slaps the table, making some paperwork bounce.

I grimace. I can just imagine how that will go over. But they have got a point. While Queenie will fast disavow anyone for thinking her a sweet butt when we visit a different charter, she's likely to speak with her fists if someone puts a hand on her. I have no doubt my woman can look after herself, but brothers in other charters aren't going to look kindly on a club that can't control their bitches. And that will blow back on the rest of us.

There'd be bloodshed and broken bones that's for certain. On our fight nights there's barely anyone who can take her. And on the firing range, we shoot beside her, but don't let her enter our competitions at all. We're men, for fuck's sake, and we have to draw the line somewhere. Secretly we know she can outshoot any one of us.

A loud sniff makes me look up in time to see Skunk wiping his nose on his sleeve, then raising his hand. "I got a suggestion."

"Hey, you got on new deodorant again?" Pothead asks from beside him. He sniffs the air. "You know, brother, for once you don't smell too bad."

"Sure have." Skunk chuckles, bringing a roll-on out of his cut as if it was a prize possession. "It's new forty-eight hour sports protection. I just have to apply it every couple of hours is all."

I don't need to ask if it's another gift from Queenie. She's made it her mission to find Skunk something that works. This must be try number fifty-two. It's the little things like this that she does which have made my brothers as well as my self have high regard for her.

"What you thinking?" Bull asks the now, I think of it, fresher smelling man, when I'm too slow to.

"She has a rag with Chaz's Queen written on it. Respectful to her, but shows ownership too."

My eyes crease and my brow furrows. Not quite a property

patch but will show who she belongs to. And it's nothing but the truth. She is my queen, and I totally worship her.

"And," Skunk continues, his gaze firmly on me, a side of his mouth suspiciously quirking. "She can carry a bag with the inscription, Chaz's Balls."

"Bag? Just a small pouch." Fire interjects.

The table erupts. Beard snorts, Legend bends his head over, his belly laughs sounding loud. Claw's trying to keep a straight face and StoryTeller's trying hard not to crack up. Mac is regarding me carefully, our newest patched member not totally sure how I'm going to react, while Pothead just takes advantage of the break in proceedings to start rolling a joint.

"You fuckin' done?" I roar, as the last of the laughter fades.

Luckily I've not completely lost my touch, as they go from yanking my chain to shifting uneasily in their seats. Skunk, in particular, seems to want to disappear into his.

"Yup," Iron states, giving the table his best sergeant-at-arms glare. "I think they're done, Prez."

Thank fuck I haven't lost my touch.

Momentarily I remember how at one point I thought I'd lost this, that I'd lost not only the respect of my club but also my patch. How I would have given it all up for Queenie.

But my brothers had come through for me. Lucky bastard that I am, I have everything.

I pick up the gavel and snarl. "Get out of my fuckin' sight before I decide to prove to you all that my balls are firmly in the right place."

I keep the stern expression and only grin when the room is empty.

EPILOGUE

TWELVE MONTHS LATER...

I rise from the chair as Queenie walks into the waiting room, trying to read the expression on her face. It's impossible to tell whether she's happy or not, but I'm sure I detect a spring in her step that wasn't there earlier. If this wasn't so important to her, I'd threaten to spank her ass for keeping me hanging.

As she approaches, I take a step toward her. Unable to hold back, I utter one word with an upward inflexion. "Well?"

She can't hold it in any longer, a beaming smile widens her face, and her gorgeous eyes sparkle. "I've got the all-clear which means I'll have my driver's permit back." She swallows as if overcome with emotion. "I can drive."

"And ride?" I've been eyeing up a motorcycle for her, knowing my old lady would relish her own bike.

After her initial announcement, it seems hard for her to find words, and I need to wait for her to blink back happy tears from her eyes. For now, I'll be content with her tentative nod as a response.

Queenie's had one year and one day clear of having one of her episodes, the stipulated time before being declared fit once again. She's been visiting this veteran's hospital on and off over the past twelve months, but since we took out Netherton, and she moved into my life, she's not once passed out.

She's become stronger and settled, taking her place by my side as my old lady, diplomatically helping me keep order in the club. None of my brothers would dare to cross her, not for concern about angering me, but for the damage she could do to them all by herself.

They've all developed an admiration for her, an affection that goes further than her just being my woman, and, a few months back, my wife. She's got a place in our club which is solely down to her. But even achieving this goal means there's still one more thing missing in her life.

It had been months ago that the brothers had first brought a suggestion to the table. As time passed and Queenie's episodes hadn't reoccurred, Skunk had brought a suggestion up at church. At first I'd dismissed it, thinking we were tempting fate, but as more months went by without issue, I'd begun to think about it seriously.

Queenie seemed content living with us. But when Story-Teller's new baby took his breath, it was easy to see, while she was offering congratulations, there was a sadness in her eyes. I couldn't give her the child she so much desired, but maybe, we could return something else to her.

We weren't hurting for money. Bikers don't need much—a decent bike and a place to reside. Our clubhouse has been renovated, our shop expanded—in part to cope for the extra business brought in by having Queenie onside. And most of us, though we staggered the purchase, have new rides. Despite our expenditure, and due to Beard's wise investments, the club's coffers remain healthy. It seems right to reward Queenie for putting the club on its affluent path.

When we arrive back from the VA, my brothers are waiting to present my woman with her own bike, a brand new sleek, black Indian Chieftain. Though we'd tried to get her over to the dark side, we knew she preferred them over Harleys. Her reaction had been just what I'd been hoping for, and within moments, we'd headed out on a ride.

Despite her undeniable pleasure in her new bike, it's the next day I'm really excited about, along with the rest of my brothers.

After breakfast, Weasel, seemingly casually, suggests a ride out. Instead of just a few takers, the whole club agrees to go, Claw remarking on the wonderful weather for a ride—which is pushing it a bit with possible thunderstorms forecast—but Queenie is as enthusiastic as anyone, not going to turn down another chance to ride. Accepting her place, she positions herself at the back, alongside Shitface the fourth—the third now riding just in front with the handle Spook, earned by him being our successful spy.

It's not far, just twenty miles, and we turn into a small airfield. As we park up, I turn my head to see Queenie handling her big bike expertly, neatly tacking it in at the end of the line. Even from this distance I can't help but see the suspicion in her eyes, nor the way she starts hesitantly walking toward me.

The sleek, black, good-looking despite its twenty years of age, McDonnell Douglas 520N which cost the club just shy of a million dollars is ready and waiting outside the nearest hanger. The colour will be the only thing in common with the military aircraft she used to fly, and I have a moment of doubt that this will be enough to satisfy her.

Before she reaches me, a man exits the hangar. He comes

up alongside, and together we wait for her to join us. Then, with a huge grin, he passes me keys, which I place into her hand.

She glances down at the keys, then at the helicopter. Instead of looking happy, she frowns. "What's this?"

"Your new ride," I tell her. Then clarify. "Well, it's yours to fly, but it's to be at the club's disposal."

"Chaz," she says softly. "I may have been medically cleared, but I can't just get in and fly."

The man by my side coughs to get our attention. "Queenie 'Helo' May? Night Stalker?" he asks. "Captain?"

She almost snaps at attention at the tone of his voice, then slumps a little. "Retired."

The man is nonplussed. He holds out his hand. "Carlton Haynes, also Captain, retired. I run this flight school along with everything else. We can do your BFR right now."

He's referring to the biennial flight review that pilots must undertake every two years to keep their license current. I've had many a chat with Carlton, the owner of this airfield, over the last couple of months. I owe him for sourcing the helicopter and for his understanding of how important it is to get her up in the air.

It's not often that Queenie is lost for words, but it seems she is now. But Carlton simply takes charge. "Follow me and we'll get that ground school session over, and then you can impress me with how you can fly."

"Queenie?" I nudge her as she remains unresponsive. Wondering whether I've made a misjudgement, and whether bringing her here has sent her back into her past, and not in a good way, I have second thoughts. "If you don't want this—"

Her face changes in an instant. "I want this."

Carlton grins widely. "Follow me." He gestures the way,

and with one glance back at me, wonder in her eyes, she goes off to take her exam.

We've exactly an hour to kill which I'd explained to the club, but none of them wanted to miss her reaction when she arrived. And hey, we're bikers, akin to machinery of all types. After the brothers with the habit have filled their nicotine-deprived lungs from a safe distance, we roam around the hangers. Despite our boy-like enthusiasm, the mechanics don't appear to resent us interrupting their work with a myriad of questions. They have a lot of their own, and a true respect in their eyes as they want to hear all about our very own Night Stalker.

We're having a barely drinkable cup of coffee from a machine, when Queenie—no, *Helo*—her demeanour all professional now, strides out of the barn closely followed by Carlson. Her raised chin lift is her only response as she catches my eye, a confirmation that, as was to be expected, any written text was a breeze.

Purposefully she strides up to the aircraft we'd bought for the club to own and her to fly.

"It's all checked and ready to go," one of the mechanics, clearly with stars in his eyes, informs my old lady. "Looking forward to seeing you put it through its paces."

She distractedly offers him a smile, her focus on the helicopter now. "I'm rusty," she warns. Then, "Can I look?" She gestures toward a clipboard he's holding and, having taken it from him when offered, approaches the craft.

"What the fuck is she doing?" an impatient Fire asks after a few minutes pass and it seems like Helo is double-checking everything. "Shouldn't she just get into the fuckin' thing and fly?"

Overhearing, Carlton chuckles by my side. "Another sign she's an ace pilot. She'll never rely on the word of anyone else and will give the helicopter its full inspection to reassure herself it's ready to fly."

Watching her more carefully, I see her complete her check of the rotors, then carefully inspect every inch of the fuselage. She's now on her knees, looking at the wheels and whatever holds them in place. Next she opens the engine compartment and gives it a thorough check.

She climbs into the cockpit, and clearly it's the controls time to be given the once-over. She yanks at the seat belts and murmurs to herself as if she finds everything satisfactory. Then she checks something else.

Carlton chuckles again. "I put a brand new fire extinguisher in it and a new first aid kit. She'll find no issues."

Finally happy with all that she's seen, she jumps back down and hands the mechanic his clipboard back. I breathe in, waiting to see some umbrage on his part, but apparently he's used to his work being double-checked, and simply bumps her fist with his when she offers hers.

At last, the moment of truth is here. With a wave of her hand, Helo heaves herself back inside, waiting for Carlton to take his place in the co-pilot's seat. She asks him some questions, presumably because it's an alien-to-her craft, and then the engine catches. The rotors start spinning, slowly at first, then faster, making StoryTeller's long hair fly.

Now it's lifting. A good takeoff? Well, it looks like it to me, but how the fuck do I know?

I feel a moment of anguish on her part, remembering the last time she flew was when she'd been shot down. Has she gotten over that now? But it seems so as the helicopter rises, gaining height.

Claw cheers, Bull claps, and Iron slaps my shoulder as she rises higher. She swoops low and proceeds to fly away, gradually becoming a speck on the horizon. When the *thwap*

thwap of the rotors can be heard again, I raise my eyes to the sky.

I don't know what a test flight normally looks like, but are helicopters supposed to fly like that? It's dipping, diving, flying at a ninety-degree angle before recovering itself. She puts the craft through manoeuvre after manoeuvre in front of our eyes. Around me I hear gasps, indrawn breaths, and a very reverential, *fuck, that bitch can fly.* Finally, it starts to lower in the sky, hovering above us, before smoothly coming to a rest in the very same spot from which she'd taken off.

Grinning broadly, I watch as the rotors slow and stop, and after a brief conversation, pilot and co-pilot get out. I half-expect Carlton to be holding his stomach and losing its contents on the grass, but no, his own grin is splitting his face.

He comes around to her, holds out his hands, and in the now quiet, I can hear every word.

"Thank you for the experience, Captain. You've got that nape of the earth flying down pat."

"Sorry about that." Helo laughs. "Force of habit. I'll have to learn to stay higher."

"Impressive as hell," he compliments her, shaking his head, then gestures behind him. "I'll go get the paperwork done now."

As he passes me, he claps me on the shoulder. "She's a fuckin' Night Stalker all right."

His comment hits me in the gut.

Have I done the right thing? We'd acquired the helicopter as a way to keep her, but it's a poor substitute from the Black Hawk she used to fly. She's got her licence to go with the freedom she got a year back. Will living with us really satisfy her now?

In front of my eyes, Helo morphs back into Queenie. Her seriousness dissipates as she smiles widely, gives a little squeal, then launches herself at me so fast I stumble as I catch her.

"Thank you!" she cries, then twists, so still in my arms she can take in the rest of the club. "Thank you all. I'll never be able to repay you."

"Sure you will," Legit calls out. "I want a ride!"

"Babe," I pull her attention back to me, then cup my hands either side of her face, unable to wait for the truth. "Is this enough? Am I enough?"

"I wouldn't be here if it wasn't for you, Chaz. It's more than enough. I didn't need this grand gesture to stay. I didn't even know it's what I wanted. But," her voice fades, and I brace for what she's going to say next. "Carlton asked me if I wanted to pilot some of the life flights or go on the search and rescue missions they fly from here. It's quite an outfit he's got."

I'd noticed the other craft with the different insignia, but with all my focus on getting Queenie back into the air, I hadn't thought much about it.

"You gonna take him up on that?"

Stupid question, but still she replies. "Chaz, when I met you I was broken. I couldn't see a way out. I wasn't a pilot. I wasn't a woman. You've given me everything back. This? This isn't what I need to complete me. That's you. It's always been you."

There's only one way I can respond to that. "I fuckin' love you, Queenie."

"I love you right back."

"For fuck's sake, enough of the sloppy shit. When are you going to take me up for a ride?" Skunks asks, with a deep yearning sigh.

I slap his head. "Enough of you asking my old lady for a ride."

ACKNOWLEDGEMENTS AND AUTHOR'S NOTE

Fire meets Fire has taken far longer to write than I had hoped, and I apologise for making you wait. I hope you enjoyed the story enough to make up for the delay.

As always, I have to thank all the beta readers who encouraged me, Sheri, Jo and Alex. My immense appreciation also goes to my long-suffering editor, Maggie Kern, and to Darlene Tallman for proofreading.

Once again I've used the talent of photographer Golden Czermak for the cover photo. As for the model, Colt Kube, what can I say? As soon as I saw your picture, the character of Chaz fell into place. The end result of the amazing cover was pulled together by CT Cover Designs.

Finally, last as always, but definitely not least, thanks to all of you, my wonderful readers who've taken a chance on this book. If it wasn't for your encouragement, I wouldn't keep writing. I have recently received messages and emails telling me how much you like my books, and I love reading everyone. A positive message inspires me to write more.

This book, like all of my works, has been to beta readers, through editing twice, to a proofreader and then to ARC readers, but there could still be the odd typo that's crept through. Please message me if you've found anything, so I have a chance to correct the book. I love to hear from readers, even if you're pointing out something I've got wrong.

If you've enjoyed this book, please consider writing a

review. Reviews are essential to us authors, and I appreciate and read them all.

The next book that I'm writing is another in the Wretched Soulz series, and is called BlackJack's Game. It's still in the early stages, so for updates about the blurb, please join my reader group or sign up to my newsletter.

Reader group:. https://www.facebook.com/groups/1852824718066605

Newsletter: http://eepurl.com/b1PXO5

Love and peace

Manda

COMING SOON

BlackJack's Game (Wretched Soulz MC)

Why can't women leave things alone? Why do they think they know best?

The Wretched Soulz had everything under control until she stuck her nose in. Okay, so maybe we were more interested in protecting our club then getting her innocent sister out of jail. But it was highly likely the two would have gone hand in hand.

Now I've been given the responsibility of keeping her alive, a woman I don't even like. Worse, she detests me. The only way I can keep her close to my side is to blackmail her. She wouldn't be with me voluntarily.

But it's my life on the line as well as hers.

I'm on the run. And all because I met my Destiny.

OTHER WORKS BY MANDA MELLETT

Blood Brothers – A series about sexy dominant sheikhs and their bodyguards

Stolen Lives (#1) Nijad and Cara

Close Protection (#2) Jon and Mia

Second Chances (#3) Kadar and Zoe

Identity Crisis (#4) Sean and Vanessa

Dark Horses (#5) Jasim and Janna

Hard Choices (#6) Aiza

Satan's Devils MC - Arizona Chapter

Turning Wheels (Blood Brothers #3.5, Satan's Devils #1) Wraith and Sophie

Drummer's Beat (#2) Drummer and Sam

Slick Running (#3) Slick and Ella

Targeting Dart (#4) Dart and Alex

Heart Broken (#5) Heart and Marc

Peg's Stand (#6) Peg and Darcy

Rock Bottom (#7) Rock and Becca

Joker's Fool (#8) Joker and Lady

Mouse Trapped (#9) Mouse and Mariana

Blade's Edge (#10) Blade and Tash

Heart Mended: A Satan's Devils MC Novella

Truck Stopped (#11) Truck & Allie

Satan's Devils MC Boxset 1 Books 1-5

Satan's Devils MC Boxset 2 Books 6-8

Satan's Devils MC Boxset 3 Books 9-11

Satan's Devils MC - Colorado Chapter

Paladin's Hell (#1) Paladin and Jayden

Demon's Angel (#2) Demon and Violet

Devil's Due (#3) Beef and Steph

Devil's Dilemma (#4) Pyro and Mel

Ink's Devil (#5) Ink and Beth

Devil's Spawn (#6)

Satan's Devils MC - Next Generation

Amy's Santa (#1) Wizard and Amy

Hawk's Cry (#2) Hawk and Olivia

Twisted Throttle (#3) Throttle and Gwen

Saving Marvel (#4) Marvel and Virginia

Satan's Devils MC - San Diego Chapter

Being Lost (#1)

Grumbler's Ride (#2)

Avenging Devil Part 1 (#3)

Avenging Devil Part 2 (#4)

Satan's Devils MC - Utah Chapter

Road Tripped (#1)

Stormy's Thunder (#2)

Satan's Devils MC - Las Vegas Chapter

Red's Peril - Part 1

Red's Peril - Part 2

Petty's Crimes

Wicked Warriors MC - Arizona Chapter

Warts an' All

Tickety Tock

Wretched Soulz MC

StoryTeller's Tale

READING ORDER

Satan's Devils MC in reading order

Turning Wheels

Drummer's Beat

Slick Running

Targeting Dart

Heart Broken

Peg's Stand

Rock Bottom

Joker's Fool

Mouse Trapped

Paladin's Hell

Blade's Edge

Demon's Angel

Devil's Due

Heart Mended (novella)

Truck Stopped

Devil's Dilemma

Ink's Devil

Devil's Spawn

Being Lost

Road Tripped

Grumbler's Ride

Stormy's Thunder

Avenging Devil Part 1

Avenging Devil Part 2

Red's Peril Part 1

Red's Peril Part 2

Petty's Crime

Second Generation

Amy's Santa

Hawk's Cry

Twisted Throtle

Saving Marvel

Wicked Warriors MC

Warts an' All

Tickety Tock

Wretched Soulz MC

StoryTeller's Tale

Fire meets Fire

BlackJack's Game (coming soon)

Blood Brothers (Billionaires and their bodyguards)

Stolen Lives

Close Protection

Second Chances

Identity Crisis

Dark Horses

Hard Choices

STAY IN TOUCH

Email: manda@mandamellett.com

Website: www.mandamellett.com

Sign up for my newsletter to hear about new releases in the Satan's Devils and Blood Brothers series.

Facebook reader group: https://www.facebook.com/groups/mandasbadboys/

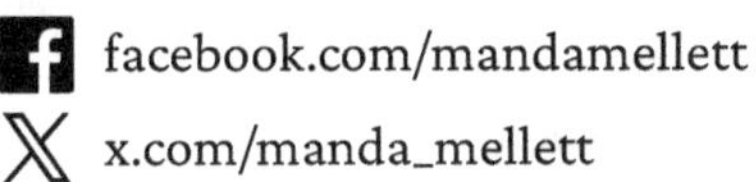

ABOUT THE AUTHOR

Manda's life's always seemed a bit weird, starting with a childhood that even today she's still trying to make sense of, then losing her parents in the late teens. Going from the tragic to the bizarre, who else could be unlucky enough to have had two car accidents, neither her fault, one involving a nun, and another involving a police woman?

There isn't enough space to list everything that's happened to Manda, or what she's learned from it. But by using the rich fabric of her personal life, psychology degree, varied work experiences, and amazing characters she's met, Manda is able to populate her books with believable in-depth characters and enjoys pitting them against situations which challenge them. Her books are full of suspense, twists and turns and the unexpected.

Manda lives in the beautiful countryside of Essex in the UK, the area's claim to fame being the Wilkin's Jam Factory at nearby Tiptree. She can usually find jars of jam which remind her of home wherever she goes. As well as writing books and reading, Manda loves walking her dogs and keeping fit. She lives with her husband of over 30 years, who, along with her son, is her greatest fan and supporter.

Manda is thankful that one of the more unusual, and at the time unpleasant, turns her life took, now enables her to spend her time writing. Confirming, in her view, every cloud has a silver lining.

Photo by Carmel Jane Photography

www.ingramcontent.com/pod-product-compliance
Lightning Source LLC
Chambersburg PA
CBHW070432170726
48291CB00002B/470

9781915106209